Every Day
Was
Christmas

BOOKS BY DONNA ASHCROFT

Summer at the Castle Cafe
The Little Christmas Teashop of Second Chances
The Little Guesthouse of New Beginnings
The Christmas Countdown
The Little Village of New Starts

Donna Ashcroft

If Every Day Was Christmas

bookouture

Published by Bookouture in 2020

An imprint of Storyfire Ltd.
Carmelite House
50 Victoria Embankment
London EC4Y 0DZ

www.bookouture.com

ISBN: 978-1-83888-216-7
eBook ISBN: 978-1-83888-215-0

To my brother Peter and his family,
Christelle, Lucie, Mathis and Joseph.
Because family matters and
I want to say thank you for mine.

Chapter One

Four missed calls.

Meg Scott pushed her mobile back into her pocket, putting into practice one of her favourite philosophies: if you don't let yourself see, hear or smell something, it won't exist. Besides, she could guess why her father was calling and had promised herself she wouldn't relent.

'So we're down to our final option.' Morag Dooley whacked a reindeer-shaped salt shaker onto a table in Meg's cafe, imitating a judge with a gavel. The black cape she wore done up to the chin and her mass of grey curls added to the illusion. Meg glanced around the small room, which was situated in the back corner of her all-year-round Christmas shop. She'd added an extra layer of festive decoration the evening before because it was mid-November – a Christmas tree, flashing white icicle lights, green and red tablecloths, and sparkly snowman centrepieces which gave her a warm fuzzy glow. The counter in the corner of the room, behind which Cora Dougall – Meg's assistant and uber-barista – stood, was lined with tinsel and displayed what was left of the cafe's decimated stock of Christmas-themed cakes, biscuits and sandwiches. The rest had been snapped up by the two dozen Lockton residents squeezed around the six tables clustered into the small space. 'I propose this year's Christmas Promise is to fix the village hall roof,' Morag declared with another triumphant whack. 'Does everyone agree?'

'The roof has to be a priority,' Fergus McKenzie growled. He was a handsome man in his late sixties with a silver beard and dark grey eyes. He grimaced at his coffee, which Morag had forbidden him to add whisky to earlier. 'The Jam Club has been coming into Apple Cross Inn every Thursday evening since the village hall closed, and they're disturbing my alone time with all their blethering.' Beside Fergus, Agnes Stuart's green eyes twinkled as she jabbed him gently in the ribs. They'd started dating over four months before and Meg knew she was used to his curmudgeonly ways.

'A lot of clubs have been forced to close since the roof started to leak, and loads of events have been called off,' Cora said quietly. 'We were going to have my new grandbaby's christening there next spring because our house is too wee – now I've nowhere to host the party.'

'Unless the roof gets fixed soon, I hear the building may be irreparable. There's talk of damp in the walls and cracks appearing in the ceiling,' Grant Stuart, a local sheep farmer and Agnes's son, said balefully.

There was a rumble of surprise from the assembled group.

Morag nodded. 'Then I think we're all agreed.' She didn't wait for a response, and instead whacked the salt shaker onto the table again.

For hundreds of years, the inhabitants of Lockton, a village set deep in the picturesque Scottish Highlands, had made a promise to do something for the community in December. The promise was then handwritten on crisp paper and hung on the twenty-foot

Nordmann fir in the village square which had sprouted in an ancient wishing well. Legend had it that any promise hung on the tree would be helped along by the various spirits who were said to live in the surrounding mountains. Whether it was through magic or the sheer determination of the locals, every pledge made by the village in almost two hundred years had been kept. Over time, the villagers had begun to hang up their own personal promises as well, and the tradition had grown.

'How much do we need to raise?' Meg asked.

'Davey knows someone in Morridon who quoted fifteen thousand for the roof,' Morag said, and Grant let out a whistle of shock.

'And that was mates' rates,' Davey Becker – owner of Apple Cross Inn – interjected. 'You wouldn't believe how much some people charge. But the offer only stands until February – after that he says there'll be way more work.'

'We need fundraising ideas.' Morag took her seat again and glared at the assembled crowd when no one spoke. 'Anyone?'

Davina Magee, who lived on a farm located a few miles outside Lockton, cleared her throat. 'Cake sale?' she suggested, and went bright pink when Morag groaned.

'Not sure it'll raise enough. Besides, we did that four years ago when we were building the children's playground, remember. The whole village had to go on a diet in the new year. Anything else?' she snapped, wielding the salt shaker menacingly.

'A naked calendar?' Matilda Tome, who occasionally worked behind the bar in Apple Cross Inn and boasted an hourglass figure, suggested, with a gleam in her eye. Morag let out an irritated huff and checked the top button of her cape was firmly secure.

Davey slurped his cappuccino before licking his lips. He was a wiry, athletic man in his mid-thirties with bright blue eyes. Like Meg, Davey was a transplant from London and had moved up a few years before, leaving behind a successful career as a music producer. No one knew why he'd made the abrupt life change, but the events he put on in his pub were legendary – and attracted customers from far and wide. 'We could host a concert on Christmas Eve in the pub? There are a few bands who owe me a favour, and a couple who've been promising to come to Lockton for a while. The ones I have in mind would draw a big crowd and I think we could charge at least fifty quid for a ticket.' There was a collective gasp. 'If we sell food too, we'll get close to our target.'

'Aye, we could offer festive cocktails and cakes.' Agnes dipped her chin, looking excited. She was in her late sixties, a pretty woman with silver hair, and she had adopted Meg as her own. Meg adored her like a mother, which, for a woman used to doing everything in her power to avoid her own family for most of the year, was a revelation.

'I know someone who runs a marquee shop in Morridon who'll give us a good price.' Grant gave the group a thumbs up. 'And I've a few heaters at Buttermead Farm we use in the winter. Set that all up at the back of the pub and we'll be able to rival Glastonbury.'

Meg clapped her hands. 'With snow and glitter instead of mud? That sounds perfect. I've got loads of things in the shop that we can use to decorate.'

'I've a friend coming to stay in December.' Davey looked thoughtful. 'He's good with his hands and he'll be working in the pub until Christmas. He might be willing to help set everything up.'

Morag scratched her chin as a hint of a smile moved across her round face. 'We could work with this idea. Cora, can you make posters and tickets?'

Cora nodded. A schoolteacher before she'd retired and started to work in Meg's cafe, she had the ability to create almost anything from multicoloured paper, highlighters and a Pritt Stick.

'We could get the Lockton knitting club to make some instruments to put around the village, to advertise the event.' Agnes nodded at Matilda, who winked.

'Then that's settled.' Morag whacked the salt shaker onto the table for the final time and Meg let out a sigh of relief when it didn't shatter. 'I'll make a list of extra tasks. You can come to the post office over the next few days to pick yours up. If you bring all the tickets to me when you've made them, Cora, I'll distribute and start signing people up.' Knowing Morag, she'd have the event sold out in a week. 'Meg, could you sell the tickets in your shop and add them to the website? And I know it's only November, but can I leave it to you to hang the village promise onto the tree too?'

Meg nodded. Her shop sold clear baubles into which promises could be inserted for that exact purpose. Besides, she wanted to hang her own Christmas Promise up tonight – and had already set the ball in motion to make sure she kept it. As if reading her mind, Meg's mobile vibrated in her pocket again.

'Are we done?' Fergus suddenly pushed his chair back and stood. 'Because there's a whisky in Apple Cross Inn with my name on it.'

'Literally.' Agnes laughed softly. 'Davey just got a batch of your new recipe from the distillery.'

'We'll need to settle up with Meg first.' Morag gave Fergus a hard stare.

'It's on the house.' Meg waved away the offers of payment for the refreshments from the villagers as she ushered them through the cafe and shop towards the exit, kissing each one in turn as they left. When the last person had gone, Meg let out a long breath as Cora flipped the sign on the door to read 'Closed'.

'You'll be bust by the end of December if you keep giving the stock away like that,' Cora complained.

'It's fine.' Meg grinned. 'Business is booming and I can afford to feed a few of my friends. Isn't that what Christmas is all about?'

'Not if it's every day.' Cora shook her head.

This wasn't the first time they'd had this conversation and it probably wouldn't be the last. Meg loved giving gifts, loved the buzz in her stomach she got from simple acts of kindness, and nothing else – not even her ex-boyfriends or lovers – had ever come close. She leaned back against the door and looked around the empty store. It was a long room with a till at the end and a door behind that led up to her flat. The walls were lined with shelves filled with all kinds of Christmas fare, including baubles, tinsel, wrapping paper and festive jam, as well as local guidebooks and whisky. Running along the centre were tables piled high with sparkly decorations, model reindeer, snowmen and an array of popular gifts. Outside the shop in the darkness, hand-carved wooden Christmas trees, which she'd bring inside soon, were lined up like soldiers in front of the glass. They'd sold a few today – and once they hit December in another couple of weeks, she'd get some real trees. Meg adored her shop, which she'd set up in homage to her favourite day of the year so she could experience it over and over again. It was the antithesis of her life when she'd been growing up – the glitter, sparkle and sheer joy of the space usually made her feel content and safe. Perhaps it was all the phone calls from her father, but today something felt off, as if an ill wind were gathering momentum, getting ready to spoil everything.

'You going out with the new boyfriend tonight?' Cora asked, heading back towards the cafe so she could gather empty plates and cappuccino mugs from the tables and pack them into the small dishwasher behind the counter. Meg would have told her to go home, but knew she'd be wasting her breath. Cora had the work ethic of an entire ant colony.

'Nope, that's finished.' Meg picked up the salt shaker that Morag had been maltreating and checked it for fractures.

'Ach, already, lassie? I thought he might be the one.' Cora sounded disappointed. 'He lasted over three weeks, and you even introduced him to your hamster.'

'He was nice, but we disagreed on movies and he was really grumpy about it.' Meg frowned when Cora let out a sigh as she slammed the door of the dishwasher closed and switched it on. 'Everyone knows *The Holiday* is the best Christmas film ever. He thought it was *Die Hard* and refused to watch what he referred to as *romantic tosh*. He didn't like Christmas much either, I should have seen that as a sign…' She shook her head, feeling a mixture of disappointment and disgust. But she should have expected it. She'd been searching all her adult years for a man she could spend time with without being disappointed, someone who'd accept her as she was. Had come close a few times, but something always made her realise things weren't right – and Meg wasn't prepared to give her heart to someone who didn't understand her, someone with whom she wasn't perfectly in tune.

'He doesn't sound like Prince Charming, but you're a little fussy, lassie.' Cora pursed her lips. 'I've told you before. You need a man with his own opinions and ideas. Find yourself a yes-man and you'd be bored within a week.'

'There's nothing boring about agreeing with someone or believing in the same things. Quarrels and conflicts get wearing over time. I should know.' Meg said the last bit under her breath as she picked up a broom, sweeping crumbs erratically off the floor. As she did, she replayed the argument from the night before in her head and her temper began to flare again. She caught the broom on the edge of one of the tables, sending the shaker Morag had been assaulting flying. Meg watched with her mouth open as it shattered on the floor, spraying salt in every direction.

'Oops.' Cora grabbed the dustpan and brush from underneath the counter as Meg dropped to her hands and knees to pick up the pieces of broken china. 'I know you're not that superstitious. But humour me and throw a little salt over your shoulder to ward off bad luck.' Cora swept up the mass of white crystals from the tiled floor as Meg followed her instructions. Then she cradled the small pieces of broken reindeer in her fingers and frowned, ignoring the insistent buzz in her pocket from her mobile, wondering if this was a sign. That the peaceful life she'd worked hard to build for herself over the last three years was about to shatter too.

*

Meg tramped along Lockton High Street in a puffy red jacket and snow boots later that evening, clutching two glass baubles in her hand. In the distance, under the moonlight, she could just make out a mountain range rising out of the horizon with thousands of stars and a half-moon illuminating its peaks. Her cheeks tingled as a chilly wind flecked with snowflakes blew into her face. She blinked as she passed Apple Cross Inn and peered briefly through the window, to see Davey and Matilda serving customers behind a busy bar while a fire roared in the corner. Multicoloured Christmas lights had already been strung across the facade of the pub and icicles dripped from the edges of the guttering and windows, glittering like tinsel in the semi-darkness. Davey had put them up earlier in the week in preparation for December, but hadn't switched any of the lights on yet.

Meg continued walking, past the red-brick post office where Morag Dooley reigned, beyond the small primary school and neglected village hall which had been roped off from inquisitive visitors, until she reached the village square which was located in the centre of the high street at a fork. From here the road split in two and went in opposite directions. One led to Morridon, a town near the coast, and the other to Inverness. The square itself was framed by iron posts and metal railings which had been painted white. In the centre, the fir tree towered up towards the sky, rising out of what remained of the ancient wishing well, whose rounded brick sides resembled a reddish-brown plant pot.

Meg took in the three baubles that were already dangling from the lower limbs. Each contained pieces of folded paper which she knew contained villagers' handwritten promises. Until Meg had discovered the clear baubles in one of her suppliers' catalogues two years before, everyone had tied their promises directly onto the tree – until the rain and snow throughout December gradually reduced them to congealed pulp. The baubles had proved a big hit, and most of the villagers had collected and reused theirs each year.

Meg got close enough to stretch up and place the village promise onto one of the higher branches. At five foot two she couldn't reach very far, but she hung it carefully and stood back to select the next spot, pausing for a moment to find the perfect location. Then she stretched a little and hung her own promise next to a bauble filled with glitter, counting that as a good omen. She pressed her eyes shut as she recited the words she'd written earlier.

'I promise to make my first Christmas alone in Lockton a happy one.' She felt her stomach clench in anticipation. 'And I promise, no matter what Dad is calling to say, that I'm not going home this year. I can't face spending another Christmas on tenterhooks, waiting for the next row. Not again.' She opened her eyes, noticing how the snowflakes fluttering around her head added a shimmer to the frigid air and how the breeze rustled through the trees, as if it were whispering something to her. She loved this time of year, and was determined to stay in Scotland for it. Her mobile buzzed, alerting her to another voice message. Phone signals were scarce in Lockton, and Meg knew if she didn't take advantage of it now, she'd have to wait until she got back to the shop. She pulled her mobile out of her pocket, checked the screen and dialled. It went straight to voicemail.

'Meg. It's Dad…' Meg waited. 'We got your Christmas card and note – you always were efficient. Your mum's not happy. In fact, she's been behaving really oddly since she read it. Things have been difficult…'

Things were always difficult. Meg steeled her heart.

'You know we love having the family together for Christmas – it's the one day of the year when we manage to get on.' The honest message was at odds with the usual jollity and jokes her dad used to deflect and hide his real emotions. 'But you're right. The time has come for us to move on. Now you're older, I've got something to tell you, something we've kept from you and your sister for too long. It might help to explain things between me and your mother… it might help you to understand why we're always at odds.' His voice was gruff. 'Meg, I—' He stopped, and there was a short silence and then a long sigh. 'On second thoughts, it might be better if I didn't leave this in a message. You may have things you want to ask… I'll try to call again soon.' He paused. 'And I might just check with your mother first.'

The message ended abruptly. Meg tried to call back, but no one answered. She was left staring at the mobile, wondering what her dad had been about to say. Perhaps telling her this secret was just his attempt to make her break her Christmas Promise this year.

Chapter Two

Tom Riley-Clark bumped up over a small snowdrift and limped his four-by-four to the edge of the road, before switching the engine off. Then he hopped out so he could check the tyre, pulling the collar of his flimsy jacket up to meet the curls of dark hair that teased his neck in a useless attempt to ward off the cold.

'Dammit.' He kicked the tyre a couple of times for good measure, because yeah, that always worked. In the back of the car his dappled basset hound, Cooper, whined and licked condensation off the window so he could peer out. 'We're not going anywhere, boy. Looks like we'll need Davey to rescue us – he ought to be used to that by now.' He pulled his mobile from his back pocket and cursed when he found he had no signal. 'Perfect,' he grumbled, popping the boot open so he could pull out the spare. It had been years since he'd helped his grandfather change the tyre in his Audi, but he still had arms, didn't he? He wasn't completely useless. At least, that's what he'd been trying to prove to himself.

He hauled the tyre out of the back and dropped it onto the ground with a grunt, pulling a face when he realised it was flat. Even after three years of being out of the music business, away from the entourage who used to efficiently organise his life, he still hadn't mastered the art of planning ahead. He cursed and lugged the tyre back into the boot. When he got to Lockton he'd find a garage and deal with it.

Tom took a moment to scan his surroundings. He was on a wide road blanketed in a deep layer of snow. To his right stood a range of jagged mountains which he'd been told offered stunning views, although today they looked bitterly cold and a little ominous. To his left, white fields led to a lower mountain range. Behind him, the road was already a puffy white as snowflakes layered themselves over the tyre tracks he'd left minutes earlier. Tom already knew he'd find nothing but snow and empty fields for at least another five or six miles – with little prospect of running into anything with two legs. Unless the legends his friend Davey had warned him about included a yeti. A gust of frigid wind blew across his shoulders, dumping slivers of icy snow onto the back of his neck. He shivered and opened the car door again so he could climb inside. He contemplated walking to Lockton for a nanosecond, before checking his mobile again for a signal.

'Looks like we're stuck until someone passes,' he muttered to Cooper, opening the glove compartment and pulling out a snack for his dog, sighing because he'd eaten all his emergency chocolate four days ago. They sat in silence, staring at the empty road as Tom tried to figure out his next move. He was about five miles from Lockton, five miles of deep snow and inhospitable road. He was stuck, empty and alone, and the whole thing felt like a mirror of his life. 'Five miles…' He began to hum under his breath, subconsciously crafting a song, until Cooper barked and Tom realised with a start that not only had he been singing, but someone had just pulled up behind them.

Tom hopped out, ignoring the snow seeping into his comfortable but not-so-sensible hi-tops. He stood for a moment, taking in the parked van, wondering if his life had just taken another bizarre turn. Or if someone was playing a trick on him?

The van was bright red with reindeer painted in vivid colours on the bonnet. Illustrated reins stretched across the front door and led towards the back, where a sleigh weighed down with a chubby, maniacally grinning Santa and dozens of Christmas presents decorated the side. The driver's door opened and an elf got out. She – at least, Tom thought it was female – wore a snowsuit with green legs and a bright red tunic top with gold buttons and a green collar that led upwards to a mass of long, blonde hair and a pointy hat. Tom stepped closer and his breath caught as the elf raised her blue eyes to meet his. She was stunning – movie-star stunning. He'd met his fair share of gorgeous women – had dated a few and had even been married to one for a while. Being a musician climbing the ladder of fame had made him attractive – and in those dark days his ego had demanded he surround himself with the rich and beautiful. But he'd never felt like this – as if his heart were about to fly out of his chest and lay itself at someone's feet, like a trout gulping for its final breath. The feeling was unsettling.

'Need some help?' the elf asked, in an accent Tom recognised as from somewhere down south, similar to his own. *Not from around here then*, his addled brain concluded as he tried to pull himself together. The elf grinned when he didn't answer, making his heart thump uncomfortably hard. He waited for a flicker of recognition, and was relieved when her expression didn't alter. 'If you tell me what you need, I'll see if Santa can deliver it.' Her full pink lips rose in a confused smile when he continued to gape. 'Are you okay?

Did you bang your head? Do you need to lie down?' She sounded concerned and Tom cleared his throat at last.

'Flat tyre, sorry. You confused me for a moment.'

'Not used to seeing elves out in the daytime?' she asked with a sunny smile. 'I get that a lot. Santa gave me the day off, we've almost finished wrapping the presents. Well, it is the first of December.' She laughed when he struggled for a response. 'And that was a joke. I'm not a nutter. Meg Scott.' She stepped forwards and held out a green-gloved hand which Tom took and swiftly shook. 'I don't really work for Santa, but I do run a Christmas shop. It's why I'm out in this weather, delivering Christmas supplies to a client in Morridon,' she added. So that explained the wheels and outfit.

'Tom Riley-Clark,' he said, annoyed when his voice came out all husky. He'd barely looked at a woman since his wife had left him and his life had imploded on Christmas Day three years before, and had no desire to feel this attracted to anyone. Least of all a Christmas-obsessed elf. 'My tyre.' He drifted off when she walked up to his car and grinned at Cooper.

'I'm guessing you have no spare?' she asked in that sing-song voice, opening the door so his dog could jump out. Did she ever stop smiling? Tom watched Meg kneel down to scratch Cooper behind the ears as he tapped his paws on the snow, looking shocked by the cold and a little put out.

'It's flat,' he said, feeling surprisingly stupid.

'Then make sure you add "new tyre" to the top of your Christmas list,' she joked.

'I don't believe in Father Christmas, I don't like Christmas and I'm not a fan of this time of year,' Tom ground out, regretting the words almost the instant they left his mouth – but he was grouchy, unsettled and decidedly off-balance. And she was leading his dog to that ridiculous red vehicle with Santa painted on the side, and opening the door. Worse, Cooper was climbing onto the back seat. Traitor. Meg stopped smiling and shrugged as something swept across her face. Disappointment? He didn't know her well enough to read it.

'Figures,' she said under her breath. 'Then believe in fate, and thank your lucky stars I came by. This road can be mighty quiet in the winter and the sun's getting ready to set.' She swept her eyes up to his face and this time they didn't sparkle. 'I can drop you in Lockton if you like. There's a hotel and a pub. You could warm up, find a place to stay and call a garage. You're unlikely to find anyone who can fix your tyre tonight.' She left the passenger door wide open as she tramped over to the driver's side.

'I'm heading to Apple Cross Inn.' Tom noticed her eyes flash with interest. He grabbed his bag out of his car and locked it before climbing in beside her. 'I'm friends with the landlord.'

'Then you'd better dig deep for some festive spirit,' Meg said as she closed her door. 'Because Davey's already put the tinsel out.'

Tom watched as she pulled off the elf gloves to expose small, slim hands and fingernails painted with tiny snowman faces. His stomach rumbled, suddenly giving away the fact that he hadn't eaten for hours. She dug into the pocket of her elf suit and pulled out a chocolate bar, handing it to him without a word.

'Thanks,' Tom said, surprised. He opened it as she fired up the engine and took a bite before pulling on his seatbelt, ignoring the Christmas tree-shaped air freshener dangling from the rear-view mirror. He was surprised by the traction of the van's wheels on the snow as they headed past his Land Rover, towards Lockton. After a few minutes of silence, Meg switched the CD player on and Mariah Carey's 'All I Want For Christmas Is You' filled the van. Tom saw her lips quirk as she concentrated on the road, and he wondered if she was deliberately provoking him. The snow was coming down in huge clumps now and the wind had picked up. The windscreen wipers were up to maximum and he could hear the motor whirring. In the back, Cooper moaned.

'He's a fair-weather dog,' Tom said by way of explanation. 'A rescue. By the way he reacts to snow, I'm guessing he hails from the Bahamas.'

'Then what are you doing in Scotland?' Meg asked. 'We're having one of our coldest winters for twenty years. You might have to think about getting him a coat. I sell dog jumpers in my shop, but they're Christmas-themed.' Cooper let out a happy bark. 'I'm thinking he doesn't share your feelings on the festive season,' she said dryly.

'He's new.' Tom stared out of the window. 'And he probably thought you were talking about food. In answer to your question, I'm here to help Davey. He needs an extra pair of hands in the pub during December. One of his bar people, Norm something…'

'Stout,' Meg filled in.

Tom nodded. 'He's had an operation on his knee and he's staying with his sister for a month.'

Meg gave him a half-smile. 'So you're the temporary barman. Davey said something about you visiting a few weeks ago. Good luck with avoiding Christmas… you couldn't have come in a worse month.' They reached the outskirts of what was probably Lockton and Tom stared out as they passed an enormous tree decorated with tinsel and glass baubles, before they pulled up outside Apple Cross Inn.

After Meg had zoomed off down the high street in her ridiculous van, Tom stood just inside the door of the pub and took in the low ceilings, green walls and small bar which was busy with customers. In the corner of the cosy room a fire roared. Beside that, a Christmas tree twinkled with red and green lights and clusters of shiny baubles. Tom swallowed and took another step forwards as the song that had been filling the room changed.

He recognised the tune immediately, the soulful mix of bass guitar, drums and keyboards – the words he'd written that first Christmas morning he'd woken with his new wife, Marnie. He'd been living in a bubble, a fame-fuelled, money-soaked, artificial world. Where nothing mattered but his next hit, the newest way to stroke his already-inflated ego. A couple of years before he'd left his band as the whole house of cards had come tumbling down – and he'd realised the sorry truth about himself and his life.

Something twisted in his gut but he couldn't put a name to it. Sometimes it was hard to articulate what he felt. Which, for a man who'd made his name transcribing every tear, laugh and minute emotion so he could add a soundtrack to it and share it with the world, was irony at its best. Tom stood for the whole three minutes and thirty-eight seconds that the song played, unable to move his feet. Cooper stayed beside him – man's best friend, and aside from Davey and his grandfather, the only real one he had in the world.

'Tom.' Davey spotted him almost the instant the song ended and strode across the pub, beaming. They hadn't seen each other for almost three years, when Davey had been both witness and saviour as Tom's life had collapsed. Davey was one of the few people who'd wanted to continue to know Tom after he'd walked away from his career – and had helped him pick up the pieces in those first few weeks. His friend looked good, younger somehow. His tall, wiry frame had filled out since they'd last seen each other, and his blue eyes were still sharp but he looked more relaxed. 'Meg just called from her van to tell me you had car trouble and to see if I could help. I spoke to a friend at the bar who has the same make and he'll lend you a tyre until we can get yours fixed. I'll help you get it sorted tomorrow.'

'Thanks,' Tom said, taken aback, not used to simple acts of kindness that demanded nothing in return. 'The pub looks good – you too.'

Davey slapped him gently on the back. 'Give it a couple of weeks and Lockton will work its magic on you. Do you want me to take you to the cottage?'

'The bar looks busy,' Tom observed. 'Don't you need some help?' There were more people waiting at the counter now, and a lone woman with curly red hair tied in bunches that trailed down her back was serving them.

'Matilda will be fine, and I didn't expect you to start working the moment you arrived. Remember my twin, Johnny?'

'No, sorry.' He'd forgotten a lot of good people he'd met in the old days; for some reason he'd always seemed to hang on to the wrong ones. None of those had lasted the course. When he'd walked away from his career, he'd been less appealing for most.

'He lives here too and makes all the food for the pub, so he'll help if it's needed. He put some meals together for you so your fridge is full, and there are tins for the dog just in case you run out.' Davey paused for long enough to scratch Cooper's head. 'I'll take you to where you'll be staying so you can settle in, and we can catch up properly tomorrow.'

The cottage was only a five-minute drive away in Davey's truck, which attacked the snow like a pro. The double-fronted building was situated in the middle of nowhere and there were no close neighbours that Tom could see. Davey parked in front and they all hopped out. The building was separated from the surrounding fields by a hip-level brick wall which framed a small garden that would probably be overflowing with wildflowers in the summer, but at the moment was swimming in snow. Davey opened a wrought-iron gate which squeaked and headed for the front door, creating a dotted pathway with his footsteps.

As they approached, Tom read the small sign above the door. 'Christmas Cottage?' he asked, shaking his head, wondering if this whole day was some kind of cosmic joke.

'Came with the house,' Davey said. 'I figure it'll go down well with the tourists.'

The heating in the cottage must have been turned on earlier, because the air was warm when they walked inside. Cooper instantly trotted through the hall into a sitting room, homing in on the grate of an open fireplace in the corner, and sniffing at the unlit pieces of wood. 'I'm thinking of offering the place as a rental,' Davey explained, switching on three large lamps which threw a cosy light across the surfaces, picking out the white painted walls. There were a couple of brown leather sofas facing the fireplace and a huge, fluffy red rug which the dog slumped onto with a weary groan. 'There are two bedrooms, both made up so choose whichever you want, a bathroom, kitchen-diner and boot room where you can store all of your stuff. It's small but perfectly formed.' He flashed an easy smile which lit his handsome face. 'I didn't have time to get you any Christmas decorations, but Meg has a shop in town if you want to pick something up – I'll pay for them. I'm guessing they'll come in handy when I rent the place.'

'I'm good.' Tom grimaced as his mind lingered on the blonde, blue-eyed elf. 'I'd rather keep the place bauble-free.' A fitting metaphor for his life.

Davey looked like he was going to say something but in the end he shrugged. 'Suit yourself. All the materials for the new kitchen are in the shed in the garden. I didn't think you'd want them getting under your feet. But please don't feel like you have to do DIY while you're staying. You're doing me enough of a favour helping out at the pub.'

'I want to.' Tom had offered to put in new kitchen units for Davey – both as a thank you for having him and because he pre-ferred to keep busy. To offset the feelings of emptiness he couldn't seem to shake.

'You've no close neighbours,' Davey continued. 'So if you want to play your music loud, feel free.' He pointed to a beautiful Gibson guitar set on a stand in the corner of the room. 'I got it out of storage. One of the bands I worked with gifted it to me when I moved up here, but as you know I'm not blessed with musical genes.'

'I don't play anymore,' Tom said, ignoring the tingle in his fingers as they conjured the feel of the taut strings. Muscle memory, intent on torturing him.

Davey raised an eyebrow. 'I didn't know that. Seems a shame to waste all your talent.'

Tom shrugged. 'You should get back to the pub. I'll come in early tomorrow.'

Davey's forehead creased but he nodded. 'How about ten? I can pick you up.'

'I'll walk. It's not that far and I'll need to take Cooper out anyway.'

'You can bring him to work if you want. Johnny loves dogs and he's not going anywhere tomorrow. Borrow anything you need from the boot room when you go outside.' Davey pointed towards the hall before heading for the front door.

After he'd left, Tom took a quick look around the house. It was cosy and clean, and would suit him and Cooper fine until the end of the month. There was dog food in one of the kitchen cupboards so he fed Cooper and wandered into the sitting room, aware all the time of the guitar standing in the corner, calling to him. Sighing, Tom picked it up and put it carefully into the boot room along with the stand and shut the door, leaning his head against it for a moment. As he did, his mobile found a signal and began to ring.

'Sonny.' Tom's grandfather, Jack Riley, sounded bright and cheery.

'How's the cruise?' Tom asked, contemplating whether he should light the fire to give himself something to do.

'A hit. I've made a posse of friends already and we've all been invited onto the captain's table tonight. I'm heading to a poker game in a minute, I've plans to fleece some guests. The weather's good – which you'd expect in the Caribbean. I think the only thing missing from this experience is your grandmother. She'd have loved it.' He paused. 'And you.'

'It was *your* Christmas present. Besides, I had business here.' Tom swallowed the ball of guilt his grandfather wouldn't appreciate, wondering if there was any Jack Daniel's in the kitchen. He didn't drink much anymore, but suddenly felt a little homesick, and bourbon always reminded him of celebrations with his grandparents. There hadn't been any of those these last three years.

'I still miss her, but I feel like she's here somewhere, watching me. She'd have got a real kick out of this boat, would have made me walk every deck at least four times trying to see if we could spot anyone famous.' Jack laughed. 'Then she'd have spent the rest of the day boasting about you.'

Tom nodded because the words wouldn't come. His grandmother had been dead for almost three years and he still found it hard to talk about her. 'How are you feeling?' He sat on the sofa and sank into the leather, shaking his head at Cooper when he looked tempted to hop up. The dog came to place his head on one of Tom's feet, earning himself a stroke.

'Good – no heart attacks, strokes or headaches if that's what you're asking. This cruise is just the tonic I needed. I'm fine, sonny. It's been three years, you need to stop worrying.'

'Worrying is part of loving someone,' Tom murmured, repeating one of his grandmother's favourite phrases, then almost kicking himself when he recognised the words.

'I recall your band recording a song about that.' His grandfather hummed a little of the tune. 'So what are your plans for Christmas?'

'Usual.' Tom frowned. 'Although I'm not sure where I'll get a Chinese takeaway around here. Not without a magic carpet.'

'Alone again?'

Tom nodded. 'Just the way I like it.'

His grandfather sighed. 'Not every woman you meet is going to be like Marnie. You'll need to take a chance on someone again at some point…'

'I loved her,' Tom said simply. 'I let her down.'

'She let you down, Tom – and she wasn't the first.' He puffed out a breath. They'd had this conversation a million times and neither of them had the appetite to repeat it. 'Where are you exactly?'

'In Scotland, visiting a friend.' Tom unlaced his wet shoes and pushed them off as Cooper went to eye the fireplace. The wind outside kicked up a notch, making the chimney whistle. 'I'll be here for a few weeks. I'll try to find a landline number so you can call me at the pub where I'll be working.'

'Are you performing?' Jack sounded hopeful.

'Nope. I'll be staying out of trouble, serving behind the bar.'

His grandfather sighed. 'Music's in your soul, sonny – and you're not going to be happy until you pick that guitar back up. I've told you that a million times.'

'And I'm still ignoring you,' Tom said, as his chest ached.

'You're supposed to listen to your elders.' His grandfather snorted. 'Then again, I didn't listen to mine. I'll have to wait until life teaches you the lessons I can't. Or your grandmother sends you a sign.'

'She's gone,' Tom said. 'And I've learned all the lessons I want.' Which was the reason he'd never pick up a guitar again. 'Talking of learning lessons, I'll be putting a kitchen in while I'm here – drawing on everything you taught me.' Tom smiled, remembering helping his grandfather with some DIY once. Then recalling the trip to the hospital when Jack had tried to slice his finger off.

'I was always better at gardening.' His grandfather chuckled. 'Jokes aside, you can't keep drifting. It's just another form of running.'

'I'm giving back,' Tom said quietly.

'You gave the world so much already with your music. You don't owe it a thing,' his grandfather said gently, before the signal suddenly cut out, leaving Tom alone, staring at the phone, wishing he was right.

Chapter Three

Apple Cross Inn was buzzing when Meg made her way into the entrance, stomping her feet on the mat to get rid of the worst of the snow. She pulled her coat off so she could hang it on one of the hooks by the pub door already heaving with jackets. It was the fifth of December and she was feeling a little put out that after days of calling her mum and dad's phones, and emailing, she hadn't been able to get in touch with either of them. After the message her dad had left a couple of weeks before, she hadn't been able to pin him down to a proper conversation. She knew everyone was okay because she'd received a direct message from her sister who still lived at home. Despite that, Meg had an uneasy feeling in the pit of her stomach.

'Here for the Jam Club meeting?' Agnes greeted Meg as she approached the bar with Cora and Fergus, who was pulling grumpy faces at everyone. 'We're in the usual place.' Agnes inclined her head towards a small room off to the side of the pub where the weekly Jam Club meetings took place. Meg had joined the sessions in the summer, when she'd put her shop on the line in a bet with Lilith Romano, owner and chef at Lockton Hotel. They'd both vowed to win the annual Lockton Jampionships and, with the help of her best friend Evie Stuart, Meg had won – and discovered a new love of cooking. She was still finding her feet in that department, but enjoyed the weekly gatherings.

'Cora's got some Christmas jam to share.' Agnes threw an arm around her friend's shoulder.

Cora sighed and pointed to the hessian shopping bag filled with glass jars by her feet. 'I made a promise to find a jam that Marcus likes before Christmas.' She shook her head sadly. 'I've tried blackberry, strawberry, gooseberry, even cranberry with a twist. He hates them all. I'm hoping someone at the Jam Club can suggest something new.'

Marcus Dougall, a policeman who serviced Lockton and the surrounding area, was well known for his dislike of all things jam-related. Cora was hoping her Christmas Promise, along with a little of the wishing well magic, would help her to come up with a recipe he'd love.

'The man's an *ee*—' Fergus clamped his mouth shut before opening it again. 'Embarrassment,' he finished, looking ruffled. 'There's not a Scotsman alive who doesn't like jam.'

Agnes chuckled. 'Fergus has promised not to call anyone an eejit for the whole month,' she explained. Her eyes shone as she patted his hand. 'It's not an easy task.'

'And Agnes has promised not to interfere with anyone's love life. So you and the rest of the single population in and around Lockton can relax, Meg.' Fergus's grey eyes gleamed as he stroked her hand in return.

'Love will find a way with or without my help.' Agnes grinned as she blew him a kiss. 'Speaking of love, I heard from my beautiful granddaughter earlier.'

'She called me yesterday too.' Meg nodded, wishing her friend Evie were here. But after meeting 'the one', Callum Ryder, when he'd stayed on Buttermead Farm in the summer, Evie had fallen pregnant and the pair had decided to spend a couple of months at Callum's home in New York. 'She's having a wonderful time.'

'They're a good match.' Agnes smiled. 'But I can tell you're missing your friend.'

Meg shrugged. In truth she had been a little lonely. She loved Lockton, but her dad's message had worried her. She didn't like talking about her problems, had only just begun to open up to Evie, and now she had no one to confide in. But she didn't want to bother her friend when she was miles from home.

Agnes gave Meg's shoulder a quick squeeze as someone sounded a bell in the other room. 'That'll be Morag, we'd better not keep her. Remember, I'm always at the farm if you want to talk. See you in a wee minute, lassie.' Agnes followed Fergus and Cora as they made their way to the meeting.

Meg felt her insides jerk in unwelcome response as Tom walked up to serve her. He looked less tired than he had a few days before, although just as dishevelled. His almost-black hair tickled the top of his fitted shirt and a five o'clock shadow darkened his jaw. His eyes dipped to Meg's sweatshirt, which had a sparkly Christmas tree printed on the front, before sliding up to her face which she'd dusted with glitter. She'd swiped extra on earlier after another unsuccessful attempt to call her dad. 'I'm not sure whether to serve you or hang a bauble on you,' he said with a smile, as he smoothed a cloth across the bar.

'I'll have a mulled wine, please,' Meg replied archly, determined to keep him at arm's length. Tom's brown eyes sparked with something that could have been humour before he nodded. 'Since you mention baubles, have you heard about the Christmas Promise Tree?' she asked. Meg watched as Tom picked up a bottle of margarita mix and added a dose into a cocktail shaker without answering, then sloshed in a dash of orange liqueur before turning his back. 'That doesn't look like wine,' Meg observed grumpily.

'It isn't,' Tom said. 'It's a thank you for the rescue and chocolate bar the other day. If you don't like it, I'll get your wine. It's on me.'

'It's not necessary.' Meg sighed, trying to hang on to her dislike. He looked good without his coat. His jeans were dark and fitted, he had long legs and a bum with just the right amount of curve. His black shirt was tight enough that she could trace his spine upwards to broad shoulders that stretched the cotton every now and again as he worked. His hair was a little too long and scraped the edges his collar. If it weren't for his feelings on Christmas, Meg might have fancied him. She ignored the tingles working their way across her skin as she watched.

'Davey mentioned the village promise and the concert you're putting on.' Tom finally answered her question.

'And did anyone tell you that you can make a promise of your own?'

Tom shook his head, threw a handful of sugared cranberries onto the top of the drink and gave it a stir, before placing it in front of her without ceremony. 'I call it The Worst Noel,' he said. 'My own creation – better not get behind the wheel of your van until you've given it a chance to wear off. Since you're not dressed as an elf, I'm guessing you're not working tonight?' Tom watched her closely.

She sipped. The drink was good, creamy with a citrus flavour and enough alcohol to make her lips buzz. 'It's nice.'

'You sound disappointed,' he said, as she put the glass back on the bar.

Meg shrugged. 'It could do with some edible glitter and a new name – something less anti-Christmas. I feel like you're trying to get me to renounce my favourite season. In case you were wondering, it won't work.'

'It was worth a try.' His eyes twinkled. 'What would you call it?'

'Elf's Delight.'

Tom snorted. '*You* can call it that if you like – I'm sticking with my name, and I'm not sure why you'd want your insides to sparkle, you've enough of the stuff on the outside.' His eyes skimmed her cheekbones.

Meg picked up the glass and took another sip. 'There's no such thing as too much glitter.' Her hormones did a little happy dance when his lips quirked.

'I'm guessing those words are tattooed across your chest?'

She gave him one of her deadpan stares, wondering why she was flirting. 'We elves never reveal where our tattoos are located. How are you settling in?' she added when his eyes darkened, making the tingles across her skin leap downwards in response. There was something about his face, something familiar. It was as if she'd known him for years. Which was crazy, and exactly the kind of thing Agnes would pounce on if she said it.

Tom shrugged. 'Fine.'

'Where are you from? I feel like we've met.'

Tom frowned. 'I'm pretty sure I'd remember you.' His eyes skimmed her cheeks again. 'I'm from down south – for the last few years I've moved all around the country.'

'Are you trying to figure out where you fit?'

'Something like that.' He nodded without looking at her. 'You? Your accent doesn't scream North Pole quite as much as your wardrobe.'

She smiled. 'I'm from London originally, I've lived in Lockton for three years. No plans to change that.' Tom put his hands in his pockets. 'So are you going to make a Christmas Promise?' Meg cocked her head. He looked so uncomfortable she almost felt sorry for him.

'I don't make promises – I've a habit of not keeping them.' Tom looked serious.

'Not trying something is the same as failing at it,' Lilith interrupted across Meg's shoulder, startling her and making Tom's chin jerk up. His expression was all relief as Lilith sidestepped Meg and leaned on the bar. Lilith was of Italian descent, in her early thirties, and a couple of inches taller than Meg's five foot two. She had a curvy body, a mouth to match it and eyes the colour of coal. She'd wound her long, dark hair onto the top of her head and wore a pair of immaculate designer jeans, a silky pink blouse that set off her olive skin and a set of boots with sky-high heels that had no business being out in the snow. 'At least, that's what my papa tells me,' Lilith added, shooting her eyes across the counter until they fixed on Meg's drink. 'What's that?'

'I call it The Worst Noel,' Tom replied. 'Want one? If you're driving I can tone it down.'

Lilith chuckled. '*Sì*. I have a lift lined up with someone staying at the hotel, so don't hold back on anything. I'm surprised you're drinking that, Meg – it doesn't even have a Christmas-themed straw.' She shook her head at the glass as the tune in the background changed to a Christmas song, and Meg noticed Tom tense. He turned away from the bar as he assembled the drink, leaving Meg feeling strangely bereft.

'You here for the meeting?' Lilith's tone was a lot less hostile than it would have been a few months before. Since Meg had beaten her in the Jampionships, Lilith had been driving some of her hotel guests to Meg's shop. They'd formed an uneasy alliance when, in turn, Meg had begun to recommend the hotel to hikers and other drop-in customers.

'Yes,' Meg said simply, sipping more of the cocktail.

'The Jam Club's started, you should—' Davey wandered through the door that led to the kitchen behind the bar and stopped dead when he saw Lilith draped across it. His cheeks flushed, and he opened and closed his mouth as if searching for his next breath.

Tom tipped his head towards the room the others had headed for earlier as he handed Lilith the cocktail and took her money. 'You don't want to miss anything.' He glanced at Davey, who was standing in the same place, gazing at Lilith. 'Besides, Davey, you were going to show me where you keep the spare red wine in the back.' He suddenly snapped his gaze in the direction of the kitchen. 'Is that Johnny shouting?'

Meg couldn't hear anyone and Davey just looked confused.

'We'd better go.' Meg picked up her drink and stepped away from the bar, steering Lilith in the same direction, reluctantly charmed by Tom's efforts to save his friend from embarrassing himself any more. 'I assume you're here for the Jam Club too?'

Lilith shook her head. 'I came to speak to Morag about a parcel I'm expecting, but I suppose I could join you for a while.'

'Cora needs some ideas for a new Christmas jam – perhaps you could suggest some Italian recipes?' Meg guided Lilith towards the Jam Club, conscious of Tom's gaze on them. Wondering why the man with the dark brown eyes and dislike of Christmas interested her quite so much.

Chapter Four

Tom drove carefully as he navigated towards the same spot on the road where he'd punctured his tyre a week before. The car was fixed now and his spare had been replaced, but he wasn't taking any chances. Snow had stopped falling for the first time in days. The downpour had been almost constant since he'd left this morning for Morridon to pick up more supplies for Davey's kitchen. He turned on the radio, snatching his hand back as if he'd been bitten when he heard a fuzzy rendition of 'If Every Day Was Christmas'. The song he'd written and recorded with The Ballad Club a few years before. It had shot into the charts immediately, but he hadn't heard it for months – he switched the radio off.

His thoughts slid to Meg as he passed the spot where she'd picked him up in her Christmas van, remembering the glitter across her cheeks when he'd served her in the pub and the sparks of warmth in her blue eyes. Then he bounced over a snowy hillock in the road and, as he did, noticed a couple of figures walking in the distance, dragging suitcases through the snow. They were moving slowly, leaving tiny wheel-tracks in their wake. As Tom drew closer he slowed the car and wound his window down. In the back, Cooper hopped up so he could press his nose against the glass.

'Are you okay?' Tom asked, bringing the car to a complete stop, suppressing a shudder at the blast of frigid air. The walkers were both women, neither very tall. One was older with short blonde hair covered almost entirely by a red beret. She wore a matching snowsuit and thick boots that wouldn't have been out of place in the Alps. She was attractive, probably in her late forties. Her mouth looked like it had spent a lot of its life making worried shapes, and as a result was framed by deep lines. A girl with the same heart-shaped face and blonde hair stood beside her, looking miserable. She had a pack on her back, a guitar bag in one hand and the handle of her suitcase in the crook of her other arm. If Tom had to guess, he'd say she was around eighteen. Her hair had been pushed inside a black bobble hat and her snowsuit looked too small – it was constricting rather than hugging her body and ended just above her boots, leaving a silver of vivid pink skin exposed to the elements.

'How far is Lockton?' the older woman asked, searching the white road as if she could conjure up a tropical oasis. You couldn't see the village yet, just the top of a hill. But Tom knew if they continued walking, it would be dark before they arrived.

'It's a way still,' he said. 'I'm headed in that direction, I can give you a lift.'

The woman moved her frown from the road to him, flicking her eyes to the back window where Cooper was staring at them. 'Is it safe?'

'He's more inclined to lick you than bite – and I'm not an axe-murderer.' Tom tried a joke but it was greeted with silence.

'I'm not sure you'd admit to it if you were,' the girl muttered through chattering teeth. Without waiting for the older woman to respond, or for Tom to help, she opened the back door and climbed up, encouraging Cooper to move to the other side of the seat as he attempted to lick her.

'Emily,' the woman squeaked, going pale. 'I know you adore animals but that dog might bite – you could end up with worms, or something far worse.'

The girl patted Cooper on the head as she took off her pack, then lifted the huge suitcase up with both hands and plonked it by her feet, pulling the guitar bag onto her lap and closing the door. 'Relax, Mum, he's really friendly. Besides, I'm prepared to risk it. It's either that or hypothermia. As you've probably guessed, I'm Emily.' The girl reached her icy gloved hand into the front.

Tom turned and took it as the older woman let out an uneasy sigh and stomped carefully around the front of the car, before climbing into the passenger side with her luggage. 'Kitty.' She gave Tom a cautious handshake before linking her fingers and placing them in her lap, glancing over her shoulder uneasily at Cooper.

'Tom.' He closed his window and switched the heat up to maximum. 'Where to?'

'Meg's Christmas Shop and Cafe,' Kitty answered. 'Apparently it's somewhere on the village high street?'

Tom nodded and set off slowly, wondering how the women knew Meg and if she was expecting them. 'Did you have car trouble?' he asked after a few moments, feeling honour-bound to fill the awkward silence. He could see the girl in the back glancing at her mobile and hoped she hadn't recognised him. He'd let his hair grow and had been contemplating cultivating a beard, but hadn't got round to it. Besides, he hadn't been recognised that often even when he had been in the business. Fans had been more familiar with the whole band and their music than the members' individual looks.

'We got a bus from Inverness airport and it dropped us in a place called Morridon.' Kitty sounded frustrated. 'I had a taxi booked from there, but the man got a call from his wife because his daughter had just gone into early labour so he had to turn back. He offered to find us another driver when we arrived in Morridon, but—'

'Mum didn't want to wait,' Emily muttered. 'She thought we could walk so asked him to drop us where we were – but it was further than we expected and we're not really dressed for the cold.'

Kitty fiddled with the collar of her puffy jacket. 'If you'd let me buy you a new snowsuit when I asked, you wouldn't be wearing the one I got you three years ago. You'll catch your death.' She glared at Emily's outfit. 'You've only just got over your last illness.'

'I wasn't expecting to make a last-minute trip to the North Pole. It's not like I need to dress like the Michelin Man in North London, and I'm as fit and healthy as you are.' Emily was looking at her screen again, her nimble fingers skipping across it. 'There's no signal.' Her tone was indignant. 'Does anyone even have a phone up here?'

'The signal's patchy.' Tom supressed a smile. 'Keep trying and you'll get one every now and again. When it appears, it's worth making the most of it.'

'How do people communicate?' Emily shoved the mobile into her pocket with a heavy sigh of disgust.

'They use their mouths,' Kitty said. 'I'm sure you'll get used to it after a while. It'll do you good to meet some new people. You spend far too much time on that phone. It's not healthy. You've been looking very pale these last few weeks.'

Emily caught Tom's gaze in the rear-view mirror and pulled a face. Then her eyes suddenly narrowed and she leaned forward, as if trying to get a better look. Tom dipped his head, hoping it put his face into shadow, and watched the road, relieved they were getting closer to Lockton. 'So you're from London?' he asked, as Emily leaned back and began to tap a tune onto the guitar case with her fingertips. It had a solid beat and Tom had to stop his foot from tapping along or his mind from forming lyrics.

'Yes,' Kitty said reluctantly, turning her head to look at the mountains to their right and letting out an almost imperceptible 'wow'. 'We left before dawn. The flight was delayed and it took longer to get here than I thought.'

'We're visiting my sister. She moved up three years ago. It was the furthest she could get from us without emigrating,' Emily joked. Her fingers stopped tapping and she frowned. 'Her name is Meg Scott. You might know her?'

'We've met.' Tom nodded, forcing back the jolt of awareness when her face filled his mind. 'Staying long?' He hoped it would be a brief trip. He could feel Emily's attention fixed on the back of his head, imagined the shimmer of confusion in her eyes as she tried to work out why he looked familiar.

'Not sure yet,' Kitty answered. 'I'm a health and safety consultant and I can work anywhere, so our plans are fluid. We've not seen Meg for months.'

'I just hope she's got decent WiFi,' Emily cut in.

'Your sister's not a Luddite.' Her mother sighed. 'At least, I hope not,' she added.

'Is Meg expecting you?' Tom wasn't sure why he seemed so determined to extend the conversation.

'Oh no, this is going to be a *big* surprise,' Emily said.

'I'm sure your sister will be delighted to see us.' But Kitty sounded worried, and they all lapsed into silence.

As the car reached the edge of Lockton, Tom let out a relieved breath. They drove slowly past the Christmas Promise Tree which was dotted with more glass baubles now, all filled with pieces of paper in a selection of bright colours. The number had multiplied in the days since Tom had arrived in the village. There were handmade decorations hanging on fences and lampposts too, and a garland had been strewn around the wishing well – complete with knitted musical instruments, baubles, snowmen and a couple of Father Christmases.

After another minute, Tom pulled up outside Meg's shop, taking in the charming grey-fronted facade and pretty gold lettering on the sign. A mixture of glass baubles and tinsel had been hung around the windows, and a dozen or so Christmas trees wrapped in white netting leaned against the glass on either side of the door. Everything outside was covered in a thin layer of snow that sparkled in the cold air. The lights were on in the shop, signalling it was still open. Tom hopped out of his car as Kitty unlocked her door and hauled the suitcase onto the snow without waiting. He opened the back and took the guitar bag from Emily, ignoring the wrench in the pit of his stomach that he hadn't been expecting. He helped her down and grabbed the suitcase, heaving them both to Meg's store where they joined Kitty.

'Thank you,' Kitty said. 'I'm sorry I was a bit miserable in the car – travelling always brings out the worst in me, especially when things don't go to plan. I was worried about Emily.' She pushed the shop door open and a ginger tabby cat darted from behind one of the nearby trees into the store as 'Jingle Bells' began to play, signalling their arrival. Then Kitty rolled her suitcase onto the dark wooden floor, and turned to hold the door open for Emily.

Her daughter stood for a moment as she checked Tom out, her eyes narrowing again as she scoured his face. He found himself holding his breath until she finally shook her head and smiled shyly. 'Thanks for helping us.'

'No problem.' He shrugged, backing away a little, catching sight of a snowman shape through the decorated windows. Emily took the suitcase and held her hand out for the guitar, and Tom reluctantly handed it over, instantly missing the familiar weight. Then he stood on the pavement, watching as the door shut behind them, muffling the sound of 'Jingle Bells'.

Tom opened his car door, and as he climbed into the driver's seat he forced himself not to turn and glance through the shop window again to see if he could catch a glimpse of Meg.

Chapter Five

Meg placed more glass baubles into the cardboard box in her stockroom, ready for when she would take them to the Promise Tree later. They'd been selling like hotcakes today as people rushed to get their promises ready before it was too late, especially now it was the eighth of December. She hummed happily as 'Jingle Bells' began to play, signalling another customer, and placed the last few baubles into the box before heading into the shop – where she came to a sudden stop. Standing beside the five-foot inflatable snowman she'd put out earlier, like something out of a bad dream, were her sister and mother.

Both women had suitcases by their feet and Emily had brought her guitar. Meg knew her sister wouldn't be parted from her instrument for more than a couple of days, which suggested this wasn't a fleeting visit. 'Mum? Emily?' Meg squeaked, putting the box down as she forced herself to step forward and accept hugs from both of them. 'I didn't know you were coming.' She kept her tone light even as her heart thundered.

'We wanted to surprise you.' Kitty grimaced.

Her mother didn't like surprises – her life was ruled by order and lists. Meg's forehead creased as she searched the shop, glancing at the door with a sinking feeling. 'Where's Dad?'

'At home.' Kitty frowned at the floor where a large puddle was forming under Emily's suitcase – snow from outside melting in the warmth. 'You should clear that up before one of your customers slips.'

'I will. Isn't Dad joining you?' Meg asked, sighing as her mother grabbed a large tissue out of her handbag and began to mop up the mess.

'He's staying in London.' Kitty swallowed. 'He's got things to do… meetings to attend.' Her tone was bitter.

Meg took in her sister's strained expression.

'I wondered…' Kitty's eyes darted to Emily as she stood holding the tissue, which was now dripping. 'We wondered if we could stay for a while. I booked a return flight for the twenty-first. We won't be any trouble. I've been meaning to visit for ages… and since you're not coming home for Christmas, it'll give us a chance to catch up.'

Meg nodded slowly. She couldn't say no. Besides, two weeks wasn't that long. And if her dad wasn't around, perhaps things would be different? Meg had stopped trying to have a relationship with her family years ago. Especially since the distance between them – even before she'd moved away – had grown. Maybe this would give them a chance to change that?

'I'm going to find a bin for this tissue,' Kitty said abruptly, heading towards the back of the shop.

'You don't have to have us here.' Emily must have read Meg's expression. She hadn't seen her sister for almost a year. They'd never been close, due to the twelve-year age difference. Her sibling had been a surprise – a late present, her dad frequently joked. Meg had recently wondered if Emily had been a bid to deal with the rifts in her parents' marriage, an attempt that clearly hadn't worked. 'I'd say no if it were me. We all know you moved up to get away from us. It's not like we're much fun to be around,' Emily said.

'Don't be silly.' Meg grabbed her sister's suitcase, surprised by the rush of affection that flooded through her. Emily sounded sad, but every attempt Meg had made to discuss their parents' marriage and the atmosphere at home had been brushed off in the past with a cheery 'everything's fine'. In the end she'd stopped asking, assuming it was only her that was bothered by it. Emily had always seemed far less sensitive.

'Ugh!' her mother suddenly shrieked from behind the till. 'That cat is down here. That can't be healthy, Meg – you run a cafe. You need to shoo it out.'

'She's a stray,' Meg soothed, heading to where her mother was now glaring at the ginger tabby curled up on a bed of silver tinsel. 'I'm hoping to find her a home,' she admitted. 'I'd have her myself but I can't because of my hamster, Blitzen. She's no trouble – she's been coming inside to sleep for the last few weeks.'

'You need to get rid of that thing before someone sees,' Kitty advised.

'It's all in hand,' Meg lied. 'I live above the shop.' She turned away from the cat and led them both into a small hallway behind the till. To their right was a tiny cloakroom where Cora and any other staff could put their possessions. Behind that was a loo, and at the back a large room they used as a stockroom. Stairs led from the hall to Meg's flat. She steered them up, pulling Emily's heavy suitcase behind her. 'How are you feeling?' Meg asked.

'I'm fine.' Emily's tone was smooth, but Meg could detect a hint of annoyance underneath it. 'Nothing wrong here, no need to fuss.'

'Emily needs to take it easy – it can take months to recover from glandular fever and she only started getting better in October.' Her mother must have overheard. 'That's why you're taking a gap year, after all.'

'I didn't want to go to university this year because I'm really not sure an accountancy degree is the right direction for me… I've never been excited by numbers.' Emily sighed heavily but didn't turn around.

'Nonsense. It's a wonderful, solid profession.' Kitty waved her hand. 'You need to take a hot bath as soon as we get settled. You must have got cold, that snowsuit's way too small, and heaven knows what germs that dog gave you.'

'Dog?' Meg asked, as Emily let out another heavy sigh.

'The man who gave us a lift had one. I'm okay.' Emily clutched the guitar case firmly in front of her like a barrier as she followed Meg up the stairs. 'I was over the dreaded "disease" before I even deferred my uni place.'

'Better safe than sorry.' Kitty repeated her favourite mantra. The one Meg remembered her saying daily during her teens. 'Besides, it's been a nice bonus having you at home for a little longer. God knows what I'm going to do when you leave.'

When they reached the top of the stairs and Meg's small, cosy hallway with its wooden floorboards, bright orange rug and white fairy lights hanging across the ceiling, Meg pulled a face. Her bedroom was at the end of the hallway facing the high street, with a clear view of the mountains. To the right sat a small sitting room, then a kitchen-diner, bathroom and double bedroom – her only spare. Could she put her mum in the same room as her sister? One look at Emily's weary expression decided it for her.

'Mum, why don't you go in there? It's all made up.' Meg pointed to the double room. 'Emily, we'll share. It'll give us a chance to catch up.' She opened the door of her bedroom and walked over to a chair on the right which was overflowing with clothes. Meg scooped them up and made space in the bottom of her wardrobe. 'I'll clear a drawer for you later. For now, put your things on there.'

Emily stood in the doorway and took in the room, and Meg followed her gaze. She'd painted the walls herself when she'd moved in with her then-boyfriend, Ned Adams, three years earlier. They were white, and had once been clear of pictures. But Meg had gradually filled each wall with photographs. Some were Christmas-themed: there was the front of her shop; Davey dressed as Santa Claus visiting Lockton primary school; and a shot of Christmas Tree Farm which lay a couple of miles outside town. The rest were of the people she'd met and places she'd been to around Lockton. Emily must have noticed there were none of their family, but she didn't comment. Instead she placed her guitar carefully on the floor and glanced at the unmade bed, and then at the hamster cage balanced on the edge of a cluttered, white dressing table.

'The bed is queen-size so there's plenty of room for us to share.' Meg pulled the duvet up, straightening the sheet and fluffing the pillows. 'That's Blitzen.' She picked up a sunflower seed from a pink earring bowl and pushed it through the bars as a plump, honey-coloured hamster waddled out. He grabbed the seed and shoved it into his mouth, then disappeared back into the sawdust shavings. 'He's the closest I have to a boyfriend right now,' Meg joked, hoping her sister would laugh.

'He's cuter than some of the men you dated in London.' Emily snorted her approval, then went to peer into the cage.

'So, why are you really here?' Meg perched on the edge of her bed, relaxing a little. Emily seemed different, a little more open than when Meg had been home for Christmas a year before. Not that her sister had been around much then. It was almost like she'd been avoiding everyone.

'I've no idea. Mum booked us on an early morning flight at midnight last night and told me to pack,' Emily explained. 'Dad had organised an appointment for them somewhere and she went mad. She's been a bit odd recently. Dad thinks it's because she's going to turn fifty in January…' Emily turned her blue eyes towards Meg. 'They're not fighting. No more than usual. It's just lots of long silences. Then sometimes everything's great.' She pulled a face. 'I really can't figure them out. Most of the time I don't try.' She exhaled, looking around the room. 'It's nice to come here though, I could do with a break – hopefully Mum will spend all of her time fussing over you. The big, bad sister who left a decent job in the city so she could run away and open a Christmas shop. She still thinks you've lost your mind,' she joked. 'Or inhaled too much glitter when you were a baby.'

'She's probably right.' Meg smiled. Her mother had never understood her, but she'd come to terms with that. In truth, they didn't understand each other. They'd never been able to communicate, at least not since she'd been a teenager. So now Meg didn't try.

'Can I get a glass of water?' Emily asked suddenly.

'I'll get you one. You unpack.' Meg headed to the kitchen before her sister could object. She tidied away her dirty breakfast and lunch things and some bowls from last night, putting them into the dishwasher and wiping the countertops before grabbing a glass from one of the cupboards.

As she did, her mother wandered in with her laptop and sat at the small kitchen table next to the window. She settled herself, smoothing the green and red Christmas-themed tablecloth, and switched on her computer. 'It's been so long since I logged on. The mobile signal wasn't good enough on our journey for me to get my messages.' Kitty sighed. 'God knows what's happened in the last twenty-four hours.' She swiped a hand across her forehead, looking worried.

'Do you want a cup of tea?' Meg asked.

Kitty frowned, but nodded. 'I found your WiFi code on the back of the router in the sitting room. I hope it's okay if I log in? It's a busy time of year and I don't want to miss any messages.' Her mother's job gave her an outlet for all her stressing, but also meant she was hyper aware of the million ways a person could hurt themselves. Her eyes darted to the glass baubles Meg had hung precariously from the lights above them.

'Sure.' Meg nodded.

Kitty continued to take in the room. It was filled with an array of Christmas ornaments on the windowsill and there were strings of lights decorating most of the kitchen surfaces. 'You certainly throw yourself into the season.' Kitty's tone wasn't critical, but she'd never understood Meg's love of Christmas, or why it made her so content. Which was ironic because the whole thing had stemmed from her childhood. When Christmas had been the one day her family had connected, although even that was getting tired now. Perhaps they'd all just got sick of pretending? 'How's your shop doing?'

'Good.' Meg switched the kettle on and found a mug. 'It's been busy. I've sold a lot of baubles for the Christmas Promise Tree and introduced a new range of inflatable characters. The trees are selling really well…' She looked up but her mother was tapping the WiFi code into her computer, then watching the mass of emails gather in her inbox. Meg let out a long breath, finished making the hot drink and placed it on the table next to the laptop. Then she picked up the glass of water and headed back to her bedroom, trying not to feel disappointed. She'd never been able to connect with her family, had always felt like an outsider, and clearly nothing had changed. She was just glad it was only Emily and her mother, and that they'd be gone by Christmas. She could definitely handle that.

Chapter Six

Meg paced the hallway of her flat, trying to block out the sound of the guitar coming from her bedroom. Emily had been playing an Eric Clapton song for the last hour, missing the same notes again and again. Blitzen had retreated into his sawdust and refused to emerge, even when offered a whole handful of sunflower seeds. Meg had suggested she put him in the sitting room out of the way, but Emily had protested so she'd left him in the bedroom. The rest of the flat felt like it had been invaded by the entire workforce of Molly Maid. The kitchen was too tidy for Meg to feel comfortable – all the surfaces gleamed, and the tinsel that had been hanging around the cupboards was now stuffed inside a clear glass vase which had been pushed to the back of the kitchen counter. All of Meg's fairy lights were secured onto the surfaces and walls with thick sticky tape – and her candles and tealights had gone AWOL.

'Of course we'll have to do a full walk-through of the building.' Kitty paced the floor as Meg popped a cup of tea on the coffee table in the sitting room. She was Skyping her fifth client of the day and almost every conversation had sounded the same. 'There are so many dangers hidden in the everyday. You're better off safe than sorry.' Kitty picked a large round ornament shaped like a robin off the mantelpiece and put it carefully on the floor. No doubt intent on saving Meg or Emily from knocking it off and doing themselves an injury.

Feeling like she couldn't breathe, Meg grabbed her coat and headed downstairs to the shop, pausing for a moment as Cora finished serving someone a cappuccino in the cafe. She took in a deep breath, smelled pine cones and hot chocolate, and instantly relaxed.

'You didnae have much of a rest,' Cora observed, as Meg began to rearrange some tinsel which had fallen onto the floor, before abandoning it when the action reminded her of Kitty. 'Shall I make you some lunch, lassie?'

'It's fine. I thought I'd pop to the post office, I've got something to talk to Morag about.'

'Your mam and sis driving you mad and you're looking for a distraction?' Cora guessed, patting her shoulder affectionately.

'I'm fine, everything's great.' Meg ran a hand across her brow, remembering she hadn't been able to brush glitter onto her cheeks this morning because she couldn't find the pot in the bathroom. No doubt her mum had put it somewhere safe. The flashing elf ornament with the spiky hat she'd left in the sitting room had disappeared too.

'Aye, I can see that.' Cora winked. 'Perhaps your da's planning a surprise visit too. Wouldn't that be nice, the whole family together just in time for Christmas? Might be just the thing your mam needs. She doesn't look very happy.' Meg gulped. 'If you see Morag, can you tell her I made that chestnut jam recipe Lilith mentioned at the Jam Club meeting – it's good.' Cora's rosy cheeks glowed.

'Did Marcus like the new flavour?'

'Ach no. But I've three more recipes to try. I'll find one he likes before the end of December.' 'Jingle Bells' began to play in the front of the store, signalling another shopper. 'Now go and get some fresh air, lassie.' Cora waved a hand towards the door. 'I'll look after the shop – and there'll be a hot chocolate waiting when you return.'

The post office was busy. Meg walked into the red-brick building and straight into the back of a queue. Behind the till, Morag Dooley rang up a couple of tins of beans and placed them into a canvas bag on the counter. The shop was dual purpose and supplied the locals with essential daily items, as well as the usual post office fare of stamps, passport forms and car tax. Anyone who needed supplies when it was closed had to travel over fifteen miles to Morridon.

Meg glanced around the shop, which was filled with shelves that showcased jams, tins, Dundee cakes, whisky and household fare. There was a small fridge packed with milk, cheese and ham, along with open baskets of potatoes, apples, onions and carrots. Next to the main till was a large glass cubicle with an opening for customers to slide their parcels and paperwork through. Morag used it when she was performing her post office duties, usually between two and four o'clock.

Meg grabbed a gossip magazine with a picture of a boy band on the front and joined the queue. A gust of cold air blew against the back of her neck as the door opened and she turned to see Davey breeze in, wearing a bulky black jacket and matching hat. His blue eyes lit up when he spotted her, and he grabbed an onion from one of the baskets and came to stand behind her.

'Ingredient emergency.' He waved the vegetable under Meg's nose. 'How about you?'

'I want to talk to Morag about something and it's been a while since I read one of these.' She waved the magazine. 'My sister used to eat them up.' Perhaps Emily still would?

Davey nodded. 'Tom mentioned your mum and sister were visiting.'

Meg looked up, surprised. 'I didn't realise Tom was on the Lockton grapevine – how did he know?'

'Gave them a lift, apparently. A heroic rescue from a frigid walk on the main road into Lockton. My words, not his,' he added. 'He was late getting to the pub and I forced it out of him – used my best thumbscrews.' Davey grinned. 'He said your mother looked like an older version of you, without the sparkles.'

Meg frowned, annoyed by the comparison. 'How's the concert shaping up?' Morag finished serving another customer and the queue moved forwards. 'I'm asking before Morag questions you. Best to get your facts straight. I heard she was once an interrogator for the police.'

Davey laughed. 'I've three artists almost in the bag – one would need to leave straight after the concert to get back to his family for Christmas Day, so that might not work out. The other two just need to confirm before we can make the big announcement, and we'll need to check if Lilith has space for them for a night or two in the hotel.' His cheeks flushed in sharp contrast to his black coat. 'I've been lucky. It's taken a while to get anyone to agree – it's a crazy time of year for most.'

'You must have a lot of good relationships if you can persuade people to work for free on Christmas Eve,' Meg said.

Davey shrugged, but his cheeks went pinker still. 'I'm owed a fair amount of favours, and it's a nice gig. Christmas in the Highlands, with snow and as much whisky as you can drink. It's an irresistible deal. Who wouldn't love it here?'

Meg's mother wasn't a huge fan – she'd complained about the snow constantly since she'd arrived the day before, citing a million reasons why they should all stay inside. Although Emily had snuck out with her guitar at least once when their mother had been on the phone.

'Do you miss the business?' Meg watched Davey's expression as he considered the question, noticing a hint of unhappiness slide across his eyes.

'Of course it's fresh, you dunderhead,' Morag rumbled from behind the till. 'But if you're worried, feel free to get yourself to Morridon. There'll be at least one bus running in the next week. Although you might have to help dig it out of the snow.' She whacked the tub of soup under the counter, out of her customer's reach, and glared as a woman Meg didn't recognise waddled to the door with her head tucked low.

'Why would I miss London when I have all this excitement!' Davey sniggered as the door behind them slammed again and Lilith strode in. She wore a red coat, jeans and boots with a three-inch heel. Davey's cheeks went beetroot and he swallowed, but this time he kept his mouth closed.

'Next,' Morag bellowed, and they all jumped and edged forwards under her dark glare. She ignored Meg and Davey – who was staring at Lilith – and focused on the Italian chef, who didn't wither under the unfriendly scowl. 'Your parcel hasn't arrived. Here's a form,' she snapped, pulling a piece of paper out from under the counter and waving it. 'I suggest you fill this out for the purposes of insurance. Your package might turn up, but knowing the eejits who work in the sorting offices over December, I wouldn't bet my whisky on it.' Lilith took the form and began to read as Morag frowned at Davey. 'Have you booked the bands?'

'Almost sorted,' Davey promised, finding his voice again. Meg waited for Morag to interrogate Davey further. To ask who exactly he had on his list of potential acts. The woman was well known for her dedication to gathering and spreading gossip – and people came from miles away to shop in the post office for their daily dose. Meg suspected Morag's news had a wider circulation than the *Morridon Post*.

'Is there nothing that can be done to find my olive oil?' Lilith sounded worried.

'You can get some here.' Morag waggled a finger at a shelf to their right, where an array of different-shaped bottles were lined up. 'It's on offer until the weekend, two for one.'

Lilith shook her head sharply. 'I need *my* olive oil. One Italian family – the Bellagambas – make it. They have an olive plantation and *only* sell the oil they make in their deli. It has a particular flavour. There's nothing on the whole of the planet that will work in my recipes as well.'

'Oh.' Davey sounded surprised. 'Um, I didn't realise oil had different flavours.'

'Ahhhh, but you are not a cook.' Davey looked taken aback until Lilith attempted a small and unexpected smile, before frowning and looking away.

'If you order more, it will probably arrive in time for Christmas. If those eejits in Morridon learn to read an address,' Morag grumbled.

Lilith raised her palms. 'The deli has sold out and there will be no more until next year. It's why I ordered so early. My mamma buys hers in October; I should have done the same.' She shook her head. 'The meals I've planned will all have to change.' She winced. 'We always eat the same courses at Christmas, ever since I can remember.'

'Who's we?' Morag asked, and then her eyes widened and she held up a palm. 'Don't answer. Forget I asked,' she snapped.

'I can ask Johnny if he has any oils. In the pub kitchen, I mean,' Davey stammered. When Lilith shook her head, he carried on. 'He doesn't boast about it, but...' He swallowed. 'Johnny, my brother, he worked in two of the most exclusive restaurants in New York before moving here. I mean, to Scotland. He... he knows his oil.' Lilith's mouth formed a becoming 'o' as she took the information on board. 'He – Johnny that is – is particular about ingredients... like you. We've fought a few times about the quality of the herbs in Lockton. He's passionate.' Davey smiled, his cheeks darkening even more. 'He convinced me.'

'*Sì.*' Lilith nodded. 'So we agree.'

'My herbs are bonnie, laddie,' Morag growled, her attention darting to a small selection of bottled dry herbs before she glowered at Davey. 'And I'll be having words with your brother about that.'

Davey paled.

'There's no alternative. The Bellagamba oil is for an Italian dish that my family' – Lilith's gaze darted to Morag as she inadvertently answered her question from earlier – 'always have on the twenty-fourth of December.'

'Can't you just pretend you used it?' Meg asked. 'If you serve it to your guests, how many will even notice?'

'My parents are coming to the hotel for Christmas,' Lilith snapped, but then closed her eyes. 'They will know. What my papa expects, my papa gets.' She tapped her fingers against her chest. 'Everything has to be *perfetto*.' Her lips pinched. 'Or their whole visit will be ruined. You have no idea…'

'I'll tell you if it arrives. In the meantime, there's not much I can do,' Morag said. The door opened behind them, bringing a fresh blast of cold air. Agnes walked inside and joined the queue.

'I've just been yarn bombing with Cora and Matilda,' she explained, giving Meg a quick hug hello. Her cheeks glowed as she pulled off her gloves and patted them.

'Bombing?' Davey looked shocked. 'I don't understand.'

Agnes chuckled. 'It's when you decorate outside with things you've knitted or crocheted.' She pulled a couple of knitted guitars from her pocket and waved them in the air. 'We've been making Christmas decorations and instruments to advertise the concert. We put a few up the other day and just finished hanging more around the village and high street. There are loads in the square.'

'Better get on with booking the bands, laddie, or the knitters of Lockton will be coming for you.' Morag frowned as her attention switched to Meg. The door opened again and this time Tom walked in. His eyebrows shot up when he spotted the assembled group.

'Is this a post office party?' he joked.

'It's the hot toddy,' Agnes said, her expression turning sly as Tom gathered bread, soup and cheddar, and put them into a basket. 'What brings you here, lad?'

'Lunch.' Tom grinned and his eyes slid to Meg, making her stomach lurch.

'Meal for one?' Agnes asked, raising an eyebrow.

Tom's eyes widened, but he nodded.

'Meg's single too.'

'What about your Christmas Promise?' Meg said sharply, and Agnes let out an unhappy huff.

'Aye.' She looked annoyed. 'And I only hung it on the tree this morning.' She grinned as her attention switched between Meg and Tom. 'I suppose I'll have to let things run their natural course…'

'Things?' Tom asked, as Meg cleared her throat. Then his eyes dropped to the magazine in her hand and his expression changed.

'Are you standing in the queue to keep warm, lass, or was there something you wanted?' Morag bellowed.

Meg put the magazine on the counter. Why had Tom looked so upset? 'I wanted to ask if you were looking to get another pet. I know you lost Petra…' Morag's face dropped as Meg mentioned her beloved old poodle which had died in the spring. 'There's a cat who keeps coming into the shop. She doesn't belong to anyone, I've asked around – I wondered if you'd want to take her on?'

'That's a lovely thought, lassie,' Agnes said.

'Aye.' Morag frowned. 'I've been considering getting another dog for a while, but a wee cat…' She pursed her lips. 'I'll pop into the shop later. It'll give me a chance to check out your guests. Cora told me your—' She clamped a hand over her mouth and rang the magazine up on the till with the other.

'Are you okay, Morag?' Davey asked. 'Is there something we can do?'

'I'm not gossiping.' Morag took her hand away and handed the magazine to Meg. 'It's my Christmas Promise. I hung it onto the tree yesterday evening and I'm not breaking it for anyone, no matter how much I want to. It's harder than I expected.'

'Aye. I hear you,' Agnes agreed.

'It's a great promise.' Davey glanced at Lilith, who was still standing next to him. 'I'm not sure how your customers are going to feel about missing out on the local updates though.' He placed his onion onto the counter and Morag rang it up before tossing his coins into the till.

'I'm sure they'll be bonnie,' she said. 'I've nae problem with people gossiping here, I'm just not gonnae repeat it.'

'Any particular reason you chose that promise?' Tom asked, his attention still fixed on the magazine Meg was holding.

'Aye. My son told me I wouldn't be able to do it.' Morag's brown eyes flashed with annoyance. 'I told the laddie, I will – and I hung my bauble in that tree straight afterwards. I haven't let a word of gossip leave my lips for…' She checked her watch and her lips pressed together. 'Fifteen hours. But I was asleep for ten of those.' She glared at Davey and Meg. 'Are you done?' she snapped. 'Because I know you've both got plenty to be getting on with. We need the bands confirmed for the twenty-fourth and Meg, why aren't you with your sister and mam?'

Meg blushed. 'I'm on my way back to the shop now,' she said, grabbing her bag and turning to leave, aware of Tom watching her – wondering exactly what had put that guarded expression into his eyes.

Chapter Seven

Meg stepped inside Apple Cross Inn that evening and took a deep, calming breath. The tables were full and Christmas music played softly in the background, mixing with the quiet hum of voices. Handbags cluttered the wooden floor, alongside dogs, who lolled by their owners' feet. It was a relief to be out of her flat, away from her mother's obsession with tidying. Away from Emily's constant guitar-playing and all the invisible baggage that came with her family. They'd eaten dinner in silence before retreating to separate corners of her home, leaving Meg feeling so alone she'd decided to come out for a quick drink.

Tom stood behind the bar, serving Davina the same anti-Christmas cocktail he'd made a few days before. As Davina walked away to join her husband, brandishing her drink, Meg studied him. He wore a crisp white shirt and blue jeans. His dark hair curled at the top edge of his collar and he'd not shaved again, so his jaw was shaded with a perfect arc of stubble that traced the edges of his cheekbones. The effect was annoyingly sexy and Meg fought a sudden urge to turn and leave, because she couldn't afford to find him attractive. Having her mother stay was a timely reminder of what happened when you and your partner weren't right for each other. If she had somewhere to go, she might have retreated. Then she noticed a couple of giggling women staring at Tom from a table in the corner by the Christmas tree. Strangely irritated, she walked up to the bar and pulled out a stool, blocking their view.

Tom did a double-take as she sat. 'Did you get attacked by a gang of toddlers brandishing glue sticks and glitter on your way here?' He smiled, clearly over whatever had upset him in the post office this morning.

Meg swiped a hand across one cheek. She'd finally found her sparkle stash in a drawer in the bathroom and had gone extra mad with the brush. 'It really is a shock that you're single,' she said dryly. 'Can I have a glass of red wine, please?' She put her felt handbag, shaped like a Christmas tree, onto the counter.

Tom blinked hard when he saw the bag. He picked up a glass and poured in a healthy dose of Blue Curaçao. The track changed to 'If Every Day Was Christmas'. The song had been used by a large supermarket chain in their latest Christmas ad, and had been on the radio and music apps constantly. Meg began to tap her foot to the beat as Tom thumped the glass on the table and marched to the back of the pub. Seconds later the tune switched to hard rock. He returned, and poured orange juice and rum into her glass. 'I hate that song,' he said, adding ice, a slice of lemon and a black straw. He slid the bright blue drink in front of her.

'You don't like Christmas music either?' Meg asked, amused.

He shrugged. 'Some tracks are okay, just not that one. Sometimes I wonder what the person who wrote it was thinking.'

Meg found her lips twitching. 'That they wished every day was Christmas?' She laughed. 'I might look them up, I'm thinking we could be soul mates.'

Tom grunted.

She considered the drink. 'Is there a reason why you keep making me cocktails?'

'You looked...' Tom's forehead wrinkled. 'Fed up when you walked in, and you're wearing way too much glitter for wine.'

Meg nodded, surprised by his ability to read her. She picked up the cocktail and sipped, relishing the interesting mix of sweet and bitter, then exhaled, letting herself relax. 'Don't tell me, you call this one' – she stared at the glass – 'I'm Dreaming of a Blue Christmas?'

Tom barked out a laugh which hit Meg right in the solar plexus. 'No, I call it The Grinch.'

'Ahhhh, you named a cocktail after yourself.' She sipped again and nodded. 'Sweet. I'm going to have my work cut out if I want to cut that ego down to size.'

'You sound like my grandma. She always tried to keep me grounded.' Tom's face fell.

'It didn't work?' Meg asked.

'She died and now that task's all mine. I'm still working on it. Some days are easier than others.' Tom picked up a glass and began to polish it as someone walked up to the bar – Matilda got there before he moved.

'I'm sorry,' Meg said simply, scanning his face. He looked so unhappy she decided to change the subject. 'How do you know Davey?'

'We go way back. You know, I think we've got this the wrong way round.' He wagged a finger between them. 'I'm sure I'm supposed to ask the questions – although I am new to bar work.'

'Ah, that explains it.' Meg nodded, grinning. 'Davey obviously forgot to explain the job. When a customer orders a drink – for instance, red wine – you're supposed to serve them that.' She picked up her glass and shook the blue liquid. 'Not whatever you feel like foisting on them at the time.'

Tom leaned on the counter. His expression was warm and he looked much happier than he had a few minutes before. 'I'll try to remember that. Can I begin the interview now?'

'Sure.' It had been a long time since anyone had tried to amuse her and Meg had always found a sense of humour sexy. It was a shame she couldn't let this attraction grow. The man had 'wrong for you' written all over his handsome face.

'Agnes said you were single, so no boyfriend?' Tom asked.

'Nope.' Meg shook her head. 'I'm too choosy, apparently.'

'Or a woman who knows what she wants.' He raised an eyebrow. 'Care to elaborate?'

She nodded. 'I'm looking for the perfect package.'

He looked impressed. 'Isn't that on every elf's job description! Details?'

Meg grinned. Had Ned ever made her laugh? Then again, her dad used jokes to hide his true feelings, so it wasn't always a good thing. 'Looks aren't important but chemistry is.' She paused as his eyes heated. 'And we should agree on most things – I'm not one for arguments.'

'Big ask.' Tom whistled. 'What about passion and the fire that comes from a good row?'

'I prefer harmony.' Her voice was soft.

'Are you controlling?'

She shook her head. 'That would be my mother. I prefer the word careful. I don't rush into relationships. There's way too much that can go wrong.'

'I'll agree with you on that point.' Tom looked at her closely, sending awareness skipping across her skin. 'What did you do before you became an elf?'

Meg tapped a fingertip on the bar. 'I worked in the city – in London – before throwing it all in and starting my Christmas shop.'

Tom nodded. 'That's an impressive résumé.'

'Thanks,' Meg said, touched. 'Do I get a turn now?'

He shook his head. 'I'm enjoying being on this end of the interrogation for once.'

'Were you a criminal before you ended up in Lockton?' Meg teased, which earned her a laugh. His eyes were dark brown and would be very easy to get lost in. She'd have to watch herself. 'I'm guessing your grandma would have put a stop to that?' She saw pain flash across his face and nearly apologised.

'Why a Christmas shop?' he deflected.

'Because it's my favourite time of year,' Meg said. 'I love everything about it. The decorations, presents – the way most families bond, play games, talk. It's magical. But it's just one day. Christmas is a step outside the real world. Why not try to live it every day, just like the song?'

'You don't think it's all a bit fake?' Tom asked, looking serious. 'Too easy to forget what's really important, to get lost in that make-believe world?'

Meg's breath caught, hurt despite herself. 'That's a lot to throw at a simple shop.'

'I didn't mean your shop, sorry.' Tom shook his head and then put his hands in his pockets. 'Favourite colour?'

It took a few moments for Meg to respond, and when she did something inside her still felt strangely sore. 'Red or green, I can't decide,' she admitted. 'You?'

'Black.'

She rolled her eyes.

'Food?'

Meg pursed her lips, considering. 'I'd have to go with turkey, obviously – or mince pies.'

'I hate mince pies.' He sucked in a breath. 'Mine's cheese. Best movie?'

Had Agnes primed him with all these questions? '*The Holiday*.' If she had, it was a spectacular own goal because it had only served to highlight their differences.

Tom straightened as someone else approached the bar and Matilda once again beat him to serving them. '*The Godfather*. I'm guessing our romance is doomed?'

Meg emptied her glass. ''Fraid so. Don't feel bad though – you lost me at "I don't like Christmas" when I rescued you in my van.'

'I guess we'll have to settle for friends,' Tom said, looking serious. Their eyes met, making Meg's insides pulse despite everything.

'Tickets and leaflets.' Davey appeared from the back and laid two piles of colourful paper onto the counter before either of them could react, dousing the sudden spark of attraction with a bucket of icy reality. 'I got the whole Christmas concert booked this afternoon. Two acts. Top Mop – they've had a couple of hits.' Meg nodded. 'And James Truman.'

Meg's eyebrows rose. 'How did you swing that?' The singer's star had been rising consistently over the last couple of years. He was clean-cut, talented and gorgeous, and his music was toe-tappingly good.

Davey polished his fingernails on his dark blue shirt. 'We're mates. He usually keeps Christmas free for his family but he's going to bring them up. He already called Lilith and she has space in the hotel, so he's going to spend Christmas there. Details are on the leaflets, so please dish out as many as you can because I promised a full house. Davina said she'd drop a load into Morridon Library.'

'The concert's going to be a sellout,' Tom said, frowning.

'You want to buy a ticket?' Davey asked, pushing the pile towards him.

'I'll be on the other side of the bar.' Tom's expression darkened. 'But I'll make a donation to the roof.' Something odd passed between the men which Meg couldn't read and she frowned. Then another customer approached the counter and this time Tom got there before Matilda, leaving Meg wondering exactly what she'd just missed.

Meg walked along the high street towards her shop twenty minutes later, ignoring the ice in the air. Her mobile began to ring and she stopped so she could pull it out of her handbag.

'Dad, where are you?' She looked longingly down the road towards her shop which was a few buildings away as she began to shiver. 'I'm standing outside and I might lose the signal if I move. Shall I call you back when I get inside?'

'No need, I only called to ask a quick question.' He sounded chirpy. 'Do you know where your mum is? She left with Emily yesterday, said they'd be away for a few days. I thought they'd be back today – you know your mother, she likes the security of her own space. I've tried calling her mobile and searched everywhere I can think of.' He sighed. 'She missed an appointment I'd set up for this afternoon. I really thought she'd come.' He sounded disappointed.

'She's in Lockton with me. Emily too,' Meg said. 'She said you were staying in London.'

'She's in Scotland?' He sounded shocked. 'When's she coming home?'

'Her flight's booked for the twenty-first.' Snow was coming down in huge flakes now, and Meg grabbed a red and green elf hat out of her handbag and pulled it on, covering her ears.

'That's weird…' He cleared his throat. 'I know we don't always get on that well, but she's been acting particularly strangely…' His tone was strained. 'We've got things we need to talk about, things we've both been ignoring.' He exhaled loudly.

'Is it about what you were going to tell me on the phone last month?' Meg asked quickly.

'Yes, but your mum would rather forget it.' Her dad sighed. 'I'll give you a buzz once I've worked out what to do.'

They said their goodbyes and Meg was left staring at her mobile. What exactly was happening with her parents? Her head began to throb as she made her way to her Christmas shop, unlocking the entrance. She paused to take in the sparkly decorations lining the sides of the room, the five-foot inflatable characters running along the centre aisle. These were her moments of security, and she had to hold on to them. There was a thump on the stairs, and Emily and her mother walked into the shop wearing coats, scarves and boots.

'We were waiting for you.' Kitty held up a glass bauble containing a piece of bright pink paper. 'Cora told me about the Promise Tree. Emily has a bauble too. I know it's snowing but can we hang them now?' Her forehead wrinkled as she glanced outside. 'Assuming we're not going to get attacked by wild animals?'

'The wildest creatures roaming free in Lockton are probably goats.' Meg unlocked the door before her mother conjured anything else to worry about. As they wandered up the high street, Emily fell into step beside her as Kitty bought up the rear. The snow was deep and ethereal flakes fell from the sky, settling on their hats and coats. 'Dad just called to ask where you were,' she whispered. 'I didn't realise he didn't know?'

Emily shrugged. 'Mum said she'd call him when we arrived – I didn't think to check.'

'He's going to call again soon. Think I should say something?'

Emily pulled a face. 'I'd leave it tonight. It's been normal today. At least Mum's been working and she seems content.' Emily pushed her hands into the pockets of her tight black snowsuit, leaving the bauble dangling so it bounced against her leg. 'If you tell her now she'll just start worrying…'

'I'll mention it tomorrow,' Meg promised as they reached the village square, and crossed the road so they could get to the Promise Tree. Hundreds of baubles now hung from the branches and swayed in the breeze. Emily reached up onto her tiptoes and hung hers.

'I promise to figure out what to do with my life,' she whispered, loud enough for Meg to hear. 'Definitely not accountancy. I just need to find something that will make me happy… the thing I was born to do.'

Kitty walked away from them, then hung her bauble on one of the lower branches. Meg heard her whisper something but couldn't make out the words. Then her mother met Meg's gaze and looked startled.

'What did you promise, Mum?' Emily asked, trotting up to join her.

'Nothing for you to worry about.' Kitty broke eye contact and turned away.

But as they made their way back towards the Christmas shop, Meg wondered what promise her mother had made, and knew in her gut something was very wrong.

Chapter Eight

The high street looked empty as Tom trudged along the pavement beside Cooper, leaving two sets of prints in the snow. It had been blizzarding all night, continuing into the morning, and even now huge snowflakes fluttered in the air before landing on the crisp, white carpet in front of them. The dog wasn't happy and stopped every few steps to shake each paw in turn, before turning to look woefully back towards home. They hit the fork where the Promise Tree rose out of the large brown well, and stopped as Tom noticed a smattering of broken baubles. The glass was framed by a torn yellow banner of delicate knitted stars. Cooper barked and scampered across the road to sniff the wool, before picking up the strands in his teeth.

'Put that down,' Tom shouted, following. But the dog was either too excited or too intent on punishing him for the walk, because he clamped his jaws. Irritated, Tom bent to pick up some of the glass as a piece of soggy pink paper blew along the ground in front of him. He caught it before it was swept off on a gust, scanning the words scrawled across it in black ink. *I promise to get a divorce.*

'Well, that's not very festive,' he said, wondering if Marnie had made the same vow to herself three years before. He pushed the note into his coat pocket and grabbed a plastic bag out of the other, placing the jagged glass inside. He stooped to gather more, shooing

Cooper away as he came to investigate. Then he heard a shout from behind, and turned just as Meg came marching up.

'What did you let that dog do?' she moaned. She was wearing her elf suit again, but this time Tom noticed it hugged her curves and brought out the becoming bloom of anger on her skin. He'd found his mind wandering to her since their chat in the pub two evenings before, and his lips turned up in greeting.

Meg glared at the ground instead of smiling back. 'I know we joked about you being the Grinch, but why would you let your dog vandalise our Promise Tree?' She pointed to Cooper, then bent to pick up a broken piece of bauble, spotting the bag in Tom's hand which she snatched away. She looked inside and groaned. 'I can't believe anyone would hate Christmas this much.'

'It wasn't me or Cooper.' Tom waved a hand at the scattered decorations, feeling a little put out. 'I was walking and found it like that. I've been clearing up the glass so I could bring it to your shop. It was probably kids. Don't you have teenagers in Lockton?'

'None who'd do this,' she snapped. 'Everyone around here loves Christmas...' Meg scoured the snow. 'I can only see one set of prints, aside from Cooper's.' There was a clear set of footprints under the tree, which Tom knew belonged to him. The rest of the snow looked crisp and untouched.

'It's been blizzarding all morning,' Tom said, tamping his temper. 'Even if a herd of reindeer had charged through here an hour ago, you wouldn't have a clue.' He took the bag from her fingers and knelt again, gathering the rest of the glass. Meg bent to pick up some pieces of paper and hung the soggy knitted decorations back onto the tree.

'You found it then.' Lilith crossed the road and crunched up to join them. She was wearing jeans and a pair of boots with heels that reminded Tom of Marnie. But the memory didn't make his heart ache like it might have even a year ago. 'I saw the damage earlier and I was going to clear it up, but I wanted to catch Morag before the post office got busy. I thought I'd give my parcel one last chance before I put in a claim. It wasn't there…' She looked unhappy.

'I'm sorry,' Meg said, as Lilith grabbed a star from the ground and hung it on one of the higher branches. 'What do you mean, you saw this earlier?' She kept her eyes fixed on Lilith, as if the mere act of looking at Tom was too much for her.

'I walked this way from the hotel about fifteen minutes ago, saw the baubles and decorations on the ground. I picked up a few over there.' She pointed to a set of railings where a saturated knitted streamer had been hung. Tom could see a couple of instruments were missing – most likely torn off. There were bits of wool everywhere. It looked like someone had been trying to rip them up. 'I saw the baubles in the snow but didn't realise they were broken or I'd have tidied the worst.' Lilith frowned, bending to pick up a piece of glass so she could toss it into Tom's bag. 'There weren't any footprints, and there was no one nearby. I think someone did this in the night.'

'I was here yesterday evening and everything was fine,' Meg said.

Lilith took in her expression. 'It's been snowing constantly, so it's going to be difficult to trace who did it.'

'We should tell Marcus Dougall.' Meg frowned at Tom. 'I'd like the police involved – even if he can't find out who it was, it'll serve as a warning.'

'Good plan,' Tom said, as Meg considered him. 'Isn't he married to Cora? Should we go back to your shop?' He did a final check for glass. 'Will you be able to replace the broken baubles?'

'Of course,' Meg said, looking around. 'I'll do it this afternoon. I think we got all the promises.' She tapped her pocket. Tom was going to tell her about the one in his, then changed his mind – sharing it didn't feel right. Besides, if the tree really was magic, which he'd overheard customers at the pub gossiping about, would that make him complicit in someone else's divorce? He had enough bad karma in his life – he'd be better off throwing it in the bin.

'I've got to get back to the hotel,' Lilith said. 'I left someone in charge of lunch, but there's a lot to do. If you find out who did this' – she waved a hand at the ground – 'let me know. I had a promise of my own on that tree.' She nodded at Meg then turned, marching quickly, despite the shoes.

Meg didn't look at Tom as they began to walk back down the high street, but Cooper kept pace beside her, probably realising she represented the fastest way out of the cold. He whined in relief as Meg opened the door to her shop and then paused. 'Cooper can come into the cafe if he behaves. You'd better explain to Cora what you found.'

Tom caught Meg's hand as they entered the shop, but dropped it again as he felt her tense, wondering why he'd felt the need to touch her at all. 'I promise it wasn't Cooper.' He was surprised by how much he wanted her to believe him.

Her mouth twisted. 'You've told me you're not so good at keeping those. But I know you're telling the truth…' She let out a long exhale. 'I'm sorry I overreacted. I was surprised to see you by the tree, but you've got nothing to gain from vandalising it. I've no idea who'd want to destroy the baubles on our Promise Tree. People come for miles to hang them. It doesn't make sense.' She headed through the shop, edging past an inflatable snowman which was almost the same height as she was. Tom followed, passing a couple browsing shelves.

The cafe was cosy, colourful and Christmassy. There was a counter on the left which doubled as a display unit and showcased an array of treats – including scones, cheesecake, mince pies and a giant Christmas cake. Behind that, Tom could see a state-of-the-art drinks machine where Cora was warming milk. The cafe was quiet, aside from a lone man with dark hair flecked with grey. He had a suitcase at his feet and was working on a laptop. As Meg spotted him, she came to an abrupt stop.

'Dad?' Her face paled. 'What are *you* doing here?' she squeaked.

'Meg!' The man launched himself from the seat and gave her an awkward hug. He was tall. Not as tall as Tom, probably five eleven. His skin was pale and he had amber-coloured eyes which contrasted with the blue of Meg's. He'd taken off his coat, which lay on a chair beside the suitcase, but his snow boots were covered in ice, suggesting he'd only just arrived. 'After we talked, I tried calling your mother but she didn't answer. Rather than put you in the middle of an argument' – he pulled a face – 'I thought I'd come up too. I managed to get on a flight yesterday evening and stayed in Inverness. A cab brought me here this morning. I feel like I've just crossed the Arctic. Cora told me you went for a walk.' He nodded as she brought him over a hot chocolate and plate of mince pies.

'Aye, your da looked cold so I thought I'd make him a snack.' Cora grinned. 'I knew you were related when he ordered your favourite foods.'

'I'll have a quick breakfast before we head up to your flat if that's okay?' her dad asked, and Meg reached for the back of a chair. She was smiling and nodding, her cheeks shining under the skylight, but Tom could tell something wasn't right.

'You're staying?' she asked, nibbling her bottom lip.

'If that's okay? Sorry to land myself on you, but it'll be good to catch up.' Her dad picked up his drink and sipped. 'Exquisite.' His eyes moved to Tom and Meg turned. She looked surprised, like she'd forgotten he was there, but there was none of the anger that had been in her eyes earlier. If anything, she looked scared.

'This is Tom Riley-Clark, he works in Apple Cross Inn. That's his dog, Cooper.' She waved a hand at her father. 'This is my dad, Oliver Scott. He's...' She paused before flashing another smile. 'Decided to surprise me.'

Oliver shook Tom's hand, then picked up a mince pie and took a bite. 'Ten out of ten,' he said.

'Do you want me to talk to Cora now?' Tom asked, leaning closer to Meg. He got a whiff of something Christmassy like cinnamon and was surprised the scent didn't make his stomach lurch.

'Um...' She looked vague. 'Let's leave it. I can do it later, I need to talk to her about a leaky tap anyway. Maybe she can get Marcus to pop over to the pub. Could you help me get these things up to the flat?' She nodded at the suitcase. 'Why don't you stay here, Dad, finish your food? I'll work out where you're sleeping.' She picked up his coat and a small bag, and marched off. Tom told Cooper to stay put – the dog slumped to the floor – then he picked up the case and followed Meg through the shop, ducking behind the till into a small hallway. She stopped suddenly and stood, staring at the edge of the banister, in a world of her own.

'Problem?' Tom asked gently, wondering why he wasn't running in the other direction.

Meg exhaled and Tom stood, feeling awkward. 'No, everything's fine.' She turned so she could give him another one of her sparkly grins. Some of the glitter had leaked onto her lips and Tom had a sudden desire to brush it off. Would she stop smiling if he did? 'You don't have to stay, I can probably manage the suitcase and other stuff on my own.'

In the old days he might have taken her advice and left someone else to pick up the pieces, but instead he waited. Because for some reason he didn't want to go. The whole thing seemed almost comic – Meg was still dressed as an elf and twenty minutes ago she'd been accusing him and Cooper of sabotaging the Promise Tree. 'I get the feeling you weren't that happy to see your dad?' Tom asked gently.

Meg's smile dropped. 'How could you tell?' She looked shocked.

He shrugged. 'Intuition… lucky guess. I don't know.' If he told her he just knew, she'd think he'd lost his mind. Perhaps he had? He was still standing here, wasn't he? Not running in the other direction like every molecule in his body was telling him to. He was all about retreat. Staying away. He wasn't in the market for another relationship – wasn't looking for anything but a way to fill the hours and atone. So why was he still here?

Meg straightened. 'Sometimes my parents don't get on.' She pursed her lips. 'That doesn't mean I'm not happy to see them… I'm going to love having them here.' Her voice cracked and she pulled a face when he cocked an eyebrow. 'You don't know me,' she said quietly, her tone filled more with surprise than anything else.

Tom shook his head. 'I don't. I'm sorry, I didn't mean to overstep. I think I was just trying to say, if you need to talk to someone…' He grimaced. What was he doing? 'Cooper's got an excellent pair of ears.'

Meg barked out a laugh and nodded, relaxing a little. 'I'll bear that in mind,' she said, still staring. 'We've nothing in common…'

Tom shook his head. 'I guess if we keep talking, we might find something. Favourite animal?'

'Hamster.'

He shook his head. 'Dog. Favourite tree?'

Meg raised an eyebrow. 'Nordmann fir.'

'I should have guessed. Mine's a horse chestnut – damn.' Tom picked up the case and Meg smiled – this time it did reach her eyes. 'Which way?'

'Up.' Meg turned and walked up the stairs and Tom followed, noticing the decorations and tinsel running along the banister. They reached a landing with bright walls and a soft red rug, and Meg took a deep breath. Someone was playing a guitar, missing the same chord over and over; it grated on Tom's ears but he tried to ignore it. 'I've no idea where I'm going to put Dad. Mum's got the spare and Emily's in with me.' She took in the five closed doors, one by one.

'Not with your mum?' Tom asked, wishing he hadn't when she shook her head. 'Lilith's hotel?' he suggested.

Meg screwed up her nose. 'There's a sofa bed in the sitting room. I have to tell Mum he's here…'

'Want me to stay?' Tom asked, hoping she'd say no – but when Meg shook her head, he felt a surprising stab of disappointment.

'I think you've done enough for me today.' She looked at him oddly. 'Thanks. For someone with such weird ideas about everything, you're okay.' She frowned.

'You're welcome.' Tom put the suitcase down. 'Good luck. If you need to talk, don't forget the dog.'

Meg nodded and smiled sadly before turning to one of the closed doors. Tom turned to head back down the stairs, wondering why he had such a strong desire to stay.

Chapter Nine

Meg knocked on the door of the sitting room. Her mother was on her mobile, pacing the rug. Her laptop was open on the coffee table and there was a steaming mug of tea set back from the edge. Piles of papers sat in tidy, symmetrical stacks on the sofa. On the other side of the room the Christmas tree had been pushed into the far corner. Kitty looked up and waved a finger, then leaned down so she could scribble 'Not long now' onto a pink piece of paper. She'd always written notes. It was easier sometimes than talking. 'Eat your vegetables' was the most common note left in the kitchen. 'Don't drink alcohol and drive' if Meg was going out. 'Fresh air cures almost everything' if she was miserable. But 'Better safe than sorry' was the classic, and could be applied to almost every situation. Meg picked up the note and nodded, then took a seat on the sofa and her mind wandered to Tom. He'd been kind and perceptive today – and she wasn't sure how she felt about that. Somehow the insight made him less easy to dismiss. Like a boring 2D card which had opened to reveal something far more interesting inside.

'Okay, dear?' her mother asked, putting her mobile on the table and dropping to her knees so she could tap something into her computer. 'I've picked up another two clients this morning. I've so much to do, I don't know where to start.' Her eyes were bright with excitement and as blue as Meg's.

Meg took a deep breath. 'Dad's downstairs.'

Kitty's eyes widened. 'What? Downstairs here?'

'You weren't returning his calls so he decided to follow you.'

'But how did he know I was in Lockton?' Kitty leaned back onto her knees. She wore an elegant forest-green suit and looked both beautiful and intimidating. 'I'd been avoiding talking to him until I worked out what I wanted to say.'

Meg swiped a hand across her mouth. 'He called the other evening and I told him you were here – he was worried,' she added, when her mother's eyes flashed. 'I didn't think he'd follow you.'

'We keep going round in circles. I want time alone to think. He never listens. Hasn't since…' Her lips pursed. In the bedroom, Emily strummed an off-key note in perfect accord with their conversation. Her mother looked hastily around the room, then into the hall. 'Where's he going to sleep?'

'I'll put him here.' Meg ignored the tightness in her chest and smiled gently. 'The sofa can be made into a bed. You can set your work up in the kitchen.' Which would leave Meg precisely nowhere to be alone.

'It's going to be difficult living in such a small space.' Kitty frowned. 'I might have to look at return flights now.' Meg swallowed the ball of anxiety. How would her father react to that? She couldn't bear them fighting about it. Not in her flat. It would be like scribbling permanent marker all over the walls, vandalising her sanctuary.

'Maybe give it a few days?' she asked.

'Hello?' Oliver yelled, and Meg headed into the hall just as Emily peered around the bedroom door.

'Dad?' She looked over the banister into the stairwell.

'Darling.' Oliver bounded up the stairs. He had his laptop bag slung over one large arm, and shifted it onto his shoulder so he could give Emily a theatrical hug. 'Surprise!' he boomed, his eyes shifting to his wife. 'You missed our appointment, Kit,' he said softly, his smile drooping.

'I told you I wasn't going. It's all too little, too late. I wanted to talk fifteen years ago. You wanted to pretend nothing had happened and make jokes.' Kitty pursed her lips and walked back into the sitting room. Then she gathered up her laptop, and carried it to the kitchen without looking up.

'We have Christmas,' her dad said quietly. 'We've always had that.'

Her mother shook her head. 'Life's a lot more than one perfect day. I'm almost fifty, I want more.' Her eyes caught Meg's and she looked away before going back into the sitting room to pick up her mug and papers. Meg's stomach felt like lead. The whole scene was so familiar. The heavy silence, the dark expressions. She glanced to the stairs, wishing she could disappear back into her Christmas shop, layer herself with yet more sparkles to block out the uncomfortable atmosphere.

'I went without you, in case you're interested?' her dad said. 'It's why I'm here.' Her mother stopped in the doorway of the kitchen and her body swayed a little, but she didn't turn – she walked inside and shut the door. 'Seems I have my work cut out. Don't worry, girls, it'll be fine. If we can't make up above a Christmas shop, there really is no hope.' Her dad glossed over the conversation with his verbal equivalent of glitter. 'Now, where am I going to get my beauty sleep?' He patted both his cheeks.

'Here.' Meg picked up his suitcase and carried it into the sitting room, before showing him how to open the sofa into a bed and gathering bedding. Then she gave him the WiFi code and he set himself up on the coffee table. Meg left him to work and pushed Emily back into the bedroom.

'What's Dad doing here?' her sister whispered.

'He wants to talk to Mum.' Meg shrugged.

'But they won't,' Emily sighed. 'They never have… It's a wonder either of us has turned out normal.' She looked up into Meg's face and tried to smile, her blue eyes shimmering. 'We are normal, right?'

Meg patted her on the shoulder. 'I know I am,' she said lightly, hoping Emily would laugh. When she did, Meg put a sunflower seed in Blitzen's cage, hoping he'd waddle out. 'Were they… I mean, has anything changed in the years since I left? I know we don't talk about it,' Meg rushed, wishing she hadn't said anything. But it was easier to ignore when she was over five hundred miles away. Now the whole thing wasn't just on her doorstep, it was in her house and she had to face it. 'You're not home much…'

Emily shrugged. 'I spend a lot of time out. But no, it's no different. Mostly they avoid each other. There's the odd fight. Christmas Day is still perfect – you know that.' She watched Meg as she bent down to peer in the cage, searching for movement. 'But you decided to avoid coming home this year? I don't blame you…' she added quickly.

'I… I'm sorry.' Meg straightened and looked her sister in the eye. 'When Dad told me you were spending Christmas Day with friends, I couldn't face it. In truth I've wanted to spend the holidays in Lockton for a while. I love that one day, but it's not enough.'

'I'm sorry too. But this…' Emily wagged a finger towards the bedroom door. 'It might be a good thing. They've been stuck for years. Something's got to give.'

'I'm sure it'll be fine,' Meg said, and pulled a face when Emily raised an eyebrow.

'You sound like Dad.'

'You're a little too wise for one so young,' Meg murmured, turning so she could take another look in the cage.

'Blitzen's fine,' Emily soothed. 'I fed him earlier, he's probably passed out because he stuffed the lot. I adore animals but I didn't realise they all had such different personalities – Blitzen's greedy.'

'True.' Meg grinned and sat on the bed. 'Mum was always too worried about allergies to let us have pets, so I guess you never got to know one that well.'

'Dad told me we had fish until I was three.'

Meg screwed up her face, reaching for the memory. She would have been around fifteen. 'Dory and Nemo, I'd forgotten about that.'

A door slammed in the hall and another opened, but the flat remained silent. It was an odd kind of quiet, as though the world had been paused and was waiting to restart. Meg's eyes met her sister's. 'Shall we go to the cafe and get a hot chocolate – with marshmallows?'

Emily's face lit. 'With sprinkles, like we used to?' They hadn't made hot drinks together in about ten years.

'I always reserve my sprinkles for special occasions,' Meg said, opening the door so she could creep into the hallway. 'But I think this might just be special enough.'

She followed Emily down the stairs, padding past the kitchen where her parents were now talking in soft whispers, thinking that perhaps reconnecting with her sister could be one silver lining to this whole thing.

Chapter Ten

Tom sanded the edge of the wooden worktop in the cottage kitchen smooth, before pushing it into place underneath the set of grey cupboards he'd hung earlier. The radio was playing in the background and the house was hot, even though he'd switched the heating off hours before. Cooper got up so he could examine Tom's handiwork, sniffing at the new cupboard before wagging his tail in approval.

'Walk?' Tom asked the dog, and was instantly rewarded with a woeful moan. 'Sorry. We both need some exercise, but there'll be plenty of treats if you don't fuss.' He scrubbed a hand over the dog's head, picked up his boots and put them by the door. Then he opened the cupboard in the boot room so he could pick up a lead, spotting the Gibson guitar sitting inside. It was still in the same place he'd put it when he'd moved in. Tom stared at the instrument for a moment, fighting the need to pick it up. He knew exactly how it would feel – the weight in his hands, the way the strap would dig into his shoulder before finding the natural dip all those years of playing had moulded. Once, merely strumming his guitar would have had people falling at his feet. He shook his head. He'd loved every moment of it. Every second of adoration. As if the simple act of playing an instrument somehow made him special and set him apart.

Meg's face flashed into his mind at that moment. The anger in her eyes when she'd seen him picking up the baubles by the Promise Tree. She didn't adore him. He wasn't sure she even liked him that much, aside from in that fleeting moment when he'd helped her with her dad's suitcase. In a strange way he found that appealing. Being disliked felt a lot more honest.

Had Marnie, his beloved ex-wife – who'd been so determined to stay Marnie Riley-Clark that she'd hidden her true feelings from him for years – ever looked at him with such passion? He doubted she'd had enough emotion invested in him to summon up any kind of strong feelings. But it had been no more than he'd deserved. He wasn't special, never had been. Music had been an illusion, had given him a gloss he'd thought was real. Until he'd been forced to face the truth. It was nothing more than a transaction with no authentic emotion underneath.

As if the world were conspiring against him, 'If Every Day Was Christmas' began to play on the radio and Tom marched back into the kitchen to switch it off. He grabbed a coat and headed for the hall, sliding on his walking boots just as someone gently tapped on the front door. Cooper wagged his tail and barked. It was freezing outside and Tom ushered Davey in, dodging the over-excited dog who was now pawing for attention. 'I need to walk him,' he explained, and Davey laughed when Cooper began to back down the hall.

'I'll join you.' Davey looked towards the corner of the room, to the empty space where the guitar had stood. 'It'll give us a chance to talk.'

Tom closed the door behind him and clipped the lead onto Cooper's collar so he could encourage him to follow. It took a couple of gentle tugs before the dog would move from the doorstep into the snow. He whimpered when his paws hit the cold, but he followed with his head bowed, looking up at Tom every now and again with a gloomy expression. 'If you keep complaining, I'll get you one of those dog coats when we next go to Meg's, to keep you warm,' he joked. 'You'd make a lovely reindeer.'

The air was frigid, but it wasn't snowing anymore. Tom had been holed up ever since he'd left Meg in the Christmas shop with her parents the day before. He ignored the stab of guilt. It wasn't like he could do anything to help, and she'd wanted him to leave. But he hadn't been back – instead he'd hidden himself away, intent on putting as much distance between them as possible. Because he was afraid of the way she made him feel. Which was ironic for a man who'd vowed to spend the rest of his life helping people.

'Jason Jones called me,' Davey said, naming the saxophone player from The Ballad Club. Tom didn't say anything as they walked along a snowy track next to the road which would lead them into a huge field that would ultimately end at the bottom of the mountains framing Lockton. 'He said he's been emailing and trying to call. He's in talks with the record company about re-releasing some of your old songs. He talked to Britney Dahl and she's all in.' An image of the band's drummer flashed into Tom's mind. 'He just wanted you to know…'

'So now I do.' As they reached the field, Tom unclipped the lead from Cooper, picked up a stick poking out of the snow and threw it – but the dog stayed put.

'They do say that after a while people begin to resemble their dogs. In this instance, I think it's the other way around. Cooper seems as determined not to enjoy life as you.' Davey adjusted his dark wool hat so it covered his ears. 'You know one of your songs is being used in a Christmas ad for the supermarket, FoodAll?'

'Nope,' Tom said as a thought occurred to him. 'Is it "If Every Day Was Christmas"? That's why I can't get away from the damn song – it seems to be playing everywhere I turn.'

'Yep, and three of The Ballad Club's other tracks are marching up the charts behind it. You're having a resurgence. Apparently the PR people want you and the others to come back to London. Jason said people are begging to interview you all. He can't go but he wondered if you wanted to. There's a whole world down there waiting for you to get back in touch.'

'Well, they can keep waiting,' Tom shot back. 'Because I'm not going back. Jason's in France making pots – in between negotiating with the record company, apparently – and Britney's opened a nightclub and had two kids. We've all moved on. As far as I'm concerned, that chapter of my life is over.' He picked up another stick and threw it hard – more for himself than for Cooper. It felt good as he watched it hit the snow and land, poking up like a long arrow.

'I get how all that attention and fame might bring you down,' Davey said dryly. They crunched across the field in silence for a while before he added, 'In all seriousness, I understand Marnie hurt you. It must have been hard finding out she'd been seeing someone else. Waking up on Christmas morning to find out your wife has left you and your present is a set of divorce papers would be enough to upset anyone.'

Tom almost laughed. In truth, it had crucified him. But the day had got far worse. He'd had a headache, he remembered. He'd been working in the studio for three weeks straight. Marnie had been hosting a Christmas Eve party. His house was filled with strangers who'd all wanted to shake his hand. He'd been like an empty vessel. Moving from day to day in a dream. Relishing all the attention, the so-called success. Until that morning, when his whole world had come crashing in and he'd been forced to face the man he was. An unhappy, lonely sucker. As far away from a star as you could get.

'Your grandmother wouldn't blame you,' Davey said gently.

'I blame me,' Tom snapped. 'My grandad had been calling all night. Twelve hours, when she was in the hospital fighting for her life after the stroke. He had to handle the whole thing alone because I was so obsessed by my music. I'd left my mobile at the studio and Marnie had unplugged the house phone because of the party. I didn't even say goodbye…' He shook his head.

'You were busy,' Davey said, and winced.

'That's not an excuse. They took me in after Mum decided having a kid was too much trouble and took off. I owe them everything. Grandma died and I didn't know until I reconnected the phone to call and wish them happy Christmas. I hadn't seen them for weeks.' He swallowed the lump of emotion threatening to overwhelm him.

'Your grandad doesn't blame you,' Davey said quietly.

'Because he's a good man. They were good people. They raised me to be the same. Shame I ended up as such a disappointment.' He stood still for a moment so he could admire the view. The blue of the sky, the snowy mountains at the horizon. The scenery in Lockton had a way of making you feel small. Making you recognise how insignificant you were. It was a lesson he needed to keep front and centre of his mind.

'Seems to me whenever I met your grandparents they were nothing but proud. I'm not sure you're seeing things clearly.' Davey let out a soft breath. 'I came to ask if you wanted to play in the Christmas concert. I saw the way you looked at the Gibson when you arrived. I see the way your foot taps when a song comes on. That faraway look you get when you're thinking – like you're coming up with lyrics because I know you can't help yourself. You're not happy, Tom. I can see that. Music's part of who you are. You can't pretend it's not important. It's not something you should turn your back on. It's like you've shut down that whole side of yourself and you're pushing everyone away. Because you can't bear for anyone to care for you.' Cooper whined, suddenly stopping in the snow and swivelling his head so he could look over his shoulder.

'He's cold.' Tom plucked a treat from his pocket and offered it to the dog, who gulped it down like Captain Scott enjoying his final meal. 'We ought to turn back. I appreciate everything you're saying. But I don't need anyone except Cooper – and I really don't need music. I'm happy serving behind the bar, helping to put in your kitchen. Doing those things makes me feel good about myself in a way that music hasn't for a long while. I'm helping – doing something meaningful with my life.'

'Giving up your soul.' Davey's shoulders slumped. 'If you change your mind, you know I'd love to see you perform. Music didn't turn you into a bad person, Tom. I worked in the business for long enough to spot one of those. I was surrounded by them for years. You were always different.' His forehead scrunched and he stopped so he could study Tom's profile. 'You had something about you. A need to perform and a desire to work harder than anybody. You were always kind and polite, regardless of who you were talking to. You didn't let people down. You gave more than you took. So you lost your head for a few years, married the wrong woman, partied a little too hard. Who didn't in their twenties?' He shrugged. 'Turning your back on the kind of talent you have is a crime.'

'Picking up that guitar would be a worse one,' Tom said, wishing he could make his friend understand. 'Music turns me into someone I don't want to be. I'll lose myself, forget what and who's important… People stop seeing me, love me for something I'm not.'

'Without it, you're going to be miserable,' Davey said sadly. 'It's like you're turning your back on yourself. Shutting everything and everyone out.'

'I disagree,' Tom said, but the words fell flat. As they walked on in silence, he wondered if his friend might be right. But he knew he wasn't brave enough to find out.

Chapter Eleven

Meg swiped a hand over her forehead as she ticked off another twenty snowman baubles on her stock list. She'd been working all day, counting tinsel, decorations and everything else she could find in the stockroom in the back of her shop, ready for a promotion she planned to kick off tomorrow. She picked up a reindeer salt shaker and spun it in her hand, watching the surface sparkle under the overhead lights. They had snowman shakers at her parents' house which were only used on Christmas Day. Last year, her dad had put on silly voices and made them dance, and her mother had laughed – the lines around her eyes deepening with something other than worry. They'd pulled crackers and told stupid jokes, the kind her dad would tell all the time. But on Christmas Day, her mum's eyes had sparkled and she'd laughed instead of frowning – the sound had been joyful and light. Her mum and dad had smiled at each other with love shimmering in their eyes. Then, on Boxing Day, they'd retreated back into their offices and silence had once against reigned, punctuated by random squabbles over nothing at all. The whole thing had felt like something out of *Groundhog Day* – the uncomfortable feelings had followed Meg up to Lockton until she'd walked into her Christmas shop and everything had been okay again.

Meg swallowed and put the shakers away, ticking them off her list. The shop was in semi-darkness when she crept out ten minutes later and found Cora mopping the floor.

'Evening, lassie.' The older woman looked at her with a frown. 'You look tired. I'm guessing you didn't take a break? No good will come of working yourself to the bone, lass. You need to have some fun.'

'You sound just like Agnes. I've almost finished. I'm working on a promotion. I just need to reprogram the till and put posters up.' Meg picked up a cloth so she could dampen it in the sink behind the counter. The tap, which had been dripping for a few weeks now, had a steady stream of water dribbling out. 'What happened?'

'Ach, I tried to turn it off,' Cora said. 'Maybe I'm stronger than I look because the drip got worse. Our usual plumber's doing a big job in Morridon and he's staying out that way because of the weather. Don't worry, I called that laddie, Tom. He was supposed to come earlier, but got held up. He's popping over in a minute.'

Meg stroked a hand over her hair, smoothing it down. She'd put some glitter on this morning, but most of it had rubbed off. She searched behind the counter, pulled out a sparkly compact she'd stashed there to stop her mother from tidying it up and patted her cheeks.

'We're lucky we don't need an electrician. I've heard tales of month-long waits. This snow has caused utter chaos around here. Do you mind if I head home?' Cora took the mop and bucket into the back. 'Marcus has been out all day, and I've a new jam for him to try. It's called Eager Elk and has cranberries and oranges in the recipe.' She looked excited. 'I think it's going to be the one. While I remember, he asked me to tell you he's had no luck tracking down your vandals. But there have been other reports of Christmas decorations going missing.' She shrugged. 'He'll keep looking – we'll want to catch the dunderheads before they do some real damage.' She tugged off her red pinafore and hung it up behind the counter, picking up her coat.

'Do you want me to drive you?' Meg checked outside the shop. Snow was still fluttering down thickly and you could barely see the other side of the street.

'Nae lassie, Marcus is going to pick me up.' Her phone pinged in her pocket. 'That'll be him now. You'd better wait here for the hot toddy. He'll be arriving any moment.' She winked. 'He's a good-looking laddie – remember, sometimes differences can be a good thing. Just look at Agnes and Fergus.' With that she swept out of the front, setting off 'Jingle Bells'. Meg stood, staring after Cora for a moment, feeling something flutter low in her belly. She busied herself putting out posters ready for tomorrow and programming the till, listening all the time for movement outside.

Half an hour later there was a tap on the door, and she went to open it. Tom was covered in snowflakes and Cooper came bounding inside, almost knocking her flying before sinking onto the wooden floor with a whimper.

'He's sulking because I made him leave the house.' Tom looked amused. 'Cora mentioned you had a problem with your tap and it was an emergency?'

Meg groaned. 'It's no emergency. She shouldn't have dragged you out, we're hardly battling a flood.'

'I'm here now, you might as well show me.' When she didn't move, he added, 'Do I need a password?' He closed his eyes. 'Let me guess, mince pies?'

Meg chuckled – Tom always seemed to find a way to make her laugh. Was that how it had been in the early days with her mum and dad? What had changed everything? Or hadn't they been right for each other from the start – how did you know? Confusion made her frown as she pointed towards the cafe. 'It's behind the counter.'

He strode ahead, carrying a large black toolbox. She watched as he stripped off his coat and hat, placing them onto one of the chairs in the cafe, before walking behind the booth. He turned on the tap and examined it more closely.

'You need a new washer, this one's perished. I've got one in the box somewhere.' Tom pulled the toolbox open and searched inside, scattering hammers, screwdrivers and other tools to the side.

'You not working in the pub?' Meg let her eyes drop to his fingers. He kept his nails short and even though his hands were large, they were graceful. He picked out a washer and gave a short cheer, grabbing a wrench.

'Davey gave me the evening off. He said he's not expecting to be busy because of the snow.' He walked behind the counter again and Cooper trotted into the cafe, pressing his body up against Meg's legs until she scratched his head.

'Have you always been good with your hands?' Meg asked, and Tom turned to stare as her cheeks reddened. 'I mean, have you always been able to fix things?' She kept her voice even, but butterflies had begun to climb from her chest into her throat.

'Is this an interview?' he asked, looking wary.

'My shop, my turn to ask the questions.' She smiled when he frowned. His face was made for dark, moody expressions. She'd always favoured smiley people – Ned had never stopped – but there was something soulful and mysterious about Tom. It made her want to scratch the surface, to find out what made him tick.

'I like fixing things,' he said simply.

'Because?'

'In some small way, I feel like I'm doing something worthwhile. Working with my hands helps me stay connected to the world.' His eyes sparkled suddenly. 'You like helping people – you rescued me when I broke down, found Morag a new pet, let your family stay. I may have found something we have in common, after all.'

'Yet you still don't like Christmas…' Meg said, with a woeful sigh.

There was a thump overhead and Tom's eyes darkened. 'Everything okay?'

Meg nodded. 'Of course.' Her voice sounded wrong.

'How are your parents getting on?' he asked.

'Same as… usual,' she stumbled, wondering why she was finding it harder to pretend each time he asked.

Tom stared at her for a moment. It was like he was reading her, seeing inside her mind, sidestepping all the pretence and lies. She broke eye contact and looked at the patterned cloth on the table in front of her, at the grinning snowmen peppered between green holly and red berries, and tried to find some solace in the festive image.

Tom came out from behind the counter and picked up a different wrench from the toolbox. His eyes skimmed her face. 'Were the toddlers out again this evening? They missed your cheeks, but you have a sparkly nose.' Their eyes met, but then he must have realised he was staring, because he walked back to the sink. There was another bang overhead. 'They staying long?'

Meg put her mobile into the deck beside the counter and switched it on, filling the room with music, masking any further noise. A Christmas song came on and Tom stiffened, but she decided not to tease him about it again. 'Mum and Emily are booked on a flight on the twenty-first, so another week, and Dad's here until they go, I suppose.' Her stomach tightened. 'The subject's a little uncomfortable so we haven't discussed it.' They hadn't discussed anything. She picked at a piece of tinsel hanging on the wall beside her, twisting the strands between her fingers. She usually loved the way the light reflected in it, creating different colours, obliterating everything else and lifting her spirits, but today she still felt unsettled.

'So you'll spend Christmas here alone?'

'That's the way I want it,' Meg said chirpily.

'Snap,' he said seriously. 'Those similarities are stacking up.' He had a sexy voice, with a deep timbre when he pronounced the letter 'r' that vibrated low in her belly.

Meg swallowed. 'Do you want a drink?' Her voice was brusque. 'Or a mince pie? I'm all out of cheese…'

'I'm good.' He gave her a half-smile. 'Almost finished now.'

Cooper came to press his head into Meg's legs again, and Tom turned as she scratched his ears. 'You know he's always around if you want to talk?' he said lightly.

Meg nodded, her eyes filling with tears – she smiled to mask them.

Tom put his tools back into the bag and Cooper whined. The dog nudged against her heels as Tom closed the lid and looked down at her. They were close, and Cooper nosed her again, perhaps trying to push them together? He'd probably decided if she entertained Tom, they wouldn't have to go back into the snow. 'I shouldn't admit to this… but if you talk to Cooper, I might listen in. I'm good at fixing things.' Deep grooves appeared in his forehead. 'Not my own problems – other people's are much easier.'

'I don't think you can make this better with a new washer,' Meg said sadly, and Tom gave her one of his rare smiles. 'You don't do that much,' she observed.

'What?' he asked, his eyes moving slowly to hers again.

She made a smiley face gesture with her finger in the air between them, tracing the arch of his mouth, making it transform into a genuine grin that took her breath. His brown eyes warmed and her heart thumped again as she swallowed. Cooper was still pressed against her, so she couldn't step back. Even though every cell in her body was warning her this man was wrong for her. She could smell Tom now, a mixture of sawdust, paint and something woody. He reached out and ran the tip of his finger across her nose, then examined it.

'Despite everything, you smile a lot,' he said. 'Do you think it's catching, like the glitter?' He showed her his finger. Some of the sparkles had transferred, making it shimmer.

'Perhaps,' she said, her voice husky.

'You've got some on your lips too.' His eyes dropped to her mouth, her stomach sank, and every inch of her body began to hum. Then his eyes lowered to take in her outfit. 'Is it magic? I'm wondering, if I kiss you, will I be happy all the time, or turn into an elf?'

She barked out a laugh and his eyes sparkled. 'Now I'd say that's a risk worth taking,' she said because he was obviously joking. 'Besides, Santa could do with the extra help.'

His face turned serious. He dipped his head so he could move his mouth lightly across hers. Not joking then. His lips were soft and full and Meg found herself leaning into them, found her hand moving up so she could stroke the stubbled surface of his jaw. It felt softer than she'd expected and she ran her fingers lightly across it before touching the ends of his hair, which curled around the tips as if determined to lock them there. He turned his head as they explored each other's mouths. He didn't touch her anywhere else. It was almost as if he couldn't trust himself, or he didn't want to get that close. She felt tingles travelling from her lips down to her toes and had to stop herself from grabbing him. She hadn't been kissed like this in a long time, hadn't wanted to have these feelings. But somehow, like a kid unwrapping a Christmas present, determined to find out what was under the layers – she couldn't help herself. Definitely couldn't stop.

Tom moved back and looked down. His top lip was sparkly now.

'I think I *am* rubbing off on you.' She pointed to his mouth when he looked confused. 'But you're not smiling anymore.' She swallowed, wondering if she was going mad, deciding she definitely was, but seemingly unable to stop the slow slide into insanity. She was drawn to him for some reason, and she had no idea why that was. She only knew she didn't want to fight it. At least, not at this exact moment. She was prepared to dismiss every reservation and sensible thought in the name of chemistry. 'Perhaps we should try again?' She stepped forwards, felt the dog move with her – determined to push them together. She lifted her head up and went back onto her tiptoes so she could reach. He was a lot taller and had to bend. Yet another mark against them. For a moment Meg didn't think he would, but then Tom must have changed his mind. This kiss was less gentle. It was as though they'd done the preliminaries, unwrapped the first layer, and were ready to go deeper. It was hotter and hastier. Tom still didn't touch her. But she let her hand snake around him, across the waistband of his trousers, tracing the muscular torso, following the line of taut muscles up the centre of his back. Heat shot through her entire body. He felt warm and solid and she wanted so much to lean into him, but didn't want to push things too far. Besides, she had no idea what was happening here, why two people with so little in common seemed so physically in tune.

This time she broke the kiss and leaned back. By her feet Cooper let out a long sigh, realising he wasn't going to get his way. She stepped over the dog, and moved backwards again until she hit the wall. Then she folded her arms across her chest.

'Well, that was…' Her eyes tipped upwards as she spotted the single sprig of mistletoe hanging like the Sword of Damocles above Tom's head. Had that been to blame for what had happened? He looked up too and grimaced before starting to pack the tools away. 'Thank you,' she said, trying to find some normality. 'For fixing the tap and for… being so kind.'

He nodded without looking at her. 'All part of the service.' He winced. 'Perhaps not that last bit.'

Meg could feel him on her lips, and forced herself not to run a fingertip over them while he was standing there. 'Why not?'

She gave him a smile, intent on proving the encounter hadn't affected her, a little overwhelmed by how much it had. 'A kissing plumber – it's definitely a selling point. I'll make sure I tell Morag and Cora. You'll get a lot of emergency calls from the members of the Jam Club.'

'I shouldn't have done that.' He looked embarrassed.

'I probably shouldn't have either, but we were in that kiss together,' she said firmly. 'So don't feel guilty about it. You made me feel a lot better this evening. Let's call it a little Christmas madness brought on by tinsel, glitter and my incredibly sexy elf outfit.' She looked down at her red trousers and green top and did a little wiggle, aiming to lighten the mood. 'Let's face it, I'm pretty irresistible.'

It worked, because Tom laughed, visibly relaxing. 'It seems I might have a soft spot for it after all.' He closed his toolbox and picked it up.

'Maybe I'll order you one of your own.' Meg followed him before she stopped. 'How much do I owe you for fixing the tap?'

'Nothing. It was a favour. All part of my quest to give back.' He headed for the door with Cooper dragging his paws, looking dejected.

Meg picked up a bauble on the way past one of the shelves. 'Then I owe you a favour in return. At least let me give you one of these.' She held the bauble up in front him, almost giggling at his horrified expression. 'Seriously, make a promise and hang it on the tree. You're in Lockton now, Tom, practically one of us. Perhaps you could promise to like Christmas a smidgen – there may be something you can find to enjoy if you think hard enough?' She grinned again, charmed by his thoughtful expression. Tom frowned, but took the bauble and placed it into his pocket. He stared at her for a moment and then opened his mouth, just as someone began to hammer loudly at the front of the shop.

Lilith stood, dripping, in the entrance as Meg unlocked and opened the door. She was wearing jeans, a bright red jumper, a long coat and sensible flat shoes which made her about six inches shorter than usual. 'I've been looking for you everywhere,' she wailed at Tom. 'I called the pub and Davey said Cora told him you were here.' Her eyes flicked between Tom and Meg and she looked suspicious. Then she noticed the toolbox in Tom's hand and let out a relieved breath. '*Grazie Dio*. I have an emergency. A pipe's cracked in the hotel kitchen. There's water everywhere. The plumber I usually use isn't answering his phone. I don't know what to do.' She ran a hand through her dark hair, looking distressed and tugging random strands from the shiny, perfect ponytail. 'The floor is completely flooded. There was a big bang, and now the fridge and freezer have gone off. The kettle won't work either.' She let out an unsteady breath. 'You have to help. I must fix it *pronto*. My guests… and what about Christmas? My parents are coming in ten days and everything has to be perfect!' Her Italian accent became more pronounced as she fired off each word in rapid succession, like bullets from an AK-47. The hysterical tirade was such a contrast to the cool, calm persona Lilith normally portrayed.

'Don't worry. I can come now,' Tom offered, ignoring Cooper's whine.

'I will too,' Meg said. When Lilith began to shake her head, she added, 'You're going to need a dogsbody to help clear up the mess.'

Lilith's face darkened. They had a long history – involving Meg's ex Ned who had dated them both for a time. Lilith had blamed Meg, accusing her of being the cheater. They hadn't put the whole affair completely behind them and Meg could tell the chef wasn't sure. 'Fine,' she snapped. 'I haven't time to argue. My car is outside. I'll drive us and drop you back later – we need to go now.'

Meg didn't wait to pick up a coat. She suspected Lilith would leave her behind and wasn't crazy about the idea of being back in her flat. Instead she trailed Tom and Cooper as they headed out of the shop, stopping so she could pull the door closed behind her and quickly lock up. Then she followed, wishing Lilith had appeared just a little later, wondering exactly what Tom had been about to say to her those few moments before.

Chapter Twelve

'How bad is it?' Davey asked from the back of Lilith's sleek, black four-by-four Maserati where he was sitting between Cooper and Meg. They'd stopped beside Apple Cross Inn to pick him up and he'd been waiting outside, dressed in boots and practical dark clothes that suggested he'd been hoping for the call. Tom had insisted Davey come – he suspected he'd need as many pairs of hands as he could get and wanted the safety of additional numbers. After kissing Meg in her cafe – then almost asking her out – he wasn't sure he could trust himself to be around her without a crowd, or at the very least a straitjacket. It was hard enough sitting in the same car. What was it about that ridiculous red and green outfit? He hated Christmas and had never harboured a secret desire to kiss an elf, for God's sake… but it was the first time in almost three years his heart had kicked up a notch.

'It's a *catástrofe*,' Lilith answered, shaking her head.

'Don't worry.' Davey reached forward to pat her gently on the shoulder as she drove through the snow towards the hotel. 'We can… whatever's happened. What I mean is, whatever's happened, we'll help.' He paused, his face contorting. '*You*, we'll help *you*.'

Lilith exhaled loudly but didn't respond, and Tom wondered what her story was. Davey was clearly crazy about her. Normally he was so calm and collected, so in control, but when he was around Lilith he turned into a babbling idiot. Lyrics began to form in his mind about unrequited love – like random puzzle pieces finding the exact perfect spot, linking together until they'd formed a picture. His fingers joined in, subconsciously tapping a beat on his jeans, picking out complementary notes like a magpie selecting the most attractive shiny objects. Until he realised what he was doing.

He swore and made his hand into a fist, then stared out of the windscreen, ignoring Meg in the back and the Promise Tree as they drove past, taking a left out of Lockton. Snow was falling in huge flakes, settling on the bright white road framed with swollen drifts on either side. They travelled in silence, absorbed in their thoughts – then five minutes later Tom saw a building in the distance. He could see it was old and had three floors. Most of the lights were on, a beacon in the darkness. Then Lilith swung into a car park and pulled up behind the hotel, screeching to a stop beside a low stone wall. She hopped out and slammed the door, then signalled at them to follow, running through the snow then down some steps, and throwing open a door before waiting beside it. Davey reached her first and followed Lilith inside, down more steps to the kitchen.

They stood at the edge of the huge room, taking a moment to review the situation. The kitchen took up at least half of what Tom guessed was an old basement, although it was obvious it had been extended. It was lit by lantern torches that had been placed on counters in the four furthest corners. There was a large white worksurface in the centre, which he suspected was where most of the cooking took place. The left-hand wall was lined with high-tech silver fridges, including one filled with wine, but there were no lights indicating they were on. Another wall held a couple of sinks and a shiny metal draining board. The floor was submerged and water streamed from a pipe to the right of the sink unit. Someone had wrapped a couple of bright blue towels around it, but they did nothing to stem the flow.

'I'm sure that bang meant the electric fused.' Lilith stepped onto the flooded tiled floor. 'I know it's safe to walk here because I already have. The rest of the hotel's on a different electrical circuit so the guests are fine. I've looked for the stopcock.' She pronounced the word carefully, her accent strong. 'I switched it off, but *nada*!' She threw up her arms, glaring at the leaking pipe as if it could understand and had simply chosen to misbehave.

Davey let out a heavy sigh and followed her into the wet, then Tom did the same, ignoring the frigid water as it seeped into his boots. He held out a hand to Meg who gingerly took it so he could help her take the last step. She let go immediately, probably registering the same flare of heat. She was still wearing her elf suit and a pair of green boots that were the perfect accompaniment to the outfit and looked waterproof. But she hadn't worn a coat and he noticed a shiver rack her body. He pulled his off and offered it to her.

'You'll get cold.'

She shook her head.

'I'm about to get on my knees in this. I'm wondering if you'll keep my coat warm and dry by wearing it? If I leave it with Cooper, he'll just slobber all over it looking for biscuits.' He gave her a half-smile. 'Please?'

He watched her face as she warred with indecision. 'Fine. But tell me if you want it back, and if you start shivering, all bets are off.' She pulled it on and tugged it around her. Then she pointed at Cooper, who was perched in a dry patch at the edge of the kitchen, watching them with a baleful expression. 'He's a smart dog.' She smiled, making his heart thump again. 'Have you any mops?' Meg asked Lilith, who was scowling at the floor.

'*Sì*, in the cupboard.' Lilith pointed to the corner, and Meg picked up one of the lanterns from the counter, disappearing inside the small room.

'That's a bad leak.' Davey knelt so he could look at the pipe, then pulled one of the towels away. He was immediately sprayed with a jet of icy water and quickly replaced the towel, turning to Tom with a grimace, his face dripping wet. 'I think that observation represented the extent of my expertise in this situation.' He was word perfect now he wasn't talking directly to Lilith. He swiped a hand over his face and grinned when Meg reappeared with a couple of buckets and mops, and put them on the floor. 'Fortunately I've never had a problem with getting my hands dirty.'

Lilith watched as Meg and Davey picked up the mops and began to wipe the floor, wringing out the water into the buckets before mopping again. The process was slow and laborious.

'You'd better get on with fixing that pipe – the words "waste" and "time" are springing to mind,' Davey told Tom, as more water leaked out to replace what he'd just mopped away.

Tom put his toolbox onto the counter. 'Show me the stopcock.'

Lilith pointed to the cupboard under the sink.

'I've switched it off – *idiota* thing doesn't work.' She turned and stared at Meg and Davey. 'I don't comprehend why you're doing this. It's cold and wet.' She frowned at them both. 'I'll pay Tom, but you barely even know me.'

'I don't want money.' Tom peered into the cupboard.

Davey shrugged. 'It's called help… giving, offering help.' He stumbled over the words and looked at her uncertainly. 'Looking out… for each other, people.' He swallowed as a tsunami of red swept up his face. 'Don't you… I mean, surely you do the same. In Italy? With your people, I mean your family?'

'No,' Lilith said darkly. 'Not in my family. We look out for ourselves.'

'Well… we do. We look out for each other here, in Lockton.' His face was a picture of sympathy.

'I still don't understand. You could be drinking red wine in your pub.' Lilith's eyes flicked to Meg. 'Playing with those pretty fairy lights you love, or spending time with your parents…'

Tom fiddled with the stopcock, checking it was turned to the right. 'This is for hot water. That leak's cold. Are there any other taps like this in the kitchen?'

Lilith pivoted on the spot so she could look around the room. 'I would ask my assistant chef, but he's staying away this evening. I only know about that one. The pipes were replaced about ten years ago when the previous owners built an extension. It could be in a different place.'

'The store cupboard's full of all sorts of things – I noticed a couple of taps on the wall behind where the mops were propped up,' Meg said. She pointed behind her before going in to look. Tom followed, and found her leaning over so she could examine a knob sticking out of the wall more closely. She turned it anti-clockwise.

'The leak's stopped,' Davey shouted. 'Give me a sec.' They waited. 'Yep, no shower. You found it.'

Meg stood and grinned at Tom, dusting her hands together. 'Lucky I'm here. I've no idea what you'd have done without me.' The cupboard was dim aside from a bright shaft of light from the torch. It lit her face, making the last remnants of glitter sparkle on her lips and nose. 'If you need any other assistance, just give me a shout.' Her eyes met his.

'I'll bear that in mind,' he said as his feet refused to move. He looked down at her. There was something about Meg that got to him. He really didn't understand it. But then he'd never met a woman who dressed like an elf, was obsessed with Christmas and seemed incapable of not smiling, even when her world was upside down.

She looked at him oddly, then pressed a hand to his chest and pushed gently, making his heart thump hard. 'You need to move, that floor won't mop itself.' She smiled again. 'You've been amazing tonight, helping me and then Lilith.'

'It was nothing,' Tom said, feeling awkward but pleased. He was used to compliments for his singing, fawning adoration for something he'd just been lucky enough to have a talent for. But this was different, because it felt real. An unexpected burst of pride warmed his chest. For the first time in a long time, someone had seen the man behind the famous face and liked him regardless. Would it be different if Meg knew who he was?

'What are you doing in there?' Davey shouted.

'Nothing.' Tom spun around and headed back into the kitchen. The water had stopped, so he made quick work of replacing the small section of pipe that had worn away. As he did, Meg and Davey continued to mop the grey tiled floor, wringing the water into the bucket and tipping it into the sink, as Lilith used a towel to finish up. When Tom was done, he switched the water back on.

'*Grazie. Grazie*, all of you.' Lilith shook her head. 'I don't know what I'd have done without you. That leak would have gone on all night. Flooded my hotel. My parents wouldn't have been able to come for Christmas.'

'That's important? I mean, to you?' Davey asked. He was still mopping the floor, but he stopped so he could look at her properly.

'*Sì.*' Lilith's eyes shifted to Davey and she gave him a small smile. Then she waded through the few remaining puddles so she could check the cupboards as Tom packed his tools away. When she got to the fridge and freezer she opened them and frowned into the darkness. 'What about these? I almost forgot. Can I put the electric back on?'

Tom shook his head. 'You said there was a bang. The circuit probably blew. You'll need an electrician to look at it.'

Lilith let out a gasp as she turned to gesticulate at the fridges. 'But my food's in there. Wine, ingredients, everything I need to feed my guests. I've only three people staying but it'll get busier near Christmas. Don't forget, the bands are staying here – I've been stocking up.'

'The closest electrician is five miles outside Morridon. We can try him, although Cora says it's hard to get hold of anyone at the moment.' Meg checked her watch, screwing up her face when she registered the time. 'Perhaps it would be better to leave it till the morning?'

'I need help now.' Lilith pulled out her mobile and scrawled through it, then quickly dialled. They watched as she squinted and listened to a message before hanging up. 'He's unavailable for the next few days, but he gave another number. I think I can remember it…' She dialled the new number, listened again and hissed, her eyes flashing. 'He's busy too. Does no one in this place need the work?' She threw up her arms. 'What about all my food? It's going to go bad.'

'It's probably the weather,' Davey said calmly, morphing into the man Tom recognised. He knew that look from his own crisis, when Marnie had left and he'd discovered his grandmother had died. The way Davey had taken over, focusing on practicalities, helping him clear his house after the party, chucking out the random strangers who'd decided to stay, making him coffee before taking him to the hospital. 'Bring everything to the pub,' Davey suggested, pouring a final bucket into the sink before admiring the floor. He wiped it once more with the mop before leaning against one of the counters. 'I've got plenty of room in my fridges.' Tom noticed Davey didn't look at Lilith – perhaps afraid he'd get tongue-tied? 'There's an empty one in my garage. I keep it for storing food and wine when we're hosting events or are likely to be busy, like at Christmas.' He made a face. 'We haven't begun to stockpile for that yet. Johnny was about to visit the cash and carry in Inverness but the weather turned too nasty. You can prepare meals in our kitchen, or Johnny can give you something from our menu to tide you over. Does the cooker work?'

'*Sì*, it's gas.' Lilith took a deep breath and nodded. 'I can use matches to light it. We can wash up by hand. I need lots of space for my ingredients.'

Davey's blue eyes sparkled. He looked like he was enjoying himself. 'We have plenty.'

Lilith frowned. 'I don't understand,' she repeated. 'But I will say *grazie*.' Her eyes skirted the room, resting on Tom and then Meg. 'For helping. I can't say I'd have done the same for you.' She pulled a face. 'I don't think I would. My family taught me different things. That the world is… I think your expression is *dog eat dog*?' In the corner Cooper barked, reminding them all he was there.

'Not in Lockton,' Davey said, his voice warm with sympathy.

'Shall we put the food into your car?' Meg put the mop back into the cupboard and Davey opened the fridge so they could start to take out the ingredients. Tom watched with his heart in his throat, trying to hold on to this feeling. Because it felt good. And it was one of the first times in the last few years that he'd begun to feel alive – aside from in that moment a few hours earlier when he'd been kissing Meg.

Chapter Thirteen

Tom was tired. He'd helped Davey, Meg and Lilith move supplies from the hotel to the pub and hadn't arrived home until after midnight. Then he'd tossed and turned, his mind filled with Meg, and woken at dawn when Davey had called asking if he'd visit Morag to help with another emergency before coming to work. He rolled his shoulders as he took the road out of Lockton towards Inverness. He drove carefully, taking it slowly over the uneven white carpet, thanking his lucky stars that his car was able to handle the tough conditions. Over the last day the roads had become impassable once you got more than five miles outside the village, meaning Lockton was almost cut off. Last night, Davey had confided he'd begun to worry about the bands making it to the concert, although he'd heard the weather was due to take a turn for the better soon. Tom had considered offering to stand in for a nanosecond, before stopping that thought. If he picked up the guitar, he was afraid he'd lose himself. Worse, Meg and the rest of Lockton would find out who he was and they'd start treating him differently. Seeing the fame and what he could give, rather than the man he was trying to be. Then he'd have to move on… just when he was starting to wonder if he'd found somewhere he could stay for a while.

Tom parked outside a double-fronted cottage with a white picket fence and large garden. A wooden gate – which sat just off-centre of the fence and opened to what Tom presumed was a pathway to the front door – had been propped up. There were knitted Christmas decorations hanging across the facade of the house, with gaps where pieces were missing. Tom squinted out of the windscreen and saw Morag peering through one of the front windows of the house, waving to him. It felt good riding to the rescue, knowing that what he did meant something.

Morag opened the door and motioned to Tom again. Behind him Cooper sprang up and pressed his nose to the glass. Tom hopped out of the car, unfastening the boot to pick up his toolbox, then opened the back door and ordered Cooper out. The dog obeyed, but complained when his paws hit the snow.

Morag met Tom when he was halfway across her garden. She'd pulled on a big bright pink coat which was buttoned to her chin, and a mismatched green bobble hat with purple gloves. She looked more like a rainbow than a person. Cooper bounded up to her, and she gave him a scratch on the head. 'Took your time.'

'Sorry. Is the gate the emergency?' Tom scoured the large garden, which was overrun with snow and ice.

'Aye. Some eejit knocked it down. Broke the hinges to boot. If I don't get it back on, I'll get all sorts of things wandering into my garden.' She scowled at the ground. 'There are bulbs down there. I don't want a load of dunderhead critters wandering in and turning them into a slap-up meal.'

'I'll get started.' Tom studied the gate. It was an easy fix and wouldn't take long.

'You should come inside first. I've made coffee and cake, and we'll have a wee dram of whisky to warm us.' She narrowed her eyes, challenging him to refuse. 'It'll fortify your bones before you come back out.' Her eyes skidded to the gap where the gate should have been. 'Vandals. It was snowing all night so I can't find any footprints. You just wait until I learn who those halfwits are, they'll wish they'd never been born.' She shook her head before heading into the house.

Morag pulled off her coat, hat and gloves and placed them on a hanger in the large hallway. She waited for Tom to do the same – his coat had a smidgen of glitter on the collar and Morag spotted it before giving Tom a smile. 'She's a good lassie, you make sure you take care of her.'

'Um, it's not—' Tom started, wondering if he was lying to himself. If so, he had a lot to think about. He couldn't keep the truth from Meg forever.

'If it's not, lad, you're a bigger fool than you look.' Morag shook her head as the ginger tabby cat from Meg's shop bounded in to join them, and Cooper grunted, dropping to his haunches, intent on making friends.

'Aye, the kitty is a doll, and I have Meg to thank for that.' Morag pointed to a door. 'Go in there, I'll bring the drinks. Zora, come to the kitchen, and you follow us, boy.' She motioned to Cooper who was wagging his tail. 'I've a special treat in the kitchen. My Petra died in March but I've still got a packet of her favourite biscuits.' The dog went with her and the cat happily trotted after them both.

Tom headed into the small sitting room. There was a fire burning in a fireplace on the far wall with two wooden high-backed chairs in front. They had pink cushions on the seats, and a large coffee table piled with magazines sat in between them. The mantelpiece was cluttered with cards and fairy lights. To its right, a small Christmas tree with hand-knitted decorations gleamed on a table. There was a dresser on the left-hand wall, filled with mismatched pottery, a few pieces of which looked like they'd been painted by a child. Tom sank into a chair and pushed his toes into the fluffy white rug on the floor. He checked out the cosy room until his eyes rested on the coffee table and mountain of magazines. He recognised the name of the top one immediately. *Sizzle* was well known for spreading salacious gossip. It was the same magazine Meg had picked up that day in the post office, and Tom had wondered at that moment if she'd recognised him. But there'd been no hint of recognition or a barrage of questions, and he'd decided he was just being paranoid. Especially when she'd continued to keep him at arm's length.

Morag's issue was dated January three years ago and had a picture of Marnie on the front – and another of Tom standing by his grandfather, shielding both their faces from the camera. His heart sank when he heard Morag's footsteps. She was carrying a tray, which she put on the coffee table.

She eyed the magazine, and pointed to a mug and one of the china plates. 'Coffee with a dash of whisky, a slice of chocolate cake and a packet of those dog biscuits for you to take home. I had another spare in the back of the cupboard.' Tom put the magazine back onto the table and picked up the drink, taking a huge sip. It was hot and the whisky went straight to his stomach before seeping out to his limbs. 'You found my magazines then?' Morag took the seat opposite. 'I get them for my shop and always save one. I reread some of the issues when I'm bored. They're popular. I have to admit, it's not every day I find one of my neighbours on the cover.' Cooper came to stand beside the coffee table, and let out a soft bark as he stared at their cakes. 'Not for you, laddie,' Morag said. The dog slumped onto the floor and she smiled. 'He's a good boy, clever. He's been an absolute angel with Zora.'

Tom let out a quiet huff, unsure of how to respond to the comment about the magazine. His heart thumped. If Morag told everyone in Lockton who he was, he'd have to leave, find somewhere else to spend December. He couldn't face all that attention. What would Meg think? Would it change the way she looked at him? Would she be attracted to the glitter of fame just like Marnie, and would the genuine affection between them disappear?

'You can take that look off your face. Lucky for you, my Christmas Promise was to give up gossiping for December.' Morag sipped from her dainty pink cup. 'Which means if you're concerned about everyone finding out who you are, you can relax.' She winked, letting her eyes drop back to Cooper.

Tom waited for the inquisition. The questions about his music and why he'd left. He could feel the tension across his shoulders and tried to chill. Instead, Morag's eyes rested on his dog. 'I've been thinking of adopting another to go with the cat. Where did you get him?'

'Dog rescue,' Tom said, still expecting an onslaught. When Morag's eyes slid to his, he braced.

'I hear you're good at fixing things and you helped young Lilith out last night.' When Tom looked surprised, she added, 'I may not be gossiping, laddie, but I've still got ears and an intelligence network that MI5 would be proud of.' She gave him a smile which lit her face. Her brown eyes studied him and Tom tried not to squirm. 'Did you learn a trade before you got yourself involved in all that music nonsense?'

Tom nodded. 'I learned from my grandfather. He's a handyman. He fixes things even now and he's over eighty.'

Morag squinted. 'Aye. It's good to be clever with your hands.' Her forehead creased. 'I've no idea why you've decided not to tell anyone who you are, but I'd advise you to come clean sooner rather than later. Some folk might consider withholding those kinds of facts as fibbing.'

Tom thought about Meg and he shuffled in his chair, feeling uncomfortable. 'I'd rather keep it to myself,' he said quietly. 'I got fed up with being fawned over. It's good being known as the bloke who serves drinks and mends things. Being famous isn't all it's cracked up to be. I'm not moaning,' he added quickly. 'I know how lucky I was. But people do far more important things than make up songs and get a lot less credit for it.'

Morag considered him. 'Well, if you're interested in my opinion, I hate that awful Christmas song you wrote – switch the radio off every time it comes on. So there'll be no fawning from me. You should try rock, or some jazz.' Her expression turned wistful. 'Agnes swears by Simple Minds. Now that's real music. You should give it a try.'

Tom barked out a laugh, delighted by her reaction. 'I'll bear that in mind, Morag,' he said, still chuckling. 'Although I've put my musical days behind me. I'm enjoying fixing things. Being the man who can.'

She nodded, her expression softening. 'There's a power in helping people. A power in putting things right. You're smart to recognise it. Too many people in this world prancing around, expecting to be admired for the wrong stuff.'

Tom grimaced. 'I was one of them.'

Her face darkened. 'But it's important to know yourself, to recognise what you need to be content. I understand why you don't want to be famous, but don't turn away from the things that make you happy. Do that and you might find you end up with nothing. Perhaps it's possible to have a little of both?'

Tom shook his head and took another sip of the coffee. 'Not for me,' he muttered. He wished, at this moment, that Morag was right.

Chapter Fourteen

'I'm sorry, Meg, but that creature is just so noisy. Does it have to be awake all night?' Kitty frowned and twisted in the kitchen chair, glancing in the direction of the hall and Meg's bedroom as Blitzen took another energetic run on his wheel. The resulting squeaks and rattles echoed though the small flat and seemed to ping off the walls, setting her mother's teeth on edge. 'You know my thoughts on pets – but this is your house.' She winced. 'It's just this constant racket…' She put her fingers to her temples and pursed her lips.

'Mum, there's nowhere else Blitzen can go. You already said putting him downstairs in the shop, even in the storeroom, could present a health and safety hazard. Meg's got some of the cafe's food in there.' Emily stood in the kitchen doorway and flicked her long blonde hair over her shoulder, frowning at her dad as he came to stand beside her. He'd been working all morning and this was the first Meg had seen of him. He looked tired and a little beaten down. He'd been in Lockton for five days now and her mother was still refusing to talk. It was like she'd given up on their marriage, just when he'd decided to fight.

'I'm sorry, darling, I have to agree with your mother,' he said, as Kitty drummed her fingers on the table.

She froze and the kitchen fell silent. 'You do?' Kitty asked, her eyes widening, her mouth curling into the barest hint of a quizzical smile.

He shrugged and looked at his hands. 'I've not been sleeping that well either.' He frowned. 'I've been thinking a lot and I've realised you're right. I don't listen – haven't for years. I'm trying to now, Kit, and I'm agreeing with you. There's a lot more I'd agree with if you'd let me.'

Her blue eyes widened even further and Meg's stomach dropped.

'I'm sorry, Meg, we really appreciate you having us here.' Her dad sighed. 'Perhaps we should move to a hotel?' He looked uncertainly at his wife. 'We could get you a room too, Emily.'

'I'd rather stay here,' Emily said, making Meg smile.

'Then I'm not going anywhere either,' Kitty insisted. 'I'm not leaving the girls.'

Meg sighed and gave them a bright smile. 'I'll speak to Davey at Apple Cross Inn. He could probably have Blitzen for a while. I don't want you to move to a hotel.' She didn't know why. Having them move out would have been a dream come true a week ago, but somehow… it was the first connection she'd seen between her parents for years that hadn't taken place on the twenty-fifth of December. She couldn't quite bring herself to let it go.

'I'm going out,' Emily said, looking unhappy. She turned and walked out of the kitchen, then Meg heard footsteps on the stairs. She got up and looked into the hall just in time to see the top of Emily's guitar case disappear downwards in a series of bobs.

She walked back into the kitchen and put her hands into the pockets of her dress. She'd been working in the shop all day and hadn't changed out of her elf suit yet. Perhaps it was because the green velvet suited her – or maybe it just made her feel safe? 'I'm going to take him now,' she told her parents. Meg headed into her bedroom and picked up a small blanket from the bed before wrapping it around Blitzen's cage. She grabbed a bag of food, popping it into her handbag, intending to leave her parents to talk. But by the time she got back into the hall, her dad was working in the sitting room and her mum was staring at her computer again.

The high street was quiet and for once, it wasn't snowing. It was early evening so none of the shops were open, but even from outside her store Meg could see Tom's car parked next to the pub and Davey loading cans of paint into his boot. She walked quickly, worried about Blitzen getting cold.

'What are you doing?' She propped the cage onto her hip, ignoring the shiver of excitement when her eyes connected with Tom's.

'This one's offered to decorate the kitchen after he finishes installing the cupboards,' Davey replied, eyeing her with interest. 'Moving out?' He nodded at the cage.

'The flat's a little small for five. Blitzen's noisy. Don't you have a spare room? Could he stay with you?'

Davey pulled a face. 'I'm sorry – I'd love to, but Johnny's allergic to fur. He can tolerate dogs, probably because we used to have one when we were younger, but everything else with four legs sets him off. He'll be sniffling and coughing in minutes, there's no stopping it. We've tried all sorts, even pills don't work.'

'I'll take him,' Tom offered. 'Cooper's only interested in things he can eat, and hamsters aren't on the menu.' He shook his head with a mixture of amusement and despair. 'There's a spare bedroom in the cottage. If I close the door I won't be able to hear your hamster and he can come downstairs in the day. You could visit now, check the accommodation's up to scratch?' He cocked his head, searching her face.

Meg swallowed, thinking about their kiss a couple of days before. In some ways it was like it hadn't even happened. Perhaps that was for the best? 'Okay.' Meg nodded, turning back to Davey. 'Did you manage to fit all of Lilith's food into the pub?'

Crimson flooded his cheeks. 'Just about – she's been coming to the kitchen every day to cook and pick things up.' His Adam's apple bobbed. 'She made tiramisu yesterday – it was the most amazing thing I've ever tasted.' He frowned. 'Don't tell Agnes I said that.'

'Sounds like a keeper,' Tom said, earning a dark stare from Davey, whose eyes flicked inexplicably to Meg.

'I'll see you,' Tom said, and opened the car door for Meg, helping her climb into the passenger seat before putting Blitzen's cage onto her knees, as awareness danced across her skin.

They took the road out of town, and as they approached the square Meg spotted a figure sitting on a bench facing the Promise Tree. The woman was staring at the decorations – and a guitar case sat in the snow by her feet. 'Could you stop, please?' Meg asked, opening the door when Tom pulled up. 'What are you doing here?' she asked Emily, who was staring blankly into the snow.

'It's pretty here,' her sister said. 'I come when I want to think. I even serenaded the tree once.' She patted a hand on the guitar. 'If I sit for long enough I can usually spot different footprints, unless it's snowing and they disappear. Those ones over there are from a robin – I've seen a big fat one flying around. It likes to sit on the baubles. I've seen foxes early in the morning and plenty of inquisitive cats.' She pointed to a deep oval print with a dot above it. 'I've been trying to work out what creature that print belongs to.' She pulled a face. 'I wish I'd brought my animal books from home. Do you remember, I had hundreds of them?' She frowned. 'I used to be obsessed, then my exams took over and Mum wanted me to be an accountant and it was easier to just go with the flow…' She shrugged. 'I've been searching footprints on Google, but haven't been able to find one like this.' She shivered. 'I'm sorry, I was being silly earlier – I was upset about Blitzen having to be rehomed. I've enjoyed having him in the flat.'

Tom wound his window down. 'Want to come back to mine before you both freeze?'

Emily's eyes flashed to Meg's.

'Tom's offered to have Blitzen,' Meg explained.

Her sister nodded. 'Mum and Dad are right.' She sighed. 'I can't remember if I've ever used those words in a sentence…' She smiled sadly. 'The flat's too small for all of us. In truth, he's been keeping me awake too. It's why I like coming here.' She patted the bench.

Meg put a hand on her sister's shoulder and was surprised when Emily rested hers on top.

'You can come and visit him at mine anytime,' Tom said. 'Why don't you get in the car before you both turn into snowmen?'

Emily nodded and picked up her guitar, following Meg as she climbed in the back and slid in beside Cooper, giving him a hug which he joyously accepted, gifting her with a big sloppy kiss.

*

The cottage was warm but bare compared to Meg's flat. She stood beside Emily in the sitting room, watching Tom light a fire while Cooper bounded around the room. They'd checked the back bedroom upstairs when they'd arrived and deemed it suitable for Blitzen's holiday. It was quiet and warm, and Meg had left the bag of food on the dresser by the cage, promising to visit the following day. Tom had offered to check in on him regularly and to put fresh food and water out.

Meg took her time looking around the large sitting room. There were no Christmas decorations, which shouldn't have surprised her, but somehow the blank walls made her feel sad. The empty bauble she'd given Tom the other night sat on the windowsill. She should have expected it, but was disappointed nonetheless. They were so different. Emily sank into one of the dark leather sofas, pulled her guitar out of its case and began to play a song off-key. Tom winced and his eyes darted towards the kitchen, before he let out a long exhale and held out a hand.

'Something's out of tune.' Tom's voice had changed, grown deeper – as if the mere act of being around music had altered his molecular state. Emily and Meg watched, transfixed, as he hooked the strap from the guitar around his shoulder and began to fiddle with the tuning pegs, flicking his fingers over the strings, testing the frets. His face changed as he worked, his eyes darkening and his body softening as he eased into the hold. Then, when he was obviously satisfied with the set-up, he began to play.

The music was fast and deep – his fingers caressed the strings, racing up and down like an Olympic athlete testing themselves. Agile and smooth, they flew across the guitar, eking out sounds that leapt through the air and caught Meg's breath, ripping a riot of emotions from her. Sadness, loss, loneliness. There was nothing light here, no festivity or joyous escape. This music grated at your soul, picked and pulled, digging for pain and unhappiness before plucking it out and waving it like a trophy in front of your face. She felt tears spring to the corners of her eyes at the jumble of emotions, felt Emily shudder beside her as they watched, spellbound. Somehow the mere act of creation made him even more beautiful – but untouchable, as if the music had turned him into something unreal, something apart from the rest of humanity.

Then Tom suddenly stopped playing. His fingers jolted from the strings as if he'd been electrocuted. He looked up, taking in their expressions, his head angled sideways, filled with confusion and regret. He wrenched the strap over his head and handed the guitar to Emily, almost shoving it into her hands and stepping away. 'I think that's fixed it.' His tone was light and utterly fake.

'That was beautiful,' Meg said, her voice husky as she watched him step away. He looked so unhappy, she wanted to reach out. 'You're amazing.'

'You're so talented.' Emily studied his face. 'Do you play much?'

Tom shrugged, looking away. 'Not anymore. I'm hungry.' He checked his watch, his movements still fitful. 'Are you hungry?' He glanced at Emily, avoiding Meg's eyes.

'I could eat.' Her sister sounded disappointed.

Cooper wandered over to sniff at the guitar, fixing Emily with a dopey expression when she began to lightly stroke his head. 'Can I take him for a walk first?' She rose from the sofa, deliberately ignoring Cooper when he let out a grunt.

'Sure.' Tom tipped his head, the tightness around his mouth easing as he shook off the remainder of the man he'd been moments before. 'He won't want to go though.' His jaw dropped as Emily walked to the front entrance and the dog followed, sitting patiently as she pulled on her boots and coat.

'I think your sister might be related to the Pied Piper.' Tom looked amazed when Emily opened the door and Cooper trailed behind her without complaint. When the door shut the room fell silent. 'How about spaghetti bolognese?' Tom asked, walking to the kitchen without looking back. Meg followed, and her eyes dropped from the stretch of the dark blue T-shirt across his back to the way his jeans sat against his bum and legs, remembering the looseness of his limbs when he'd been playing. He'd been hypnotic. How could one man do that and then morph into this? He looked uncomfortable in his own skin.

'That really was something,' Meg said, watching him. Something was tapping at the edges of her brain, a memory she couldn't quite reach.

Tom shrugged and pulled the fridge open, gathering ingredients, putting the small breakfast bar between them. Meg hadn't been to the cottage before so hadn't seen the old room, but the grey cupboards and chrome hob and oven looked good. The worktops were dark oak and had been smoothed at the edges and then waxed. She could see a pile of tools in the corner of the room and a few cupboard doors propped up against the wall, which explained the gaps. Tom put the ingredients on the breakfast bar as Meg pulled up a stool and sat, watching as he grabbed a knife and chopping board. 'Would you like a beer or some wine?' He looked up, finally meeting her eyes. There was desperation in his expression.

'What, no anti-Christmas cocktail?' She gave him a small smile that said, *I'm not going to ask what just happened, but I hope you'll confide in me anyway.*

He offered a tight smile in return, which didn't meet his eyes. 'I'm saving those for the pub. I have wine – red or white?'

'Red, please. Can I help?'

He nodded and poured her a glass, popping a lid off a bottle of beer before sipping from it. Then he pulled out another chopping board and knife and slid them to her – along with a handful of mushrooms and carrots – keeping the counter as a barrier. Perhaps he was afraid she would leap over it and pin him to the ground to demand answers. He began to chop, and they lapsed into silence. Meg quickly washed her hands and then sliced the mushrooms before letting her eyes slide around the room. It was clean and sparse but it could be cosy. Her eyes shifted to the ceiling, to a small silver hook. It would be the perfect spot for a sprig of mistletoe or sparkly decoration.

'Before I forget.' Tom yanked one of the kitchen drawers open and got out a set of keys, putting them on the counter. 'Feel free to pop in anytime to check on Blitzen. Even if I'm not around.'

'Aren't you afraid I'll go through your cupboards, or check out your underwear drawer?' she joked, peeling one of the carrots.

'Will you?' He quirked an eyebrow and gave her a rare smile. The first genuine one she'd seen from him since he'd picked up Emily's guitar.

'No promises. Santa often gets us elves to do recon when he's not sure what to put into someone's stocking.' She cut the carrot into random shapes without looking at him.

He laughed as he finished chopping the onion and garlic, and pulled a pan out from under the counter before switching on the hob. 'Is that so?' He had his back to her and she admired him as he added the onions and garlic to the pan and began to stir. She sipped her wine, relaxing. 'You can tell Santa I've got everything I need to be content.' There was an edge in his voice, as though something was slightly off.

Meg glanced around the room. 'You need decorations – it's too bare. At least a tree in the sitting room.'

Tom grunted, and an idea began to form in Meg's mind. A way to say thank you for having Blitzen. She had a spare Christmas tree at the shop and a selection of baubles that would be perfect. He might think he didn't like Christmas, but no one hated decorations. Especially when someone else did all the work. She imagined his smile when he came home to find the house decked out, and grinned.

'You got the veg?' He turned and studied the carrots and mushrooms she'd chopped before raising his eyebrows. 'Too challenging?'

She giggled. 'I never learned to cook – and I've no natural inclination. Agnes has been showing me the basics and I'm getting good at jam. Chopping isn't one of my talents.' She pushed the board towards him.

'Oh, I don't know.' Tom considered the shapes. 'I can see a spaceship, that's a guitar, and maybe… is that one of the windows from the Sistine Chapel?'

'Nope.' Meg laughed. 'That's obviously a star.' She pointed to a piece of carrot. 'A Christmas tree and one of Rudolph's antlers.'

'Figures.' Tom slid them into the pan. 'I like how you find fun in the simplest things,' he observed, as Meg hopped off her stool so she could watch as he added tomatoes, herbs and mince.

'Thanks,' she said, disarmed. 'And thanks for inviting us over, and for having Blitzen to stay.'

He lifted a shoulder. 'He can visit for as long as you like. At least while I'm here.'

'You're leaving?' Meg sipped her wine, feeling oddly unsettled. Tom was wrong for her. But she had all these feelings she didn't understand and she was drawn to him, despite their differences. Was that what had happened to her parents? Too many raging hormones disguising the fact that they weren't really compatible? Was she going to make the same mistake? Was falling for the wrong person simply part of her DNA?

'I don't know yet.' He stirred the pan with his back to her. 'I'm thinking of staying but I haven't fully decided. I've got feelers out for other jobs. There are charities looking for handymen in Devon and a friend's renovating his garage. He lives in Whitby and he's got a place I can stay.'

'Isn't it odd, not having a base?' Meg's smile dimmed as she thought about Lockton without Tom in it. He'd only been around for just over two weeks, but having him here felt right.

'Sometimes.' His expression clouded.

'Are you avoiding something?' Tom flinched. 'I'm sorry, I'm prying. It's just… The music, the way you held the guitar. You looked so natural, but you don't play. That's what you said. I suppose I don't understand. If I was that good at something, I'd never want to stop.' She let the words drift between them, and he let out a sigh and turned so he could look at her.

He folded his arms. 'I was really smart when I was younger. Super smart.' Meg nodded. 'I got a scholarship to a private school that was local to my grandparents. I lived with them – my mum pushed off when I was ten, she wasn't interested in being a parent.' He recited the words by rote, like he'd said them a hundred times.

'I'm sorry,' Meg said slowly, trying to imagine that. Her parents had been so wrapped up in themselves and their unhappiness, they'd essentially ignored her and Emily most of the time. But being dumped so young, that was a whole different matter…

Tom's shrug was nonchalant. 'She got into drugs when she was a teenager and—' He blew out a breath. 'That's not important. I got bullied when I joined the school. I had a stupid haircut, my eyes were too far apart, I was rubbish at sport.' Meg looked into his eyes, saw humour there and acceptance. 'Then after I'd been at the school for about four months I got used to the bullying – learned to tolerate it.' He shrugged. 'This music teacher made me try out a guitar in one of our lessons. I'd never played an instrument – aside from a recorder which I was terrible at – and I was embarrassed and annoyed.' His lips thinned. 'I wasn't looking to be the centre of attention and I hated the idea of making an idiot of myself in front of anyone. They didn't need more reasons to tease me. But… I don't know, I started to play. I'd been watching the others, studying the way their fingers moved over the strings and which notes made which sounds.' He paused. 'It's the way my mind works. I like figuring things out.' He pointed to the cupboard doors on the floor. 'It's why I enjoy working with my hands. I copied what I'd seen. I wasn't brilliant. But I was good enough for that teacher to insist I came in at lunchtimes so he could teach me properly.'

'Then you got good?' Meg asked.

He nodded. 'Very – and suddenly, all those kids who'd been bullying me were looking at me differently. People started to talk to me in the corridors. Girls were interested.' He looked embarrassed. 'Which, for a teenage boy who'd been left by his mother because he was too much trouble and was living with his grandparents – used to everyone treating him like a pariah – was pretty great. So I practised and practised, became more and more popular…'

'And?' Meg asked when he stopped.

Tom exhaled. 'Nothing. I realised one day that people didn't like me for who I was. I still didn't fit. Underneath it, they all disliked me just as much. But I got to like the way being adored felt.' He pulled a face. 'It changed the way I was. Turned me into someone *I* didn't like very much. So I gave music up.' There was a finality to his voice but Meg could feel there was more to the story. He turned away so he could stir the sauce.

'Well, I think you're great on the guitar, but I still don't adore you,' she said evenly, keen to make him smile. When he laughed, she did too.

'Which is one of the reasons why I like you,' he said, turning again so he could look at her.

At his words, her whole body seemed to shudder to life. 'You do?'

Tom's eyes were warm, less defensive now. He hadn't completely raised the shutters on his world, but this was progress. He reached out to run a finger down the edge of her face, skimming her cheekbone, stopping at her chin, leaving a trail of tingles which multiplied and fluttered outwards. 'Yes,' he said, inspecting his finger, chuckling when he found a few flecks of glitter sparkling on the pad. 'You're real. So different from everyone else. You don't pretend to like people because you like everyone – and you don't pretend to be something you're not.'

'I'm not perfect,' Meg whispered as Tom moved closer.

'Is anyone?' He swallowed and she stepped forward until their feet were almost touching. Then Meg reached a hand up so she could slide it into his hair and pull his face down. His lips were soft, and at first they moved slowly. Neither of them seemed to be in a hurry. Perhaps they were still exploring each other, intent on holding themselves back. Tom drifted his hand so it caressed the dip in the small of her back, easing her closer. Meg could hear the food bubbling in the pan beside them, imagined the same bubbles rising up inside her as her skin began to prickle. Then he gently pressed the tip of his finger into her back again until their bodies met. She rose up to her tiptoes and slid her arms around his neck. Now she could feel the hard muscles across his chest, could smell the woody shower gel he used, and wanted to tug at the bottom of his T-shirt so she could pull it over his head. Her legs were shaking now as the power of the kiss shot through her, her breathing growing heavier as Tom began to explore, sliding his hand to the slope of her waist, down to the curve of her bottom. He pulled her closer still as their kiss deepened and grew hotter…

Then there was a bang as the front door opened, a crash as it closed and the quick splatter of paws as they hit the floor and Cooper entered the kitchen. They sprang apart with surprise. Emily followed Cooper inside, her face pink and her hair wet. 'The walk was wonderful – he's a clever thing and good company. That smells amazing.' She must have picked up on the atmosphere because she stopped and then began to back away. 'I was thinking I'd go and practise on the guitar. See if I can be even ten per cent as good as you, Tom.' She stopped in the doorway. 'I got a text from Mum as I reached the garden. She asked where we were. I told her we wouldn't be back for dinner.' She turned and headed into the sitting room.

Meg looked at Tom again. Her heart was thundering now. He gave her a crooked smile. Should they discuss what had just happened?

'How are your parents?' Tom made the decision for her.

Meg smoothed her fingertips across her hair, trying to iron it into submission or to give her shaking hands something to do. 'Fine.' The words were automatic, and when he frowned she grimaced. 'In the interests of being real, I will tell you I don't know.'

Tom stared at her, his eyes fixed on her face, as if committing every tic and pulse to memory.

'They don't always get on.' She let out a sigh and shut her eyes briefly. 'It's usually so much easier to pretend.' Her gaze scanned the kitchen, imagining how it would look with tinsel hanging in the window, or some small reindeer figurines sitting on the windowsill with candles flickering inside. She had a silver Christmas tree that would look perfect on the kitchen counter, and that hook in the ceiling should definitely be holding sprigs of deep green mistletoe.

'Reality has a habit of catching up with you,' Tom said, watching her. 'Why are they in Lockton?' he added, before she could ask what he meant.

'I don't know. I only know something's changed – but somehow nothing has. They're very different. Perhaps they always were. I don't want to make the same mistake.' Which begged the question, why had she just kissed Tom? Worse, why did she want to do it again?

'I think mistakes are part of life. You can't avoid them. The only thing you can do is stop yourself from making the same ones.' Tom turned away from her, back to the pan. He looked sad and she felt sorry for him. Her mind flicked to the small boy whose mother had left him, the child bullied at school – was that why he hated Christmas? Could she do something to change that? As Meg watched him she began to warm to her idea. Maybe Tom would hate Christmas less once he saw just how beautiful it could be. The cottage was a blank canvas, begging her to paint it with glitter, baubles and fairy lights. She had a sparkly star which would be perfect over the fireplace. She could come into the house when he was working – use the key – put up a tree, some mistletoe and sparkles. There was something so comforting about a bauble, the smell of a Nordmann fir and the twinkle of fairy lights. If she could give Tom a little Christmas magic, show him he wasn't really alone, then that's what she'd do. But she wasn't going to let herself think about why his happiness mattered so much to her.

Chapter Fifteen

Apple Cross Inn wasn't open yet because it was early, but the kitchen was busy. Tom put a couple of leftover lemons from the pile he'd been chopping for the bar into the fridge and watched Johnny battle with a pile of carrots. They were perfectly diced and reminded Tom of the crazy shapes Meg had created when she'd been in his kitchen yesterday evening. He sighed as Lilith wafted in through the back door, bringing with her a rush of cold air. This was the third day she'd visited the kitchen since the flood.

'It's the talented Miss Tiramisu.' Johnny barked his new nickname for her as footsteps echoed on the stairs and Davey appeared, his face flushed and his eyes sparkling bright blue.

'Woah…' He stopped dead when he saw Lilith. She'd dressed up in a pink silk shirt which set off her olive skin, and a pair of jeans that she must have needed a shoehorn to get into. Her heels were spiky and added a good few inches to the length of her legs. Tom wondered how on earth she'd made it to the pub from her car – not to mention why she looked so glamorous for a morning in the kitchen. 'Wow.' Davey gaped before shaking himself. 'You look very… it's…'

'Are you here to make another spectacular dessert?' Johnny jumped in, saving his brother from stuttering anymore.

'*Sì*.' Lilith nodded, her eyes sliding from Davey to the counter. 'What are you cooking?'

Johnny tossed the carrots into a pan. 'Cottage pie. It's a pub favourite. Easy to make and popular with the customers – I might be the expert in the kitchen, but Davey has a few tricks up his sleeve, including a secret ingredient for this dish which he'll add to the pan when I'm not here. It'll make it taste even more…' He kissed his fingers dramatically. 'I might have to pay you to find out exactly what it is later.' He gave her a teasing grin as he stirred the contents of the pan.

Lilith looked back and forth between the brothers. 'You don't share your recipes?' She frowned. 'I thought you shared everything. Isn't that the way of things in Lockton – family and community above everything else?'

'Not since Johnny stole my formula for the perfect custard to go with rhubarb crumble, and used it to steal the heart of the girl I'd fallen for,' Davey joked, relaxing into easy banter as his tongue untangled itself.

'You were in love?' Lilith's neat eyebrows met, lining her smooth forehead.

'He was sixteen at the time,' Johnny said dryly. 'And the girl dumped me two days later for a boy who'd just passed his driving test. So all the subterfuge and heartache weren't worth it.' He thumped a hand over his heart. 'I never got over it. I haven't been able to eat custard since. Although the whole experience got me into cooking, so I suppose it was worth it in the end.'

'I think you deserve a broken heart for stealing your brother's love,' Lilith said without humour, her dark eyes darting back to Davey.

'It's almost time for you to do your magic.' Johnny grinned and patted a hand on Davey's shoulder. 'Need us all to disappear into the bar so you can add your secret ingredient?'

'Tom and Lilith can hide their eyes,' Davey said, blushing as Lilith continued to stare at him sympathetically. '*You* have to turn your back.' He pointed at his brother. 'I don't trust you not to look and try to use my recipe to steal another of my girlfriends.' Lilith shook her head as Johnny turned, making a performance of leaning his head onto one of the shiny silver cupboards hanging on the wall. She put a hand over her eyes – she had tidy pink nails which were free from polish. Tom watched her move one finger a few millimetres so she could watch Davey, before she slid it back into place when he yelled, 'No peeking!' in Johnny's direction. Tom put his hands over his face too, and listened to the clatter of a cupboard and the sound of the fridge door opening and closing. Then Davey said, 'You can look.' He was standing by the hob and stirring the pan. He handed the spoon back to his brother with as much gravity as a gymnast passing the Olympic torch. 'It's okay, Lilith, I forgave him a long time ago.'

Lilith nodded and watched as Johnny pretended to punch his brother on the cheek, and Davey countered before they ended the exchange with a big affectionate man-hug. Her expression was bemused but he saw longing in her eyes. Then Davey took a teaspoon out of one of the drawers and scooped some of the mixture up, before handing it to her. She savoured the meat for a moment.

'*Bene.*' She nodded. 'It is very good.' She cocked her head to one side and flashed Davey a megawatt smile, which even from this distance Tom could see had an immediate and almost nuclear effect. 'Perhaps we can swap our secret ingredients. I will share my family recipe for tiramisu and you can teach me how to make this?' She put the spoon in the sink and leaned back against the counter. 'I could surprise my parents. I think this would even satisfy Papa, and he usually only eats Italian food.'

'Um… okay.' Davey's eyes darted to his brother. 'You'll need to leave the kitchen if I do tell her,' he said.

'Ah yes, if I'm to share my family recipes I won't be able to have you in the room either, not now I know you're not to be trusted.' Lilith looked serious. 'Perhaps we can meet here again tomorrow?' she asked Davey.

'Sure.' He beamed.

'For today' – Lilith wiped her hands onto her jeans and headed for the fridge – 'I have some crab. I will make a linguine sauce when I get back to the hotel. I wondered if I could put together a minestrone soup here? I have containers in the car.' Her eyes scanned the main counter. Johnny had spread himself out; there were half-used ingredients, pots and pans everywhere. He was a great chef, but not the tidiest worker.

'I'll help you clear up.' Davey picked up a saucepan and put it into the dishwasher.

'I've finished all my prep. Now it'll just be baked potatoes and sandwiches – so I'll get things cleared up in a tick.' They watched as Johnny picked up more pans and helped Davey straighten everything. As they worked, Lilith looked through the cupboards, picking out a large copper pan and testing the weight of the knives before selecting one. By the time the men had finished, she'd chosen her tools and lined them up by the sink. Johnny finished wiping the surfaces and flashed them a grin. 'Time for me to put my feet up until the rush arrives. Unless you need a sous chef, Miss Tiramisu?'

'I'm… I'd like to help. I mean, if you need anyone,' Davey stumbled, his eyes darting from Tom to Johnny as if only just remembering they were still in the room. 'I've always wanted to know how to make a decent minestrone.'

'Tom, I noticed the fire in the bar is almost out.' Johnny jerked his head towards the door and winked. 'I'm going to put my feet up.' He waved and left the kitchen without waiting for anyone to respond.

'That's true.' Tom cleared his throat. 'I noticed we were running low on wood.' No one spoke, and Tom watched Lilith pick up the equipment and vegetables she'd assembled earlier, so she could lay them on the large metal counter. She slid a chopping board towards Davey – her cheeks pinkened as their eyes met.

'You can slice?' she asked, and Davey nodded.

'I… um, I'll go now. I guess I'd better hurry, we'll be opening the pub in half an hour.' Tom grabbed his coat, disappeared into the hall and through the back door, before either of them had noticed he'd gone.

Snow had stopped falling a few hours before, but there was plenty piled up at the edges of the pub cark park. Tom crunched through a drift on the right, past a few parked cars belonging to the staff, to where Davey had a small locked shed tucked away behind a long brick wall. Tom slid off his coat and hung it on a hook inside the shed. Here, a small silver axe had been fixed on the wall and he grabbed it, before picking up a large tree branch from a pile of uncut wood laid out on a plastic sheet on the ground. Outside, well away from the cars, a tree stump had been set into the snow. He placed the branch on the stump and brought the axe down in a satisfying whack, splitting it in two, feeling his shoulders loosen as he chopped another few pieces. As he worked, he tried to keep his mind off Meg, blocking that look on her face when he'd kissed her, ignoring the tune that kept popping into his head and the desire to write it down so he wouldn't forget. He'd always found physical work helped him to think; the easy, unconscious movements got his mind racing and artistic juices flowing. Marnie had once teased him about disappearing to his 'creative place' in the earlier days of their marriage – but by the end she'd hated it, calling it his mistress. A mistress that had all but destroyed their relationship. Now that place felt bad and he forced himself out of it. When he had a large enough pile, he grabbed a canvas bag from the shed to carry it in before locking up. As Tom crunched his way towards the car park and back door of the pub, he noticed a blur of prints on the ground leading from the woods. Perhaps someone going for their daily dog walk?

Curious, he followed them, making his way along the edge of the pub towards the high street and the front of Apple Cross Inn. As he approached the pavement, he saw shards of tinsel and three baubles lying in the snow. Tom picked up the baubles, frowning, and took a few more steps, following the abandoned tinsel around the other side of the pub. Here, a string of solar lights had been ripped from the wall of the building and lay in the snow in two halves. As Tom fully rounded the corner, he saw a tall man dressed in a policeman's uniform talking with Agnes.

'The dunderheads have been vandalising decorations all round town!' Agnes picked up some red and green baubles from the snow and hung them by their ribbons back onto the hooks Davey had banged into the pub's facade. She was dressed in black boots, thick trousers and a dark coat. The only splashes of colour in her outfit were from a knitted bright pink bobble hat and matching scarf and gloves. 'Morag told me someone pulled her fence right off its hinges. We've not had any trouble on Buttermead Farm, but I've felt like something's off. Like someone's been watching me when I've been walking around the fields.' Her eyes widened. 'Perhaps it's ghosts. There are legends about them, although I don't know why they'd be bothering us at Christmas. The only folklore from this time of year concerns the Promise Tree.' Her attention flashed to Tom as he joined them. Beside Agnes, the policeman scribbled notes onto a pad. He was a tall man, with a round belly and ruddy cheeks.

'Hello, laddie.' The man held out a hand. 'I'm PC Dougall, or Marcus when I'm not in uniform. I heard you were visiting from the Lockton grapevine – that is, from my wife, Cora.' He beamed. 'Cora mentioned you were with Meg when she found those baubles under the Promise Tree…' He checked his pad. 'Six days ago?' Tom nodded.

'Right he was.' Agnes's green eyes flashed with annoyance. 'Seems to me we've got a plague of crime this festive season. People have been talking about decorations being torn down and disappearing all over the village. Question is, what are you going to do about it, Marcus? CCTV, or do you want some of us villagers to patrol the area in packs?'

Marcus sighed and tapped a pencil against his mouth, before sweeping his attention across the front of the pub. From here, Tom could see another half-dozen baubles lying in the snow, a series of green and red blobs. None of them looked broken, but judging by the spaces on the walls, they'd been knocked off. 'Investigations are ongoing, Agnes. I don't think we need further help at this point. I've interviewed all the teenagers in Lockton and they're as shocked about this as you. There are a few rentals I haven't been to yet, but I'll go when the snow's cleared. I'm just not sure what the motive is. An obsession with sparkly things, or a dislike of Christmas?' His attention darted to Tom, curious and piercing. 'Cora told me you're not very keen on the season?'

Tom opened his mouth.

'The laddie's fine, Marcus. He's been fixing things all over town. He isn't your vandal. Don't go looking for trouble in the wrong places. This'll be something else.' Agnes's expression darkened. 'I've still got my suspicions about ghosts…'

Marcus raised a bushy grey eyebrow. 'Whatever it is, it needs to stop,' he said. 'I've taken photographs, and I'll bag these lights and take them to the station.' He pulled a plastic bag and some gloves from his pocket, before bending to pick up the lights, shoving them into the bag. 'I've already dusted for fingerprints. Best thing you can do is keep your ears and eyes open. I'll keep you posted.' He swept his gaze down the street. 'We don't get much crime in Lockton. I'm not going to let it continue – especially if it interferes with the fundraising for the village hall roof. How are the concert plans coming along?' His attention fixed on Tom again.

'Oh,' he said, surprised. In truth, he'd been keeping away from the whole affair. 'I'm not sure…'

'They're coming along fine, Marcus,' Agnes interjected. 'Davey said the bands have worked out their sets ready for next week, and Morag told me we've almost sold out of tickets, despite the snow. Johnny's sorted the menu for the night and' – her eyes slid to Tom – 'I hear you're going to set up the marquee soon, and Grant's serviced all the heaters.' He nodded; Davey had mentioned something in passing. 'We've plenty of chairs in the village hall for the crowd.'

'Cora says you might be playing – I heard you're good on the guitar?' Marcus had dark blue eyes which were a little too penetrating.

'Um.' Tom's heartbeat picked up a notch.

'Don't worry.' Agnes patted his shoulder. 'That'll be the Lockton grapevine. I think Meg's sister mentioned something in the cafe about you having a go on her guitar. No one's expecting you to perform. Being in the limelight isn't for everyone.' She shot him an understanding look which made him feel like a fraud.

'I'll be helping at the bar – I'm not planning on getting on stage.' Even if the thought of performing sent a shiver of excitement down his arms.

Marcus nodded. 'Let me know if you see any more of this.' He pointed to the baubles. 'We don't want vandals ruining the concert. I'll keep you informed of any developments.' He gave Agnes a reassuring pat on the back and headed back up the high street towards Meg's Christmas shop.

'I'll help tidy up.' Agnes shot Tom a smile and bent to pick up the decorations.

Tom set the bag of wood on the pavement and helped. It took a few minutes to rehang them but they were left with two empty hooks. He checked his watch. 'I'd better get back to work. The pub opens soon.'

Agnes gave him a wink. 'See you later then, laddie, I'll be back in this evening with Fergus for one of those cocktails. You'd better fill Davey in on what happened here. Perhaps you should pop in later for a chat with Meg.' She winked. 'I'm not matchmaking, but I've a feeling about you two…'

'I think you're mistaken,' Tom said, wondering again if he was lying to himself.

Chapter Sixteen

Davey and Lilith were giggling when Tom returned to the kitchen. He stood by the door, out of sight, waiting for an opportunity to interrupt. In front of the couple sat piles of chopped vegetables. Lilith drew a bottle of oil from a large bag and waved it in front of Davey. 'I have a little of my Bellagamba left.' She held the small glass bottle up to the light, and even from this distance, Tom could see there was only a dribble in there. It looked thick, golden and expensive. 'I thought I'd use it for the soup – there's not enough for much else.' She let out a long sigh. 'I heard from the electrician that he won't be coming to the hotel for at least another day because of the weather. With that and my oil not arriving, I feel like my parents' visit is going to be a disaster.' She puffed air into her cheeks before letting it out slowly.

'It's important to you?' Davey asked. 'Them visiting? I mean, I imagine it is…' He exhaled and tapped his long fingers on the counter. 'Johnny and I, we lost our parents a few years ago.'

'I'm sorry,' Lilith said.

Davey shrugged. 'It's just the two of us now. But I know how important family is. You must miss them?'

'I…' Lilith frowned. 'I haven't been in Scotland for that long so I've not had time to miss them yet.' She gave him a half-laugh. 'They wanted to wait until I'd found my feet before they came.'

'They must be very proud,' Davey said. 'Owning and running Lockton Hotel, that's impressive.' The cooking and time alone must have helped him relax, because he seemed less tongue-tied and awkward now.

Lilith shrugged. 'They bought the hotel for me.' She looked embarrassed. 'I ran a small deli near our home before. It was just outside Rome and I loved it, but…' Her lips thinned. 'Papa wanted to sell. He was offered a lot of money for the lease, and…' She shrugged her slim shoulders. 'It was good business. He thought the hotel would be a chance for me to prove myself. My family are very successful. My brother' – she pronounced the word with a sharp edge that made her sound annoyed – 'runs his own chain of restaurants in Rome – he's a very big deal. He started the deli and turned it into a thriving business before I took it on.'

'He sounds impressive too,' Davey observed, no doubt reading a lot into Lilith's admission. Tom had too. He understood about living up to something – it was easy to let the whole thing turn into an obsession.

'He is, *very*. Handsome as well, with a beautiful wife and three *bellissima* bambinos.' Lilith nodded a few times, as if she were counting his accomplishments. 'My sister too – she is brilliant, beautiful, with a sharp wit. So, I want everything to be perfect when my parents arrive.' She wagged a finger at the pan.

'I'm sure they'll be proud of what you've achieved.' Davey turned so he could look at her properly. Tom stayed where he was, caught between wanting to listen and not wanting to disturb the moment. He knew how Davey felt about Lilith – this was the first time his friend had been able to string a complete sentence together in her presence.

She puffed out her cheeks again. 'I'm hoping they'll…' She sighed. 'Well, see what I'm capable of at least.' She gave him a dazzling smile which looked a little fake. 'Otherwise Papa may want me to sell and I'll have to search for a new opportunity. I suppose I might enjoy having a deli again.'

'Oh…' Davey looked crestfallen. 'So the hotel still belongs to your parents?'

Lilith pulled a face. 'It's mine, but they're very involved.' She forced out a small smile. 'If the hotel doesn't do well, they want me to hire a manager with experience so I can learn. It's something we are due to discuss on their visit. As Papa keeps reminding me' – she made quote marks with her long fingers – 'there is no room for emotion in business – or life.' She frowned.

'That's…' Davey's forehead wrinkled as he searched for the right word. 'Tough.'

'It's all I've ever known.' Lilith's expression darkened as he studied her. 'I need to sauté these vegetables in some of this oil.' She turned away and heaved the large pan onto the hob, before flicking on the gas and picking up a wooden spoon from one of the drawers. She poured in the remainder of the oil. 'Would you watch it for me while I go to my car? I've left some fresh herbs in the boot. The dish won't be the same without them.'

'I can go?' Davey offered, looking pointedly at her shoes.

'No. I'm more comfortable doing things for myself.'

Davey watched her leave and Tom stepped out of the shadows just as Johnny appeared from behind him. 'Has the Italian beauty gone already?' Johnny sniffed and looked in the pan. 'That oil smells so good…' He winked at Davey. 'The cook's almost as irresistible. You falling for her now you've had some time alone?'

'I…' Davey brushed a hand across his brow. 'I wasn't sure when she first arrived, but she's really great.'

'You look worried.' Johnny leaned against the counter and folded his arms. They were twins – not identical, but their hair and eyes were the same colour and they had almost exactly the same expressions.

'Lilith's parents bought her the hotel,' Davey said, his voice low. 'If this Christmas doesn't go well, if I'm reading things correctly, they might make her take on a manager or even sell up.' He patted his fingers on the counter, looking annoyed. 'I wish there was some way I could help. She's not having the best luck. Perhaps she could get more involved in the concert and I could pay her to do that, buoy her up to her parents when they arrive…'

'Are you in rescuing mode again, Davey?' Johnny asked, his tone light, but Tom could tell there was a subtext to the words which were a lot more serious. 'I thought you'd got over that since leaving London.'

'Lilith doesn't need rescuing – she's about as helpless as a tiger shark.' Davey turned away from his brother, pulled another pan from the cupboard then thumped it onto the counter.

'I'm not interfering, mate,' Johnny said. 'I just don't want to see you get hurt. There was a long line of women in London you spent your life trying to save, remember. The one thing they all had in common was that once you had, they left you high and dry.' He shrugged. 'Or the relationship didn't work out once the drama was over. I don't want to see you get used again.'

The groove in Davey's forehead deepened. 'This isn't the same…'

'You've helped with Lilith's kitchen emergency, loaned her ours, she's using the fridges. Now you're cooking together and talking about the problems she has with her parents – and again you want to help. Don't get me wrong.' Johnny held up a hand to stop any protest. 'We'd do the same for anyone. It's a way of life in Lockton. But make sure you're not mistaking a woman in need for something else. I know how soft your heart is, I know you like her, but you've been taken advantage of too many times.'

'This isn't the same.'

'I'm just going to say the name Crystal Armitage and leave it at that.' Johnny's eyes flicked to Tom's. 'She got her hooks into Davey – mined him for every contact in the music business he had while she stayed in the basement flat in his town house.' He made quote marks with his fingers. 'Because her evil boyfriend had kicked her out and her mean, horrible parents hated her. Turns out, they all got fed up with her using them and wanted her to stand on her own two feet.' Johnny shook his head slowly. 'She was that desperate to make a name for herself.' Davey's lips thinned. 'I'm not saying Lilith is Crystal, but you need to be careful. That woman used everything you gave her, and when she got her first music contract, she left and didn't look back. Not even to say thank you.' Johnny turned to Tom. 'She was the final straw for him in London – the reason he left the business when he did.'

Tom had always wondered what the story was. Davey had been at the peak of his career. Then he'd suddenly retired and bought the pub in Lockton, changed his whole life. In many ways it was a mirror of his own journey. Except Davey deserved better.

'I'd been thinking about coming up to Scotland for a while,' Davey began. 'But she wasn't the first person to take advantage, you're right. It was a pattern I'd fallen into. But it's a very different thing offering to help someone out when their kitchen has flooded, to being expected to launch a stranger's career. Lilith's not like that.'

'*Sì*,' Lilith said from the doorway, her eyes dark and her lips turned down. 'I'm not.' She took a deep breath and flashed a megawatt smile in Johnny and Davey's direction. 'So, shall we finish this soup so I can get out of your way?'

Tom crunched through the snow on his way home from the pub at the end of his shift six hours later. It was early evening and the sun had set a while ago, but there was enough light from the moon and brightness from the snow that he didn't have to worry about using a torch. It was cold though. He pulled his coat tighter and patted his arms. He still had to walk Cooper when he got home. He could see tall trees in the moonlight, their branches laden with ice, and the jagged tips of mountains on the horizon. He'd left the lights on in the cottage when he'd popped over at lunchtime to check on Cooper and Blitzen and could see them glowing further up the road, just in front of the trees. He stumbled as he got closer and noticed blue, green and red lights flickering through his windows, which hadn't been there earlier. His heart thumped as he drew closer. There was a Christmas wreath made of holly with plump red berries hanging from the knocker on the blue front door. A welcome mat with a red-nosed snowman beamed up at him from the floor of the porch, and Tom deliberately stood on its face. He put the key in the lock, dreading what he'd find, and held his breath.

The sitting room had been turned into a Christmas grotto – there was a large rustic star hanging above the fireplace with white lights highlighting each of its sharp points. Snowmen, reindeer and Santa ornaments grinned inanely as he pulled off his boots and coat and slung them onto the floor. Cooper came bounding up to greet him, spinning around with excitement as he got further into the sitting room, trying to catch his tail. The noise on the wooden floor was almost enough to drown out the Christmas music playing in the background. He'd left the radio on when he'd gone out so Cooper had some company, but he hadn't set the station to this. He marched into the kitchen to switch it off, almost doing a double-take as he spotted the huge sprig of mistletoe hanging from the ceiling, and the metal fir tree candle holders on the counter. Running across the windowsill, edged with red and silver tinsel, were a set of grinning elves.

Baffled, Tom walked back into the sitting room. 'What the hell?' There was a tall fir tree in the corner. It had been decorated with a mass of multicoloured baubles, and yet more lights shone out from between the branches. He let out a soft exhale and marched back into the kitchen, grabbing a bottle of Jack Daniel's and pouring himself a stiff glass before glugging it down in one. He couldn't explain why the decorations made him feel so empty and alone, why the mere sight of the lights had his hand shaking. He knew it was Meg. Had known from the moment he'd seen the soft glow on his walk. He wasn't angry with her – he knew it had been done with the best intentions – but he couldn't live with these memories in his house.

The whole thing reminded him too much of Christmas Day, that moment when he'd woken to find Marnie gone, the divorce papers under the tree, wrapped up as a festive joke present. She'd wanted to hurt him – payback for those years he'd put his music first, the lost connection in their marriage. Then the calls from his grandad, the guilt as he battled with the emptiness in his chest, trying to figure out the quickest way to the hospital and how to get Marnie's friends out of his house. Thank God Davey had been around and had stepped in to help.

He shouldn't blame Christmas, but the whole thing was so utterly fake. The promises people made to each other and themselves, the way families gathered together, pretending they loved each other, pretending they were better than they were. As if the decorations, the food, the millions of wrapped presents could somehow hide reality. It was such a stark reflection of the way he'd lived his life. Except that fame had been his Christmas – and love had been his gift. But none of it had been real. The scales had dropped from his eyes overnight, and when he'd looked for love and friendship when he'd most needed it, he'd found it had all been an illusion. Perhaps because he didn't deserve it? Never really had.

He swallowed and poured himself another, smaller drink, sipping it slowly as he wandered around the house to see where else Meg had been. Had she been dressed as an elf as she'd tried to infuse Davey's house with festive spirit? What had she expected? That a few lights, a sprig of mistletoe and spray of tinsel would change his mind? He could see how she used Christmas to hide behind her true feelings – to pretend life was perfect. Perhaps she thought she could do the same for him? He slumped into the sofa, trying to relax, and Cooper came to rest a paw on his leg, picking up on his mood. He stroked the dog's head, trying to ignore the star's twinkles and the way the lights on the tree flashed on and off in a rhythmic sequence.

He'd woken up under a tree three Christmases ago, or at least close to one, slumped on the sofa in all his clothes because he'd been sitting alone playing the guitar – surrounded by a crowd of people invited by his then-wife. Most of them he'd barely known.

Tom's fingers tingled as his mind began to pick up on the beat of the Christmas lights. The Gibson was still in the cupboard and he imagined himself playing – could hear the notes in his head. But he couldn't let them in. Couldn't trust himself to let music into his life again. Who knew where it would end? Who else he'd end up letting down.

He shook his head and rose, pulling the plug on both sets of lights before heading through the kitchen towards the garden. There were at least a dozen boxes in Davey's shed. He could pack this all away, put it on the doorstep under the porch so it didn't get wet. Then he'd figure out exactly how he could get the whole lot back to Meg without hurting her feelings.

Chapter Seventeen

Meg made her way down the road towards Tom's house the next morning, carrying an inflatable snowman in a bag. She'd decorated his house yesterday afternoon, dancing to 'Jingle Bell Rock' on the radio, but even as she'd finished she'd realised the garden looked bare in comparison. If Tom was at work this morning, she'd put the snowman up and give him another surprise to come home to. To show him she'd been thinking of him.

She grinned as she drew closer, her eyes skimming the horizon – admiring the mountain peaks, jagged and imposing against the blue sky, the white fields and trees laden with shimmering snow. She loved this weather, but it was good that a milder spell was meant to be on its way, otherwise the Christmas concert might be affected.

Meg was just a few steps away from the cottage's garden when she came to a sudden stop. There were two large cardboard boxes on the porch, and next to those a six-foot Nordmann fir stripped bare of all decorations. 'He didn't…' There was a pool of ice in the pit of her stomach as she approached the house, tramping up the pathway. Tears pricked her eyes as she fumbled in her pocket for the key, noticing, as she found the lock, that the wreath she'd hung on the door knocker yesterday afternoon was gone. Along with the mat she'd left to welcome Tom home.

Numb, she opened the door and Cooper greeted her with a loud bark. He scurried around her heels as she pulled off her coat and boots and padded into the sitting room, chewing her lip. The tree was gone. All the decorations on the mantelpiece. The beautiful star she'd taken out of her own collection because she'd wanted to make the house feel like a warm hug when he got home. The only decoration that remained was the empty glass bauble on the front windowsill. Meg's hands curled as she wandered into the kitchen. He'd taken the mistletoe down; no doubt it was boxed up outside. The icy pool in her stomach hardened as she made her way back to the sitting room and slumped onto the sofa, scouring the bare surfaces. Cooper let out a sigh, reading her mind, and came to rest his head on her lap. She'd worn her elf outfit again, another deliberate attempt to make Tom laugh – to see that shine and warmth in his eyes when he let his guard down. She just felt like an idiot now. Her emotions were raw, worse than when she'd discovered Ned had been cheating on her with Lilith. Which made no sense at all…

'Stupid,' she muttered. She knew how Tom felt about Christmas, but this was like a rejection. She was all about the sparkle, warmth and joy of the season. She'd tried to bring it to his house, wanting to surround him with those good feelings. She sensed he was unhappy and lost. Had wanted to offer kindness and love – just some of the feelings Christmas gave her. But he'd chucked it away – because he didn't want it. Because he'd meant what he'd said that day in the pub: the whole season was fake. Perhaps he thought she was too?

Or maybe they'd just got a little too close the evening he'd kissed her, and he was putting a stop to anything further developing.

Taking a deep breath, Meg got up, ignoring her wobbly legs and the headache that had begun to throb behind her eyes. She popped upstairs to check on Blitzen, dropping a few seeds into his bowl before picking up his cage, wrapping it in the blanket she'd used when she'd brought him over, and heaving it under her arm. Perhaps Agnes might let him stay instead? She popped the spare keys onto the kitchen counter, gathered her bag and headed back out into the snow. Knowing that whatever happened, she was going to avoid Tom Riley-Clark from now on.

The high street was almost empty as Meg made her way along it, towards her Christmas shop. Her heart was heavy but she was determined not to focus on it, so paused a few times on the walk to admire the knitted decorations and dazzling lights, blocking out all thoughts of Tom. She stopped momentarily to take in the Promise Tree. She'd sold dozens more baubles over the last few days and it was heaving with the villagers' promises. Hundreds of globes swung in the wind and she tried to spot hers – as she did, her dad walked up to greet her.

'You were out early?' he said, glancing at the cage under her arm with a frown. He pulled up the collar of his thin blue coat and patted his arms. 'I thought I'd take a walk before work so I could clear my head. Your mum's still not talking to me.' He frowned and pointed at the tree. 'I hung a promise on there this morning in one of your baubles. Do people ever manage to keep them?'

'Sometimes…' Meg shrugged. 'I promised one Christmas I'd make enough money to buy a new van for the shop, and I did.'

He nodded, looking up again. 'I've made a lot of mistakes with your mother. We were so right for each other once.'

'You were?' Meg's tone was surprised and her dad laughed.

'Love isn't always black and white, Meg – sometimes there's a lot more going on under the surface. I've always tried to ignore that. I wonder if you're a chip off the old block?' She was going to ask what he was talking about, but there was a cough behind them and they both turned. Her mother was standing a few metres away looking awkward – in her hands she held a blue hat and scarf. She held them out to Meg's dad.

'You forgot these.' Her mouth made a worried shape. 'You don't want to get cold, you might pick up a bad chill.' Her dad took them and opened his mouth, but she turned away. 'I've got to get back to work,' she muttered, walking back down the high street towards Meg's shop.

Oliver wound the scarf around his neck and pulled on his hat, watching her. His expression was a mixture of pure bemusement and longing. Then he looked up at the tree. 'Perhaps there's something in your tree after all. I'll see you later, love…' He smiled and nodded, then walked in the direction of the fields that framed the boundary of Buttermead Farm, passing Lilith as she opened the gate and stepped onto the high street.

The Italian's cheeks were pink. She carried a battered yellow knitted garland and three glass baubles. 'Don't accuse me of being the vandal,' she snapped, before Meg could finish processing what had just happened between her parents and comment. 'I was feeling mad this morning and needed to walk all the feelings off, along with a slice of tiramisu I ate for breakfast. So I hiked through four fields to get to the village and found these on my way. It was as if someone had left a trail leading to Lockton.' She shoved them under Meg's nose, before pointing back the way she'd come.

'Were there any clues?' Meg asked, taking one of the baubles so she could study it.

'I think I saw footprints but they were mostly filled with snow.' Lilith's brown eyes dropped to the bundle under Meg's arm as the cage shuddered.

'It's my hamster,' Meg explained, as the wheel inside the cage began to squeak. 'Long story. Have you come to pick up some food from Apple Cross Inn? How's your kitchen, is the electricity back on?'

A shadow passed across Lilith's face. 'The electrician had a cancellation and he's due later this morning. I sent someone from the hotel to collect the food for today earlier. We'll get the rest when the work is done. I needed a walk, to clear my head. I'd only headed into town when I found these.' She held up the decorations again. 'I was going to drop them into your shop before I walked back.'

'We should call Marcus, point him to where you found them.' Meg looked around. 'There could be clues to the identity of the vandal that you didn't spot. Do you want to come straight to the Christmas shop – I'll make you a drink and we can wait for Marcus?'

Lilith frowned as her eyes skimmed the facade of the pub. 'If you insist on speaking to PC Dougall I'll come to the cafe, as long as it won't take long.' A gust of wind swirled between them and the baubles knocked together, making a musical tinkling sound.

Lilith's gaze darted to the tree. 'There are so many now. Do you think anyone ever keeps their promise?' she asked, echoing Oliver's question from a few minutes ago.

'I think so,' Meg said, looking up too.

'What was yours?' Lilith asked, surprising them both. 'I'm sorry. You don't have to say if it's private…' She turned suddenly and headed down the high street.

Meg caught up and they walked side by side. 'It's stupid,' she confided, wondering why she was. Perhaps she was missing Evie? Whatever the reason, she needed someone to talk to, especially after her visit to Tom's and the strange moment between her mum and dad. 'I promised I'd be happy spending my first Christmas alone.' She sighed. 'Which is ironic, since my whole family is now living in my flat.'

'I don't understand.' Lilith's forehead wrinkled. 'Why would you not want to be with your family?'

Meg sighed. 'Let's just say there's a lot of expectation put on that one day. In some ways, as much as I love it, it's always been a strain. Not when I was younger. Everything felt different then. But over the last few years. My parents pretend everything's okay and we're this wonderful, happy family – and we all play our parts. But we're not. Haven't been for as long as I can remember. And the minute Christmas Day is over, everything reverts. It's hard to explain, but my mum and dad need to work out what they want. I don't think having Christmas together is helping with that. My sister figured that out way before me… I suppose one day can't fix everything, not if it's really broken, even if I wish it could.' She frowned. Why was she confiding in this woman? She'd just blurted out her deepest, darkest feelings. It had only been a few months since Lilith had been trying to run her out of town. Lilith let out a soft laugh; it was sad and so at odds with her usual persona that Meg's eyes darted to her profile. She was a pretty woman, usually so prim and perfect – so difficult to read – but today she looked troubled. 'Are you okay?' Meg asked, expecting Lilith to snap her head off.

Instead the chef gulped and looked over her shoulder at the baubles. 'I promised to impress my parents – to make this Christmas our best ever. To find a connection with them that I've never had. Now my kitchen is broken and the oil I need to make their favourite dish is somewhere between Lockton and Rome. Then I thought… I thought perhaps…' She stared at Apple Cross Inn, then let out a laugh which sounded more like a hiccup. 'Looks like neither of us is going to get what we want.'

'I'm sure your family will understand,' Meg said softly.

'Are you?' Lilith turned so she could study Meg. 'Because I'm not. I've been wanting to spend time with them for so long…'

'And here I am, desperate to get rid of mine,' Meg joked. 'Perhaps we should swap?'

Lilith's expression warmed. '*Si*. Perhaps we should.' She shivered suddenly. 'It's cold. Shall we go and get some of your awful coffee? You should really buy Italian beans.' She turned and marched off at speed, crossing to the opposite side of the road as they passed Apple Cross Inn, heading to the other pavement again only when they got close to the Christmas shop.

Lilith waited for Meg at the entrance and then followed her into the cafe, watching as she put Blitzen's cage onto one of the seats.

'Morning, lassies,' Cora greeted them. She looked surprised when Lilith sat. Probably because she hadn't made any scathing comments about the decor.

'Two cappuccinos and a couple of slices of rainbow cake, please, Cora,' Meg requested, as Lilith held up a hand to protest. 'At least try some. Agnes made it, so it'll be delicious. Cora, is Marcus around? Lilith found some decorations by Buttermead Farm, and I thought he might want to check it out.'

'I'll give him a tinkle. You two, sit.' Cora went to the counter as Meg sank into a chair, hanging the bag containing the inflatable snowman onto the back. Lilith peered inside it and raised an eyebrow.

'It was for Tom.' Meg felt a pinch in her chest as she said his name. 'But he didn't want it.' She swallowed and looked away, fighting the tears that pooled in the corners of her eyes. 'He hates Christmas.'

'Ahhhh.' Lilith nodded and glanced around the cafe. 'I see. And this is something you can't forgive?'

Meg sighed. 'You either work or you don't. There's no in between. A square peg won't fit into a round hole no matter how much you want it to – or try to squeeze it in. I know that. Having my parents staying is a timely reminder.' Although had she just seen the first hints of a thaw? Meg frowned, feeling confused. What had her father meant about the world not being black and white?

'*Sì.*' Lilith studied her with a cool expression. 'I suppose. These men, they are difficult to understand. I wonder sometimes why we bother.' They sat staring at the tablecloth for a few moments, until Cora brought over their coffees and cakes.

'Marcus said he'll be here in ten minutes,' she addressed Lilith. 'So don't go running off yet, lass.' She left as another customer entered the shop.

Lilith sipped some of the coffee and put it down without pulling a face. She sliced a tiny piece off the cake and bit into it, nodding. '*Sì*, it is good.' She paused as she nibbled some more. 'You've known Davey long?' she asked suddenly.

'He arrived about six months after I moved here.' Meg chewed her lip, waiting for Lilith to continue. It was obvious something was bothering her, something to do with Davey or Apple Cross Inn. 'He's a good man – he'll help anyone with any problem no matter who they are,' Meg added, and watched as Lilith's shoulders sagged.

'That's what I thought.' She sighed.

'Something wrong?' Meg asked gently.

'I'm not as good with people as you,' Lilith said. 'I don't know how to read them. I see how well you build your friendships. With Agnes and Evie Stuart, with Davey, Morag, Johnny, even Tom.' Her forehead creased.

Meg sighed, tracing one of the snowmen on the tablecloth with her fingertip. 'I don't always get it right. To be honest, most of my relationships – especially with men – have been a complete disaster. Tom and I don't fit, and look at Ned.' She gave Lilith a wry smile. 'I followed him from London to Lockton, gave up my whole life, and he cheated on me with you.'

'Then perhaps we were both taken in by the wrong man. I thought Ned was a good guy. I thought you…' She trailed off and then shrugged. 'I didn't have any close friendships when I was growing up. I didn't learn how to separate good from bad. My family… they like to work.' She nodded. 'That's important to them. People are not important – feelings are for the weak, and doing well no matter what is the true measure of success. And success in business above all else is what I was taught to value.'

'I understand that – my shop's important to me,' Meg said. 'It's my life. Pretty much all I ever wanted for as long as I can remember.'

Lilith winced. 'And I tried to take it away from you in the summer.'

Meg shrugged. 'I think we can blame that whole sorry affair on Ned.' She picked up her coffee and held it between them. 'Thank goodness he moved away after he got found out. Perhaps we should make a toast to him – our cheating boyfriend who brought us together and is now firmly consigned to our pasts. I'd like to think we've both moved on.'

Lilith looked unhappy, but she picked up her cup and clinked it against Meg's, and they both sipped. 'I'll toast to that.' Her dark eyes still looked troubled. 'But I'll add a new one. To a life without men – they really aren't worth the trouble.'

Meg nodded and tapped her cup gently against Lilith's again before taking a long gulp. 'They really aren't,' she agreed, ignoring the sharp stab of pain that shot through her heart.

Chapter Eighteen

Meg finished unpacking the boxes of decorations she'd picked up from Tom's yesterday afternoon, and hung the last bauble on the shelf as the shop buzzed around her. Under the counter, Blitzen clattered on his wheel out of sight of her mother, who had no idea Meg had hidden him there. She'd called Buttermead Farm earlier and left a message asking Agnes to have him to stay, but hadn't heard back. The flat had been quiet last night and Meg had gone to bed early, curling up beside her sister and trying to get some sleep. But she'd tossed and turned, her head filled with Tom and her parents.

'Your three-for-two special is going down a storm. We're selling out of everything and it's only the nineteenth,' Cora said happily, showing their collection of Christmas plates to a woman carrying a basket already piled high. Meg looked up as 'Jingle Bells' began to play in the front and her heart stopped as Tom wandered in, looking awkward.

He spotted her immediately, too late for Meg to make a dash for the back. She put her hands in the pockets of her skirt and watched him approach.

'I came to apologise,' he said simply, ignoring any preliminaries and getting straight to the point. His dark eyes studied her, his face pensive. He was always so serious – so different from her. She should have known before now that it wouldn't work. 'I wanted to tell you I'd taken the decorations down yesterday, but the boxes were gone when I got home from the pub.' He frowned. 'The shop was closed when I called by and your mobile was switched off.' He looked so unhappy her chest felt tight.

'I closed early.' She swallowed. 'It's fine, really,' she lied, giving him one of her brightest smiles when he frowned. She'd layered on so much glitter when she'd got up this morning she wondered if the sparkles might blind him. Hopefully they'd at least hide the misery in her eyes. 'I've already put everything back on the shelves… there're plenty of people who'll be happy to use them, so it's no problem.'

'What you did was…' He sighed, pulling a face as he thought, the skin crinkling beside the corners of his eyes. 'Kind. It surprised me. I'm not used to people doing things without expecting anything in return. It threw me and I hurt you – and hurting people is the complete opposite of what I've been trying to do for the last three years. But the decorations brought back memories I wasn't ready to deal with. Things I've been trying to avoid.' A woman with a huge stomach waddled past them and gave Tom a curious look. He coloured and turned his head away from her.

Meg rested a hand on her hip. 'What happened – did Santa bring you a Barbie instead of an Action Man and scar you for life?' The joke fell flat but she was angry, more upset than she'd expected, and it had made her hit out. 'I didn't mean that.' She sighed, gripping her hands into tight fists, making herself smile at him. 'I'm sorry.'

He shook his head, dismissing her apology. 'Not necessary, and that's not why. If you come to my house for dinner this evening, I'll explain. I want to explain.'

Meg took a step away from him. She was tempted, but knew now it would be a mistake. 'I'm sorry too, Tom, but I think we're done. I appreciate the apology, but I've known all along this wasn't going to work. We're just too different… and I'm not prepared to take this any further.'

'Because I like cheese and you like mince pies – or because I took down your decorations without explaining why?' he asked, looking disappointed. 'This isn't about liking Christmas.'

'It's about being the same,' Meg said. 'Or about being so different we make each other unhappy.'

Tom shook his head. 'You're looking for excuses. We both know why.' His eyes shot up when Meg's mum appeared from the back. She was dressed in her puffy coat and a woolly hat and stood for a moment, looking into the shop, frowning. As she did, Cora appeared from the cafe with two pink baby booties dangling from her fingers. She approached the customer who'd stared at Tom earlier and beamed.

'These will do for your new bub. I've got some at home for my oldest grandbaby. I hung them on my tree the first year she was born, and on every Christmas since. She's fifteen now. I have the same for all my grandkids – even the one I barely see.'

Kitty's face clouded, and even from here Meg could see her eyes fill. Then she marched from behind the counter and out of the shop with her head angled down.

'I need to go,' Meg mumbled, without looking at Tom. It was harder to walk away from him than she'd expected and she felt tears start in her own eyes as she did. But when she turned back as she reached the counter, he was gone.

*

'I found those footprints I saw by the Promise Tree on Google,' Emily said, holding her mobile skywards as they walked out of the shop ten minutes later. After Tom and her mother had left, Meg had dashed upstairs and pulled on boots and a coat, grabbing her sister as she headed outside. She hadn't explained where they were going, unsure of how her mother would react. 'I'm sure they're from a reindeer,' Emily continued, sounding excited. 'You know, Meg, I've remembered while I've been staying here just how much I love animals. Mum's so anti them, I'd given up any idea of getting close to one – but now I'm thinking about applying to do a different degree.'

'Like what?' Meg stopped outside the shop and glanced at her sister.

'Perhaps veterinary medicine,' Emily admitted. 'I might need experience to get in.'

'Wow.' Meg smiled. 'A vet. That would suit you.'

Emily beamed before her smiled dimmed a little. 'It might be easier to get experience here.' She looked around. 'If I did, I might end up staying in Lockton for longer...' She pulled a face.

'That would be fine with me.' Meg nodded. It would be great to have Emily around for longer. Although her mum might not agree. She looked up and down the high street. She hadn't watched her mother leave, so had to guess which way to go. She wouldn't normally follow her, but Kitty had looked so stricken. It had been a moment of pure honesty that Meg had rarely seen and she couldn't ignore it. Besides, it was good to have something other than Tom to focus on and she had to keep busy. 'Let's head for the Promise Tree,' she said.

'Perfect!' Emily sang, oblivious. The ground was thick with snow and there were drifts of sparkly white on either side of the pavement, so the going was slow. 'The prints were beside the tree and under the bench which means it must be close. Do you get a lot of reindeer around here?'

'There's a herd somewhere in the Highlands, apparently. But I've never seen one in Lockton,' Meg admitted. They passed Apple Cross Inn and Meg kept her eyes fixed firmly ahead, wondering if Tom was now serving at the bar. She'd have to avoid the pub, at least for a while, until her heart didn't thunder in her chest and her eyes didn't fill when she thought about him. She spotted her mother in another few steps, sitting on the bench facing the Promise Tree. Her shoulders were hunched and she was staring at the ground with her hands clasped firmly in her lap.

'Mum?' Meg said softly as they approached. Emily walked up to the tree with the phone in her hand and bent to peer at the ground. 'Are you okay?'

Kitty looked up. Her eyes were glazed, her mouth set down. 'Of course.' But her tone was anything but.

'What's wrong?' Meg sat on the bench beside her.

'Nothing.' Kitty shook her head.

'Was it the pink bootie decorations?' Meg pressed, frowning when her mother flinched. 'Mum, isn't it time you told me what's going on? There's something very wrong between you and Dad. Can we just stop ignoring it?' She looked at the snow layered on the pavement, surprised by her own wish for honesty.

There was a pause, then Kitty let out a long exhale and nodded. 'I lost her fifteen years ago…' She looked down at the snow too. 'I was only four months gone but we weren't expecting to have another. She was a surprise. Another present, your dad said.'

Meg slumped in the seat, feeling her stomach turn over. 'I didn't know…' she said, frowning.

'You were only fifteen when it happened; Emily was three. We barely held it together, your dad and me.' Her mother looked up suddenly, checking for Emily, who was still out of earshot. 'It happened near to Christmas, but we were determined to make that one day okay… and after that, it was the only day we could be normal.' She sighed. 'It's why Christmas is the way it is in our house.'

'You never said.' Meg gripped the bench, glancing over at her sister, but Emily was too far away to hear.

Kitty shook her head. 'Your dad didn't want to talk about it. It was the only way he could handle it. I needed to though, I felt so guilty. I slipped on some ice, and lost her because of the fall.' She swallowed. 'Just a silly accident. It wasn't anyone's fault. Just one of those things. Although I've learned to be a lot more careful since. By the time your dad wanted to talk…' She shrugged. 'It was just too late. But it changed everything. We used to be so happy.' She shook her head.

'You were?' The words came out shocked, even though they echoed almost exactly what her dad had told her. Emily glanced over, before crossing to the other side of the street so she could peer at the pavement. 'But you're so different,' she said.

Her mother's smile faded. 'It's funny how little children remember. All those moments of joy that somehow disappear into a black hole, all those memories that evaporate over time until they simply don't exist. We were happy until then. Not perfect, but life was a lot more like Christmas. You didn't know I was pregnant– no one did because we wanted to wait. But it left a mark in our marriage we never really dealt with.' She lowered her head sadly. 'It's too late to do it now.' Kitty looked up then, into Meg's eyes. Hers were so blue. Meg had often thought they were cold, but there was nothing cold in them now. 'If you find someone you care for, listen if they want to talk. Be honest in return – don't run from what you want, or what hurts. Because the words you don't say can cause just as much pain as the ones you do. All those unsaid feelings and thoughts freeze in time, turn into silences that become impossible to ignore. They eat you up, twist you inside out, until there's almost nothing left.'

'But Dad wants to talk now,' Meg said softly, swallowing.

Kitty nodded sadly. 'He's fifteen years too late, darling. I'm fifty next month. I want to move on. There's nothing left for us to talk about.' She stood suddenly, then patted Meg's shoulder. 'I'm sorry. For so many things. But it's time for everything to change. I think you realised that before I did, when you made your Christmas Promise this year.' Then she walked away, back down the high street towards the Christmas shop, leaving Meg staring after her, wondering what to do.

'Here!' Emily shrieked suddenly, making Meg jump. She had dropped to her haunches and jerked her head round to stare into a bush bordering the fields just a couple of metres down from the Promise Tree. 'I can see something staring at me.' Emily tried to push her arms into the greenery but ended up with a huge dollop of snow on her head. 'It's running away. I can see it now, it looks like a reindeer. I was right.' She stood and leapt up a few times, trying to look over the hedge as Agnes and Fergus walked up the high street towards Meg.

'Is the lass okay?' Fergus asked, frowning at Emily as his dog Tag trotted up to join her on the other side of the road. 'She looks like a right bampot with all that jumping in the air.'

'She's fine.' Meg nodded.

'She's young, Fergus, remember when you were like that? Because I do.' Agnes winked before turning to Meg. 'I went into the shop earlier. Cora said you'd gone for a walk. I picked up your message.' She grinned. 'We'd love to have Blitzen for a stay. Tiki hates other birds, but she loves anything furry and she's been hankering for some company these last few weeks. You can bring him over tomorrow, I'll be home all afternoon.' She linked an arm through Fergus's and her eyes danced as she looked up.

Meg nodded, her eyes filling with tears as she looked away towards the Promise Tree. She'd almost had another sister; the whole thing felt surreal. All that pain, all that deceit colouring their lives, for every day since she could remember. Her whole life felt like it had just been turned upside down. Would it ever turn the right way up again?

Chapter Nineteen

Buttermead Farm was positioned a couple of miles outside Lockton, framed by a glorious mountain range. It was a sheep farm with a large area devoted to three yurts, which the Stuart family rented out during the summer months. Behind the yurts sat Bonnie Lochan, a clear blue lake, which provided the setting for a number of local legends dating back to the seventeenth century. Meg drove her Christmas van slowly down the single-track lane towards the farm, trying not to think about Tom. He'd been in her thoughts constantly since he'd left her shop the day before. After her conversation with her mum, she wondered if she should have given him a chance to explain.

'Are you sure Blitzen will be okay?' Emily sounded stressed. She sat in the passenger seat, glaring out of the window.

'Agnes promised to take good care of him. Mum's...' Meg paused. She hadn't confided in Emily, unsure if her mother would want her to. There seemed little point in sharing the tragedy now and she wasn't quite ready to admit her parents' marriage was over. 'Mum's a little fragile right now and I don't want to upset her more.' The flat had been quiet since her confession and Meg didn't want to rock the boat. Her mum and dad still weren't talking, but despite everything, she'd seen those tiny glimmers of love over the last week and a half when they'd been together, and still felt there might be hope. For them, at least.

Emily gripped the cage as they pulled into a parking space outside the farmhouse. It was a pretty building with a sloping roof and windows with flower boxes underneath. In the summer they were filled with vivid floral arrangements; today they were piled high with snow. Meg tramped to the door, but before she could knock it was opened, and Agnes was enveloping her and Emily in a hug. 'Wonderful to see you, lasses. Is that our wee guest?' She stood back so they could enter the large kitchen. It was a beautiful room, with a chandelier dominating the ceiling hanging over an oak table where Meg had spent many hours with Evie. Agnes had laid the table with a Christmas cake, mince pies and a pot of tea. 'Make yourself at home, lassies.' She took the cage and set it onto a dresser next to a huge Santa ornament so Blitzen could face into the kitchen.

'Time for a snack!' Tiki, her African grey parrot, squawked from the corner, ruffling her red tail feathers. She stood on the top of a metal cage and turned around a couple of times before eyeing the hamster.

'Is Blitzen going to be safe?' Emily chewed her bottom lip.

'Aye, they'll get on like a house on fire. Ignore the wee bird, she's having you on.' Agnes put 'Waterfront' by Simple Minds onto her mobile, and the parrot instantly relaxed.

Meg's mind drifted to Tom as the tune filled the room. He hated Christmas music. He'd talked about his experiences at school, but beyond that he hadn't explained anything about his life. He'd wanted to though – but she'd said no. Was that wrong?

'Take a seat so you can enjoy some cake. I made it especially. There's tea too, to warm you.' Agnes pointed to the table and shook her head when she looked outside. 'This weather's getting worse and I've heard news of even more storms coming, so all those tales of better weather turned out to be false. Davey told me yesterday he's worried about the concert going ahead, we've only another four days. The marquee's going to be erected tomorrow and all the tickets are sold, but there's talk of the airports closing if things get worse. I'm even worried about Evie and Callum making it back from America.'

Meg frowned as she pulled up a chair. 'Who'll play in the concert if the bands don't make it? What about the fundraising?' Everyone had worked so hard.

Agnes shrugged. 'The whole thing will be off, lassie. We'll lose the village hall if the roof doesn't get fixed. But there's not much we can do about the weather. We'll just have to hope the predictions are wrong,' she said, just as her son, Grant, came bursting in from outside.

'Something's been messing with the yurts.' His ruddy cheeks glowed from the cold. 'I checked and the snow's all flattened around the doors. I thought it was Miss Daisy at first.' The small pygmy goat spent most of her life glued to Evie when she was home. 'But she's settled in the barn – has been most of the day. It's almost like something was trying to get inside one of them.' He patted his coat, swiping the light dusting of snow from his shoulders. 'I'm worried it's the vandals.'

'Show me.' Agnes tugged on a set of bright red wellies. 'Want to come?' she asked Emily and Meg.

'Sure.' Meg saw her sister glance warily at the hamster cage.

'He'll be fine, lass,' Agnes soothed. 'Tiki won't hurt Blitzen. Poor thing has been squawking at the angel on the top of our Christmas tree for the last two weeks, desperate to get a peep out of it. She craves company – she's not going to eat it now it's here.' She pulled a knitted hat over her silver bob, adding a pink puffy coat as Emily and Meg got ready and followed them out.

You could get to the Buttermead Farm yurts via a gravel track which led from the farmhouse towards the lochan. The view was breathtaking, with rolling hills and mountains framing the farm on either side. Three yurts rose out of the horizon, surrounded by snow. They were made of white canvas with slatted wood criss-crossing the outside, leading up to a tented point which ended at a clear plastic window affording a generous view of the sky.

'I'm going to check down here!' Grant headed along the path towards the lochan as the women stopped so they could wander around the outside of the yurts. Meg spotted tiny prints immediately. They were everywhere, scattered away from the path. A flash of silver caught her eye in the snow by one of the fences and she went to investigate, digging into the icy powder, pulling something out and holding it up. 'It's a bauble and there's an "AC" painted on the front, just like the ones outside Apple Cross Inn.'

'Aye, and me and your hot toddy found some had gone missing from the pub three days ago,' Agnes said, as Meg's stomach flipped. Would Tom haunt her conversations forever, just like Agnes's ghosts?

She turned, spotting a streak of green, bending so she could tug a string of knitted bunting out of a drift. It was stiff with ice but Meg recognised it immediately. 'That's from the high street.'

'Aye, I recognise those neat stitches. That's Cora's knitting. Means the dunderhead vandal must be hiding somewhere on the farm…' Agnes twisted round, checking in every direction and craning her neck. 'There!' she yelled suddenly, marching to the left before ducking through a low hedge into the adjoining field.

Meg and Emily followed. 'You think the vandal's hiding on the farm?' Emily asked, as Agnes bent to pick up a bright pink bauble from the snow. She waved it in the air, her eyes flashing green before she began to walk again.

'I can't see any signs that a person's been walking up here.' Meg scoured the snow. She sped up, stumbling over bumps and drifts until she caught up with Agnes. They were halfway across the field now, heading for a barn Meg knew was mostly empty in the winter.

'I've an odd feeling we'll find what we're looking for over there.' Agnes pointed to the wooden structure. 'I told Marcus I had a sense something was watching me, and I got the strongest feeling around this field. If you're afraid of spirits and spooks, you might want to go back to the kitchen.' Meg and Emily shook their heads. 'There are lots of legends – not one that refers to a kleptomaniac ghost, but we might be about to discover one exists.' Her eyes sparkled and she turned to march in the direction of the barn. Even from here, Meg could see the wooden panelled door was ajar and there was a peppering of prints leading inside.

The building was dim despite the six windows scattered across the sides. It was freezing, but dry. Meg followed Agnes, crunching on the straw bedding which lined the ground. As her eyes adjusted to the semi-darkness, she spotted about a dozen shimmering baubles in the far corner, almost hidden out of sight. There was a wall erected across the back of the barn which blocked most of their view of what was inside. Meg's throat tightened as Agnes approached it. 'Stop,' she warned, feeling her heart thunder. 'Something might be hiding…'

'I'd say that's very likely, lassie,' Agnes said. Then she clapped her hands and gasped in delight. Because standing in the corner on the other side of the wall was a golden brown reindeer.

Emily moved closer, slowing a little as the creature looked up. 'It's him. The reindeer I saw in the field yesterday.' She gently scrubbed a hand over his head, pausing a couple of times to make sure he wasn't spooked. 'I wondered where he disappeared to. This is wonderful.'

'He's very tame.' Meg moved closer, ready to spring if the creature turned nasty, feeling fiercely protective of her sister.

'Aye. There's a herd lives the other side of Morridon who're good with people and reasonably tame. This wee poppet must have got separated.' Agnes examined him. 'He looks fine – I'm guessing he's found plenty to eat and he's not injured.' She scowled at the pile of baubles in the corner. 'What he's doing with those, I can't work out. I've never heard of a reindeer stealing ornaments in my whole life.'

'Perhaps he's as obsessed with Christmas as Meg?' Emily joked, running her hands over the reindeer's soft pelt again and letting out a hum of pleasure. 'If he picked up a bauble in his teeth, I suppose he could carry it. It explains why we found so many pieces abandoned in the snow – he probably dropped them. It can't be easy.' She shook her head, smiling. 'He really is incredible.'

Agnes stood surveying the decorations. 'At least we've a solution to our mystery vandal. I prefer it to any other explanations.'

'What should we do with him now?' Meg asked.

'Get him back to his herd,' Agnes said. 'He'll need his family – especially at Christmas.' She gave Meg a wink. 'I'll bet they're wandering somewhere around here looking for the wee bairn.'

'Oh.' Emily let out an unhappy sigh.

'He can stay here for now.' Agnes patted her shoulder. 'I'll call Cora, Marcus and Morag in a minute – between them we'll track down the herd and figure out how to unite them.' She scowled at the surroundings as she looked around. 'This place could do with a little cheering up. It's not very Christmassy, and I've a mind this wee laddie will appreciate it.' She flashed Meg a smile. 'You can leave that to me and the rest of the knitting clan.'

Meg nodded and smiled, but as she made her way out of the barn with her sister, heading back towards the farmhouse, she wondered if a few sparkly decorations couldn't make up for family – or love – after all.

Chapter Twenty

'We've had an order,' Cora said, as soon as Meg and Emily returned to the Christmas shop. It was busy and customers were milling around with baskets, picking up presents and decorations, and chatting in groups. 'From Tom.' She winked.

'I'm going upstairs.' Emily waved at Meg and Cora. 'I want to do some research on this reindeer herd to see if we can find out where they are now.'

'Aye.' Cora nodded. 'Marcus filled me in on our wee vandal when you were driving back from Buttermead Farm.' She chuckled. 'That's a turn-up.'

Emily frowned. 'I hate to think of the reindeer alone at the farm. Agnes is right. We all need our family around this time of year. I'm just beginning to realise how much they matter.' She patted Meg's shoulder, then went behind the till and up the stairs without another word.

'What does *Tom* want?' Meg asked, following Cora into the cafe and pulling off her coat, ignoring the irritating flutter in her stomach. 'I can't imagine there's anything in this shop he'd be interested in.'

'Aside from you?' Cora grinned. 'He bought a few things while he was here and asked us to put together a box of Christmas decorations, along with something to go in his garden. He asked if you could deliver it personally.'

'Why?' Meg muttered. They'd said their goodbyes the day before. She'd made it quite clear there was no future for them. Her heart contracted.

'Of course I told him you'd be delighted.' Cora frowned at Meg's expression. 'I've packed some of your favourite baubles, tinsel and a mile of fairy lights, and included a reindeer sweater for his wee dog because Cooper hates the cold. Oh, and I made a special spiced strawberry and apricot jam for Marcus, and popped some in the box. I had a brainwave about what to serve it with. My husband hates all the recipes I've tried so far, but he's sure to love this. You'll understand when you see.' She grinned. 'We got a delivery of mistletoe yesterday afternoon, so I put a sprig into the box in case you had any ideas about how to use it.' She winked. 'Anything you want to add?'

Meg frowned. 'There's no need for mistletoe. I'm not even sure I should go…'

'What are you afraid of?' Cora asked softly. 'Because from where I'm standing, lassie, this is an apology pure and simple. Question is, are you going to accept it?'

Meg let out a sigh. 'I don't know.'

'At least listen to what the hot toddy has to say. Seems to me you owe the lad that much when he's bought this much stock. If you won't, I've got to wonder why. Are you so caught up in the idea of a perfect man that you can't see what's right in front of your nose? Or so wounded by your parents that you've forgotten how to listen – or forgive?'

'I'm—' Meg faltered, digesting Cora's words – hearing an echo of her mother's from yesterday. 'How did you know about my parents?'

'You think I didn't see through all that "it's fine" nonsense?' Cora raised an eyebrow. 'I've been around longer than that, lassie.'

'Okay.' Meg frowned. 'I'll see what he wants, but I'll be back before you lock up.'

'We'll see.' Cora smiled as Meg headed upstairs to change.

It was snowing as Meg parked her Christmas van outside Tom's cottage. She sat for a moment and turned up the song on the radio, trying to absorb the sentiments in the words about forgiveness and love, before shaking her head. She grabbed the boxes out of the boot and stomped up the pathway. Then she stopped, momentarily stunned, as she noticed that the Christmas tree Tom had dumped onto the porch had gone. She saw smoke billowing from the chimney and frowned. Perhaps he'd chopped it up and burned it in the fire? She reached for the bell, but then the door swung open and Tom was standing in the doorway.

Meg's eyes dropped to his torso and her jaw fell open. 'Are you making fun of me?' she asked, swallowing a stab of hurt as she stared at the Christmas jumper stretched across his broad chest. She sold them in her shop – this one had a reindeer on the front with a bright red nose.

'Of course not.' Tom tugged her inside before closing the door and taking the boxes out of her hands. Cooper skidded up and Meg stared at him, because he was wearing reindeer antlers now.

Had she taken a wrong turn out of Lockton and ended up in a parallel universe?

'I… I wanted to apologise again. I thought…' Tom looked down at his top – the red glitter did nothing to detract from his pure masculinity and Meg's stomach clenched. 'If I stepped into your world for a moment – showed you I've realised what an idiot I've been – you'd agree to come back into mine. It was supposed to be a symbol, proof that I've realised a few Christmas decorations can't hurt me. I wanted to make you smile. It wasn't supposed to make things worse.'

Meg put her hands in her pockets as she followed him into the sitting room. The fir tree was standing back in the corner – stripped to its birthday suit and sparkle-free.

Tom hefted the boxes onto the large rectangular coffee table. 'There are reasons why I hate Christmas. I want to explain, but I've realised you're right. A single day isn't to blame for anything. I wondered if we could turn back the clock and you'd help me decorate the house again?'

Meg frowned. 'When I found the boxes on the porch, saw what you'd done with the tree, I thought…' She swallowed. 'I overstepped, I get that. But we feel differently about a lot of things, and when I see how miserable my parents make each other… I'm not looking to repeat their mistakes.' Her eyes met his. 'For once in my life I'm not going to smile and say a few sparkles and Christmas decorations are going to fix this – not when so much isn't being said. I've spent a lot of years hiding from my feelings, pretending everything's okay – even when it's not. I need to stop. I've realised that since my parents arrived. It would be better if I left now. I don't want to complicate things by letting us get close again.' She took one step back towards the door, then stopped when Cooper came to rest his head against her leg, effectively blocking her exit. Her feet felt heavy and her chest throbbed. She didn't want to go. 'Okay.' She sighed, scratching the dog's head. 'I'll listen before I leave, give you a chance to explain. I owe you that.' She'd use the lesson her mother had given her before she got in her van and left Tom behind for good.

'Thank you.' He put his hands in his pockets, drawing attention to his long lean legs, and looked away. 'I woke up on Christmas Day three years ago and my wife, Marnie, had left me. I loved her.' He swallowed. 'At least, at the start of our marriage, but…' He shook his head. 'I don't think she ever loved me. She was looking for what I could give her, but it was never enough. *I* was never enough.'

'I'm sorry,' Meg said, watching the darkness spread across his eyes. 'That would… I can imagine why you wouldn't want to relive that.' Perhaps it did explain a few things – at least why he hated Christmas. Although it was clear from the set of his shoulders that he was holding something back.

'That's not all.' He read her mind. 'My grandmother died on the same day. I'd been so wrapped up in my work, so obsessed by the way it made me feel, I'd missed all my grandfather's calls. She died and I wasn't there.' His voice was matter-of-fact. 'This woman who raised me when my mother wouldn't. One of the few people who gave me love without expecting anything in return.' His forehead creased.

Meg stepped forwards, wanting to reach for him, but he held up a hand.

'I know it's stupid to connect those things, but when I saw the decorations in the house, it brought everything back,' Tom continued. 'Then I realised after we talked, after I saw those people in your shop, that I can't blame Christmas for what *I* did – or think that shutting it out, avoiding all those memories and pretending it doesn't exist will change anything.' He paused. 'I've done a lot of things I'm not proud of, Meg, and I've been trying to put that right. Hurting you, it made me realise I've been moving backwards, not forwards. Hiding from all the wrong things.' He shrugged. 'Christmas… music…' He cleared his throat. 'You.'

Meg's heart thumped. 'I thought you were angry. You hate Christmas, you told me as much. When I saw all the decorations piled outside, I thought…' She let out a long sigh. 'It was such a rejection. Like you were saying you didn't want *me* in your life.' Her eyes filled.

'I'm sorry,' he said simply. 'I… I used to be good with words, I used to say all the right things. They'd just be there in my head whenever I needed them.' He clicked his fingers. 'Now they're gone. I reach for them and all the wrong ones come out. I need you to know I never intended to hurt your feelings…'

'Okay.' Meg nodded. 'I'm sorry too.' Perhaps her mother was right about listening. Perhaps honesty could turn things around, after all? 'Is that it?' she asked, sensing there was still something he wasn't telling her.

'No.' Tom didn't look at her. 'I want to decorate the house again – with you – swap all the bad memories for better ones. I'd like to prove I'm finally ready to move on.'

She raised an eyebrow. 'You'll embrace Christmas music too?'

His lips twisted. 'As long as I get to choose the songs. I'll even make you mulled wine if you ask for it.'

'Deal.' Meg nodded, bending to take off her green boots. She unbuttoned her coat slowly and put it on the sofa, then pulled up the sleeves of her top.

'Just like that?' He looked surprised.

'Unless you want to tell me anything else?' She cocked her head, still sensing something was missing. Tom shook his head firmly and Meg nodded again. 'Then that's it. I learned a long time ago not to hang on to resentment. Or at least, to try not to. But you should know Cora picked out *a lot* of baubles, so if you're going to have second thoughts you'd better say now – because I'm not packing these away again.' She opened the box; it was piled high with tinsel, lights and a multitude of colourful decorations, with a single sprig of mistletoe in the centre of the mound.

Tom let out a low whistle as Meg began to unpack the box. 'What's first?' he asked.

'Music and wine.' Meg grinned.

An hour later the tree sparkled, Meg's star took pride of place over the fireplace, mistletoe hung in the kitchen and Cooper was slumped in front of the fire wearing the reindeer jumper. The dog seemed delighted with the outfit and had even complained when she'd tried to take it off. Meg put Cora's tub – which had been at the bottom of the box – onto the table next to their glasses and opened it, then laughed when she found four perfect doughnuts. 'These are a gift from Cora. Her Christmas Promise was to find a flavour of jam that Marcus would enjoy. I'm guessing he's going to love this idea.' She picked one up and bit into it, feeling the sugar scatter over her lips. 'That's amazing,' she hummed. 'The jam's so sweet.'

Tom laughed. 'Policeman – doughnuts. That's inspired.' He took a bite and chewed, nodding.

The music changed on the radio, clicking over to another Christmas song with a strong guitar solo. Meg saw Tom stiffen.

'I'm not prying,' she said softly, licking the last of the sugar from her fingertips, watching his eyes track the movement. 'But I saw the guitar in the boot room when I was putting the boxes out of the way. You talked about hiding from your music…' She knew she was on to something when a muscle pulsed in his neck. She didn't know why she was pushing, except she could feel something was still hidden between them. She wasn't looking for perfection now, just honesty and truth.

'I did…' Tom sipped his wine. The light was shadowy. Flickers from the fairy lights lit his profile, picking out the edges of his jaw and shadows under his eyes. She swallowed, feeling the bubble of emotion as it rose, even as she tried to hold it back.

'Will you play for me?' Meg asked. She waited while he sipped his beer and considered. Intuition told her this was important so she didn't push.

In the end, Tom nodded, then got up and disappeared into the hall. Meg heard a door open and close. Then he walked back in with the shiny red guitar she'd seen on the day she'd decorated. 'I've not played properly for years.' He tugged off his jumper and tossed it onto the floor. His T-shirt rode up, exposing the bottom of a washboard stomach and the trail of dark hair leading from his bellybutton down. Meg tried to ignore it but her hormones still jerked to attention. 'A lot of people have been telling me not playing is a mistake. That I've been denying myself. I must admit, I've missed it. I wonder if it's one of the reasons I've found it so difficult to express how I feel.' He slid the strap over his shoulder and his fingers began to tease the strings.

He didn't look up, but Meg saw his face soften as the music took over. Felt her skin prickle in response at the sounds he drew from the guitar. He was a thing of pure beauty; every inch of his skin seemed to glow. Meg felt her breath catch, and shuffled on the sofa as every cell of her body began to heat. It was like she was being seduced, like the notes were pumping through her blood, drawing her to him. Tom's body loosened as his fingers raced across the strings, making everything in the room – even the decorations – melt away. Then he closed his eyes and began to sing.

There was something haunting about his voice – something Meg connected with on a visceral level. Something almost familiar. His song was about broken hearts and lovers who used, about putting money and fame ahead of everything else and losing your soul. Then about the power of stepping back, of denying yourself. Meg held her breath, felt goosebumps rise across her skin as it prickled and hummed. Then the song ended and she slowly stood, unable to help herself. Perhaps Tom could read her face, because when he opened his eyes he didn't say a word. Instead, he pulled the guitar slowly from his shoulder and placed it on the floor. Then he reached out and grabbed her.

The kiss wasn't slow and it wasn't particularly expert. They slammed into each other, pressing their bodies together as if their desires outweighed any need for sensitivity or skill. Meg's heart was racing. Beating so hard she could hear it filling her ears – blocking out all semblance of sanity. Which was a good thing, because if she could think she'd be pushing Tom away and heading for the door. But it was too late for that. She moved her hands down to the bottom of his T-shirt, then yanked it up and over his head, before dropping it on the floor. Now she could see the chest she'd been drooling over earlier. It was hard and muscular and there was that trail of hair dipping downwards. She put her hands on his skin, slid them across his belly before he took over, whipping her arms to either side so he could unpop the red buttons that lined the front of her elf outfit. Once they were undone, he whipped the sleeves off her arms and shimmied the top down so it was hanging from her waist.

'You're beautiful,' he murmured, tracing a broad hand across her belly and then up to her back so he could undo her bra. He discarded that too, tossing it over her shoulder and throwing it so it landed with a soft thud onto the wooden floor. 'With or without the glitter,' he added, letting his eyes streak across her skin, resting momentarily on her breasts which were puckering in the cool air.

'Do you think we should move?' Meg asked, stepping forwards so their skin brushed, aware of Cooper sleeping by the fire. She tipped her head in the dog's direction just as his ears pricked up.

'Bedroom.' Tom grabbed her hand and guided her into the hall, before closing the door. The hallway was small and freezing away from the fire. Tom looked down and smiled, before turning Meg round and lifting her onto the bottom step. Now their faces were level. 'I might undress you here,' he said, pulling her in for another kiss.

Meg wasn't sure what was happening to her. She was used to her skin heating from someone's touch. The flood of arousal when she was kissed. But this felt different. Usually she held back, waiting until she was sure she was compatible with a lover. She didn't jump into bed with just anyone. Years of watching parental wars had taught her the power of the wrong kind of love. And no amount of feel-good hormones were worth that. Still, waiting hadn't helped her up till now.

But with Tom she felt different, less in control. He kissed her again. Slowly. Now their faces were level it was harder to pretend this wasn't happening. That he wasn't having such an effect on her body. Her arms slid around his neck, pulling him closer, and she felt his fingers move to the buttons at the waist of her elf outfit, dealing quickly with the clasp before pushing the zip down. Then she felt the material fall as the cool air hit her legs, scattering goosebumps across the surface of her skin, making her shiver. She concentrated on the feel of Tom as she ran her fingers down his back, letting them rest for a moment on the waistband of his jeans before moving them towards the front. She felt his stomach contract as she reached the button, his body jerk away, and then felt it press into her. As if he couldn't control his own reaction and he wanted more. He hummed against her mouth, taking the kiss deeper, and then grabbed hold, pulling her closer as he dug his fingers into the soft skin of her bottom, stroking around the outer edges of her pants, making her squirm. She couldn't remember what colour her underwear was and hoped she'd put on a silky matching set this morning, rather than comfortable cotton. Some of those had Christmas patterns on. It had been so long since anyone but Blitzen had seen her without her clothes, Meg barely even noticed what she wore. Tom didn't seem to care – he let his fingers slide underneath the material as they trailed gently up and over her bottom.

Meg undid the button of Tom's jeans and pushed their bodies apart, shoving them over his hips and down. He wiggled and they fell, then she felt him move, knew he was pushing the legs down and off because his warm hands temporarily left her body. She held on until he was undressed, kissing him gently, not wanting to let go… wondering if she ever would.

Chapter Twenty-One

Meg's skin was like silk. Tom hadn't touched another woman since his divorce. Hadn't particularly wanted to. He'd always loved sex, but with Marnie it had become less about give, take and the expression of love, and more a demonstration of power, a satisfaction of needs. She'd needed constant reassurance and when his hadn't been enough, she'd looked elsewhere. To another musician, to be exact – someone slightly more successful. The idea still hurt. Not because he still loved her, but because it was so clear now she'd never really cared for him. That music had been his value all along. But with Meg it was different. Because she didn't know who he was.

Meg wouldn't spin him a line: you got exactly what you saw. A woman smothered with glitter, obsessed with Christmas, with a soft heart who wanted to spread happiness and joy wherever she went. Ironically, despite the crazy outfits and make-up which some might see as armour, she was vulnerable, and her strength was in letting him see that. Because it was there in everything she said, every kind act or word. Meg didn't hold anything back and she didn't lie. She was unlike any of the women he'd known – aside, perhaps, from his grandmother.

She stepped backwards on the stairs and grabbed his hand, pulling him upwards one step. He smiled into their kiss, wondering if the sparkles on her face were rubbing off again; a physical manifestation of what was happening to him. The stirrings and faint sense that his life might be beginning again. Perhaps he was ready to risk letting someone get close? But not completely, not yet. He wasn't ready to tell Meg who he was. Too afraid it might change everything. He wanted – needed – her to know *him* first. Wasn't ready to trust this was real.

Meg backed up another step, pulling him with her, her hands moving down his body, across his chest, making his heart pump harder until he could barely hear above the rush of blood. He grabbed her, lifted her up and felt her legs knot around his back. He thought she'd protest, but instead she deepened the kiss and wrapped her arms around his neck. He grinned, delighted. Marnie was as light as a feather but she'd never have let him pick her up – she'd have complained about being too heavy. Yet another reminder of how different they were.

When he reached the top of the stairs he thought about setting her down – there was a rug on the floor they could sink into, and his body was pumping with so many needs he wasn't sure he'd make it to the bedroom. But then Meg let her legs drop to the floor and she turned to tug him down the long corridor, passing the spare room where Blitzen had stayed, before opening the door to his bedroom and pulling him in. The curtains were open and the moon threw light across the bed and floor. Meg ripped back the covers and then stood, facing him.

'Second thoughts?' he asked, walking in to join her.

'Not really.' She smiled and let her eyes shift downwards, then shook her head. 'Nope. I'm just taking a moment to appreciate how quickly we've gone from fighting over decorations to bed. I'm not normally that…' She tossed her head and Tom saw a hint of glitter in the moonlight. 'We're very different, and being here – let's just say I'm breaking all my rules.'

Tom wanted to touch her but he stopped himself. 'Can differences be good sometimes?'

Meg gazed up at him, moistening her lips. But instead of shaking her head and turning away – which he half expected – she fell back on the bed, grabbing him and pulling him on top, somehow manoeuvring herself up so they were face to face. 'I'm beginning to wonder that myself.' Her body was warm and soft, but he held himself up so he didn't crush her. Then he leaned down to give her a long kiss, rolling them both to the side. He eased backwards and pushed a strand of blonde hair from her face, let himself look into her blue eyes. A song began to form in his head. And this time he didn't shut it out: he let the music play in his mind as he kissed her again.

Meg's hands ran down Tom's sides, across his chest, before reaching the top of his boxers which she pushed off. He made quick work of her underwear, breaking off the kiss so he could throw them onto the floor. He grinned when he got a quick flash of a snowman's nose on her pants, but decided not to tease her. Instead he eased her back, letting his hands drift slowly down. Her breath quickened, as goosebumps marked her skin and his fingers traced her curves. Their kisses, which had been slow and gentle until now, began to heat – then Meg pushed him onto his back and climbed on top.

'Protection,' he whispered. 'In the drawer. I wasn't expecting…'

She pressed a finger to his lips and leaned across to open it. 'I'm not going to judge you for being prepared,' she murmured, before slipping it on. Her golden hair shimmered around her shoulders as she arched up and then bent to kiss his neck, tracing her tongue across his skin and chest before she took him inside. Tom's vision blurred as she began to move, taking it slowly as the heat continued to build. When it was almost unbearable, he gripped her thighs, thrusting up to meet each movement. Then Meg moaned suddenly, her body shuddered – and he let himself go.

He pulled her down onto his chest and kissed her cheek as they caught their breath. The song that had begun in his head filled it again as Tom fell asleep.

Tom yawned and stretched, trying not to wake Meg, who was sprawled across his chest like a sparkly blanket. He squinted into the darkness. The moon was still high, and there were more stars out than there had been earlier. The house felt chilly and the heating was off, which meant it was after ten. Cooper barked downstairs and Tom eased himself from underneath Meg, who stirred and let out a sigh. He picked up his boxers and pulled them on, feeling a strange confusion of contentment and guilt. Then he frowned as Cooper's barks grew louder and hurried downstairs. The dog was woofing at Meg's handbag, which she'd left inside the small hallway. It was ringing, the insistent chirp coming – he guessed – from her phone. Cooper whined and Tom let him outside, grabbing the mobile as it stopped, started up and then stopped once more. Meg's dad was calling, and he'd been trying for a while judging by the seven missed calls. Cooper batted his head against the door and Tom let him into the house again, thinking about making coffee to ease Meg out of her slumber. But when the mobile rang once more he picked it up.

'Meg,' Oliver barked. 'Where are you? I've been calling for ages.' He sounded panicked. Cooper sniffed Tom's feet, tickling them with his nose.

'It's Tom.'

There was a pause before Oliver said, 'Is Meg there?' There was confusion in his tone and Tom waited for him to ask more.

'She's busy at the moment.' Tom winced. Would Meg mind if her father knew she was here? 'I'll get her to call you back in a minute.'

'Tell her it's urgent.' Oliver's voice was tight. 'Tell her Emily's disappeared.'

Chapter Twenty-Two

It was approaching midnight and freezing outside as Tom, Meg, Oliver, Kitty and Cooper tramped up the high street from Meg's shop towards the Promise Tree, checking the snow for prints. They hadn't had a blizzard for the last day, although a big dump was due later, so the snow on the pavement had either been gritted or trodden down. There weren't many clues as to who'd been walking recently, but the soft glow from the street lights and the moon gave them enough light to check.

'What happened?' Meg asked her dad as he sped up to join them, leaving Kitty alone with Cooper, who was sniffing the ground at the edges of the pavement. Meg's mum hadn't said much at all since they'd turned up at the shop. Her face was ashen and she kept clenching and unclenching her fingers.

Oliver's forehead crumpled as they stopped to look through each of the windows of Apple Cross Inn. The lights were off inside and it was unlikely Emily would be hiding in the shadows. 'Your mum told me about your conversation.' He let out a long exhale as they continued down the street, and Tom wondered if he should be listening in. 'About the baby. She told me she's been unhappy for a while, that what we have together isn't enough.' He lowered his voice. 'I told her I wanted things to change. I said I loved her. That I went to a marriage guidance appointment I'd booked for us both because… I think we can get through this. I might be fifteen years too late, but I don't want to lose her.' He let out a sigh as Tom stared at the ground, pretending he wasn't listening. 'I assumed Emily had gone to bed. We hadn't seen her after dinner, but the door to the kitchen was open and she must have heard us talking. At least some of it.' He grimaced. 'I checked in on her as I was heading for bed, but she was gone. Her guitar is missing but she hasn't taken anything else. Not even her phone. I tried calling her a few times before I realised she'd left it on your dresser. She's not dressed properly – all she has is that silly snowsuit that's too small for her.' He swallowed, his eyes shining with fear. 'It's so cold and there's more snow due tonight. She could be anywhere.'

Tom reached out to take Meg's hand. She wore gloves, but her fingers were stiff and unyielding – it took a couple of moments before she unbent them and gripped his tightly in return. Tom felt a surge of something in his chest – a burst of emotion. It had been years since he'd felt this type of connection. Even in the hospital after his grandmother had died, he'd been so racked with guilt he'd disconnected from everything. His life had imploded and he hadn't known how to process the emotions. So he'd shut them out. It was only now he was beginning to let himself open up.

'I should have told her about the baby,' Meg said. 'I thought it would be better to keep it to myself. But withholding the truth, even for the right reasons… that's lying, isn't it?' The guilt was evident in her voice, and Tom tried not to think about what she was saying. Or connect that situation to theirs.

'It's not your fault, Meg—' her dad began.

'You're not to blame,' Kitty interrupted, catching up with them. 'I am. I lost one child and I'm in danger of losing another. Because I didn't face up to how I felt. I wasn't honest. You didn't want to talk.' She looked her husband in the eye. 'And I blamed you. I couldn't forgive you even when you wanted to put things right. I just wanted to run, to pretend it hadn't happened, to hide in my work... To protect myself and my babies. But you can't, can you?' She swallowed as a tear trickled down her cheek. Oliver reached out and caught it with his finger, then wiped it away. 'Why is running, pretending everything's all right, or ignoring it until the silence almost destroys you, so much less terrifying than facing up to what's happened?' She shook her head as her voice wavered. 'I've ruined everything.'

'It takes two to make a problem, Kit,' Oliver said softly. 'This is not all on you. But we can put it right together. I don't think it's too late. Emily's going to be fine.' Tom could see that the lines around his eyes had deepened with worry – he knew he didn't entirely believe what he was saying.

'You're always so calm. I need calm today.' Kitty's brow knitted as she gazed at him, then her eyes dropped from his face. 'We have to find Emily.' Her voice broke as she looked at the high street. 'It's so cold. She was sick a few months ago. What if—'

'She's going to be okay.' Oliver squeezed Kitty's shoulder and she nodded slowly. Then she turned away and began to shuffle along the pavement, searching the ground for clues, before she reached the Promise Tree where she stood, staring up into the branches, frowning. Until Cooper began to bark. The dog was pawing at the hedge on the other side of the road and whining.

'Of course.' Meg nodded suddenly, her blonde hair shimmering in the moonlight under her red hat. 'I know where Emily is. I should have realised. I was so scared I didn't think…' She smiled, her face transforming. 'We need the car – it's too far to walk in this weather and Emily will be freezing.' She crossed to the pavement and grabbed hold of Tom's hand, before leading them back towards her Christmas shop where his car was parked.

'Take a left,' Meg directed, before speaking to Agnes on her mobile, as Tom drove along the high street and turned onto a narrow track with a sign for Buttermead Farm. It was dark and the car shuddered as it bounced over a huge drift of snow.

Oliver and Kitty were sitting in the back with Cooper between them. The dog moaned as the car negotiated another bump and a pinprick of light appeared in the distance. Tom followed Meg's directions until five minutes later he pulled up outside a large farmhouse. 'We need to be quick. It's too cold to wait.' Meg jumped out and slammed the car door without looking back. Cooper nudged his nose against the window as she ran up to the building and knocked.

'Where's she going?' Oliver opened the back of the car and sprang out. He helped Cooper and Kitty down as Tom grabbed a lead and fixed it to the dog's collar, in case he decided to run off. He had a small torch in the glove compartment which he grabbed.

The farmhouse door swung open and Agnes appeared, wearing a puffy pink coat with a knitted scarf wrapped around her neck. She switched on her torch and set off down a gravel pathway away from the farmhouse, with Meg and the rest of them running after her. They couldn't see much, though the moon was out and Tom's torch lit some of the track, picking out piles of snow and a few spiky bushes. He shivered as he paused so Kitty and Oliver could keep up. He didn't take his eyes off Meg, but still almost missed her as she followed Agnes to the right and ducked through a gap in a hedge before disappearing. Cooper groaned as Tom broke into a trot, trailing them into a field where the snow was much deeper. The dog hesitated, then shadowed Tom as he raced after them.

'Where are they going?' Oliver shouted as he and Kitty caught up. Tom pointed to a midway point across the field where Meg and Agnes – lit by the moonlight – were approaching a barn. The three of them broke into a run again, stumbling across icy branches and roots buried in the snow. When they arrived outside the barn they were all panting, their breath like long ribbons curling in the air. 'What is this place?' Oliver rubbed his arms and shivered.

'We found a reindeer here earlier,' Meg explained, pointing to the door of the building. 'I think this is where we'll find Emily.'

Oliver glared at the structure, frowning.

'A reindeer?' Kitty said. 'She could catch—' Oliver patted her on the shoulder and shook his head.

'She'll be fine, Mum,' Meg soothed.

'Aye,' Agnes interjected. 'This one's a sweetheart and as tame as my goat. He's taken a shine to your lassie – I think that girl has a gift.' She glanced at one of the windows. 'There's a light. I'll guess Emily's come to wish her new friend good night.'

The barn door was closed but as they approached, Tom could hear the soft strum of a guitar. Agnes opened the door and then they saw a light shining inside. Cooper jerked the lead, tugging it from Tom's fingers, and shot into the building. The guitar stopped abruptly and Tom heard Emily squeak. They followed the light into a stable and found her curled up on a pile of straw next to a large brown reindeer. She had a lantern torch, which spread an arc of light around the room. It was Christmas-themed so Tom guessed she'd taken it from Meg's shop. Her lips were bluish and she was shivering.

'Oh my god.' Kitty dived at Emily and wrapped her into a huge hug as Oliver pulled off his coat and draped it around her shoulders, then Meg went to hug her too. Tom took in the surroundings. The walls of the barn had been decorated with red, white and yellow knitted bunting with mini Santas, snowmen and stars. Hung in between were glittery baubles – and the room had been finished off with a string of white fairy lights.

'You've been busy.' Meg put her arm around Agnes. 'We were only here this afternoon.'

She shrugged. 'Ach. I just drove around once you'd left and collected up a load of decorations the Jam Club had been working on – everyone contributed, so it didn't take long to hang them up.' The reindeer got to his feet slowly and walked up to sniff her fingers, probably looking for food. 'Fergus thinks I've lost my mind.' Her cheeks coloured as she stroked its head. 'I've started knitting a string of reindeer; I thought that would make the wee thing feel at home. I asked around, but we've not had much luck tracking down his herd.'

'I found something when I got back to the flat earlier today.' Emily untangled herself from Kitty, and Oliver and Meg stepped back. 'I was searching the internet.' She glanced at Tom suddenly with an unreadable expression, making his heart thump. Then she looked away. 'I saw a couple of posts on Twitter about a herd being spotted close to Morridon.'

Agnes frowned. 'That's a fair amount of ground to cover. I'll ask Fergus if he's heard anything around his way. We might need to take a drive tomorrow. If the snow holds off.' She frowned at Emily. 'I don't think you should sleep here tonight, lassie, it's too cold. Besides, reindeer might look cuddly, but they're not particularly good room-mates.' She wrinkled her nose.

'I…' Emily sighed, eyeing her parents who were now staring at each other. Meg's dad began to tremble, cold now he'd given her his coat, and Kitty pulled off her scarf and wound it around his neck. 'I'm sorry. I wasn't thinking. I just needed time to digest.' Emily looked at her hands.

'It's okay, love.' Oliver went over to put his arm around her. 'We know what you overheard. I'm sorry.' He shook his head as he glanced at Kitty, his expression sad. 'I don't think either of us realised what we've been doing to you both. Let's go back to the flat. I think we need to get some sleep, and your mother and I need to talk.'

Kitty swallowed, then nodded, her eyes filling with tears. When Oliver reached out a hand and offered it to her, she tentatively took it and Tom heard Meg sigh.

He took a small step back as feelings simmered in his chest; an odd sense of discomfort. Because while Meg's family were finding their way back to each other, perhaps considering facing their problems with truths, he wasn't ready to face his. And he wasn't sure exactly where that left him and Meg.

Chapter Twenty-Three

Meg stood on the doorstep of her shop and watched Tom drive away in his Land Rover, with Cooper staring at them from the back of the car. He'd been quiet on the journey, and she'd felt like something was off, but there'd been little chance for them to discuss anything with her whole family in the car.

'Tired?' her dad asked, looping an arm through hers as they followed Emily and her mother into the shop.

'Very.' Meg sighed, rubbing her eyes. 'It's been a long night.'

As Kitty ambled down the left-hand aisle, she stopped suddenly so she could look at one of the shelves. It displayed Agnes's various jams as well as bottles of Scottish whisky, some from Fergus McKenzie's distillery. She picked one up and held it to the light, and the brown liquid sparkled like liquid magic. Then she glanced at Meg. 'Can I take this? I'll pay you tomorrow.' She looked pensive.

'It's on the house: consider it a celebration,' Meg said, her eyes drifting to Emily. 'I thought you only drank at Christmas though?' Kitty rarely indulged because she thought too much alcohol spelled accidents – which meant Meg's father had almost stopped drinking too. 'And I've never seen you have whisky.'

Her mother shrugged. 'Your dad always used to like a tipple in the evenings. I thought perhaps he might want to have one now?' She cleared her throat, her eyes darting around the shop, anywhere but at him. Meg felt something in her stomach stir, something warm and hopeful.

Beside Meg, Oliver let out a little cough of his own and nodded. 'I'd like that very much,' he said. 'It's been a long time…'

Kitty's gaze darted to his and her lips settled into a familiar worried arch. 'About fifteen years, if I'm counting correctly.' He nodded, his smile dimming. 'Then a drink is overdue,' she said. 'I'm making no promises, Ollie, but I think it's time we finally talked. Meg, I have a feeling we might not make our flight tomorrow.' She checked her watch and grimaced. 'It's been a long night.'

'You can stay as long as you like. In fact, I'd like it if you did.' Meg swallowed, realising she meant it.

Then her mother turned and headed for the stairs, and her dad followed. And for the first time in years, Meg detected a little bounce in his step.

After their parents had gone into the kitchen, Emily pulled Meg into the bedroom and shut the door, before leaning against it and frowning. 'I'm sorry about tonight, I shouldn't have run off. I must have ruined your evening.' Meg waved the apology away. 'I overheard Mum and Dad talking—'

'I'm sorry,' Meg interrupted. 'I just found out about the baby myself – but I thought they wanted to keep it to themselves.'

Emily shrugged. 'They didn't mean for me to overhear, but I'm glad I did. It explains a lot. I just needed some space to process the information, it was such a shock. I thought we were leaving tomorrow and suddenly I wasn't ready to go. But I've realised running away doesn't solve anything.' She closed her eyes.

'Perhaps this time it did?' Meg shrugged, her eyes drifting to the door. This was the first proper conversation she remembered her parents having in years. It was only four days until Christmas and she realised she wasn't dreading spending it with them. Perhaps because they were finally being honest with each other?

Emily scrubbed a hand over her mouth, looking worried. 'I've got something to show you, Meg. Something you need to know. Something I found' – she checked her watch and winced – 'earlier tonight. I tried to call before I left, but you didn't pick up and I didn't want to leave a message.'

'I was at Tom's,' Meg explained, as Emily pursed her lips. 'I'm sorry.'

'It's okay. I suppose I should have guessed when he turned up with the rest of you.' Emily tugged off her dad's coat and dumped it onto the chair in the corner of Meg's room, before grabbing her laptop and jumping on the bed. She pulled a blanket over her knees, shivering a little, and switched it on. 'It's going to make what I tell you a bit worse.'

'It is?' Meg asked, turning to look at her sister properly.

Emily pulled a face. 'I was looking through social media, searching the news for anything I could find about reindeer herds in Scotland. I put on some music and this ad popped up – for an album.' She tapped her fingertips on the laptop. 'I don't normally take much notice. But there was something familiar about this band. Like an itch at the edge of my brain I needed to scratch. Something's been nagging at me since I got to Lockton and met Tom, you know?'

Meg nodded, with a sinking feeling in the pit of her stomach as she realised she'd felt the same. A sense that something wasn't quite right. She'd ignored it of course, but it hadn't gone.

'So I clicked the link, and you know that song, "If Every Day Was Christmas"?'

'Yes.' Meg's voice was rough. 'Tom hates it.' She turned, feeling a sudden urge to keep her hands busy, and pulled off her boots and skirt, then grabbed some black pyjama bottoms and tugged them on.

'I don't see why – since he wrote it,' Emily said dramatically, spinning the laptop around on her knee. The screen was filled with a black and white album cover featuring two men and a woman. The picture was arty and atmospheric. One man was holding a guitar, his head angled away from the camera, but Meg would have recognised that profile anywhere. Especially since she'd been feathering kisses along it last night.

'I don't understand…' Her heart thumped and she swallowed a lump of emotion as it threatened to burst out of her throat. 'Is it really him?'

Emily nodded. 'Tom Riley-Clark – there's absolutely no doubt. I found more pictures.' She flicked to another tab and about twenty photos loaded. Full body shots: in one Tom was shirtless; in another he wore jeans, a black shirt and held a guitar; two featured him in a dinner jacket; and in four he stood by a tall, stunning woman with dark hair and laughing eyes. Tom looked disconnected in all of them, apart from the ones where he was playing. In those he looked so alive his face almost glowed. His expression matched the one Meg had seen earlier – when he'd been playing the guitar for her. Her thoughts were jumbled. She'd known Tom was holding himself back but she'd never guessed it was anything like this. She blinked, feeling stupid. Was this about trust, or did she just not matter enough for him to tell the truth?

'I'm sorry, Meg.' Emily frowned. 'The band's called The Ballad Club, I googled them. They were making a name for themselves, had a few songs in the charts, getting a good following. They made four albums in total. Then the whole thing imploded about three years ago. There's loads of stuff about them breaking up – Tom's ex-wife left him on Christmas Day apparently, and there was a death in his family, I can't remember who.'

'His grandmother,' Meg croaked. At least he'd told her that much.

'Anyway, he just disappeared. Upped and left his whole life. There are a few stories about him being spotted. His ex did a lot of interviews before interest dried up. At least, until the last few weeks. Now that song is back in the charts and the record company have re-released an album, so there's a lot of media interest. I knew he looked familiar, right from that first moment in his car.' She paused, reading Meg's expression. 'He didn't tell you, did he?' Her voice was kind.

'No,' Meg said, looking away. 'He didn't.' She pushed away the jolt of hurt, gathering her emotions as she glanced back at the screen – at the man she thought she knew. At the man she'd slept with earlier. 'I could feel it though. I knew he wasn't telling me something.' She huffed out a breath. 'No wonder he's so good on that guitar.'

Emily nodded. 'I thought the same. Maybe he was afraid of how you'd react? I don't know. People do weird things sometimes for the right reasons. But I don't understand what he's doing in Lockton, working behind a bar.'

Meg nodded, letting her shoulders relax, thinking about her mum and dad in the other room drinking the bottle of whisky. Finally talking after all these years, sharing their pain, perhaps even finding a way through it. 'I think I should give him a chance to explain. Tell him I know? There's no point in prolonging it. I'll say I just found out, see what he says.'

Emily nodded. 'He cares for you, any idiot can see that. If you tell him you know, perhaps he'll open up.'

Meg nodded as her eyes welled with tears. 'I've got the morning off tomorrow – I'll go to the pub, see if we can find some time alone.'

She just hoped Tom would tell her before she admitted she knew – but most of all, she hoped he had a very good reason for hiding the truth.

Chapter Twenty-Four

The marquee was huge and took up most of Apple Cross Inn's car park. The gig was in just three days, and preparations were in full swing. As Meg made her way around the side of the pub, she took a moment to stop and listen to the sounds coming from inside. Snow – heavy and dense – fell from dark skies and fluttered around her head, landing on her eyelashes and nose until she brushed it off. Feeling her heart thunder in her chest, she steeled herself to confront Tom. She'd worn her favourite elf outfit this morning – it had a short skirt that floated around her legs and a furry white border that was soft to the touch – hoping it would make her brave. But her boots still slowed as she approached the marquee and her heart still pounded as she ducked through the flap. She could see Tom at the far end, setting up a wooden stage, while Davey darted in and out, running a cable along the floor and plugging in heaters. Music was playing from a speaker somewhere and, despite the fact that it was snowing, the air inside felt warm. Meg swallowed as she approached Tom. Her feet faltered on the black plastic squares that had been laid on the ground. She stood for a moment, watching him screw a metal leg into the stage as Cooper whined and sank onto the floor.

'There's a treat for you in the pocket of my coat, if you'll just let me finish this.' He grabbed a screwdriver from his toolbox without looking up.

Meg dropped into one of the plastic chairs facing the stage and waited while Tom finished working, trying to figure out what to say first and in no hurry to begin the conversation. She swiped a fingertip across her cheek and watched as a shower of glitter floated onto her tights. Wishing she could get lost in it like she always had. Or head back into her shop so she could pretend everything was okay. But somehow this felt different – these feelings were much harder to ignore. Perhaps they were just too strong?

Cooper spotted her and scampered over just as the music changed, clicking to 'If Every Day Was Christmas', as if they were part of some cosmic prank. Meg watched Tom's shoulders tense but he continued working, oblivious to her presence. She'd googled him after her conversation with Emily last night and found out a little more about his life. The years on the road, the band members who'd gone their separate ways and the Christmas when he'd just disappeared. The pictures with his ex-wife had been interesting. The woman had been stunning, with dark hair and eyes, model-thin with a penchant for dramatic gold jewellery, colourful floaty tops and tight jeans. She'd clearly loved being photographed but they'd rarely been pictured together, and there had been rumours that they'd lived almost separate lives. But one article had mentioned the song he'd written for her, just after their wedding. The song that was playing now.

As if he could sense her, Tom suddenly spun around. The look he gave her was pure happiness and Meg felt a punch in her gut, realising with surprise exactly how far she'd already fallen. She flashed him a dazzling grin in return, tumbling back into her usual pattern of pretending everything was okay. Then Davey returned with another heater from the pub, and Meg saw him hesitate as he heard the music and spotted her. Even from here she could tell Davey knew. There was something about the tension in his neck, the way his eyes lowered, and her blood cooled. Was she the only person in Lockton Tom hadn't been honest with? What did that say about her – and them? Had she been kidding herself that they might have a future together all along?

'Meg,' Davey said quietly, and gave her a quick hug. 'Come to figure out where to put all your decorations? There's plenty of space.' She nodded just as Matilda shouted something about a call on his mobile from inside. 'No rest for the wicked.' He gave her a tight smile, putting the new heater onto the floor before heading back towards the bar.

'It's good to see you,' Tom said after a short pause, searching her face, perhaps reading some of the emotions she was trying so hard to hide.

'You too,' she replied, meaning it.

'Your family all right?' He cocked his head, looking concerned.

'All good.' She nodded. 'Mum and Dad took a walk first thing. I watched them leave and they were holding hands.' She shut her eyes for a moment, still expecting the image to disappear. 'Normally they barely touch each other. But they talked for hours when we got home last night, drank half a bottle of whisky and when I got up they were still chatting in the sitting room.'

'So they missed their flights this morning?'

'They want to stay.' She blinked. 'Looks like I'll be spending Christmas with them after all.'

His eyes scanned her face. 'You don't look very happy about it?'

Meg looked at her hands, which were sparkling now, and nodded. 'I am, actually. I just keep expecting the whole thing to implode. There have been so many years of silences and fights, of nothing really being said. It's… weird. I'm not sure I completely trust it. I suppose I should.' She offered him a fake smile. 'It's much easier if I pretend everything'll be all right. But there's a power in honesty. I don't think either of them have been particularly honest with each other until now. Until they were, I guess their marriage didn't stand a chance.' She let the words drift between them, intending for them to burn.

Tom swallowed and nodded as Cooper came to lick his face and whine. 'He's bored,' he said, beginning to rise. He walked over and leaned down so he could give Meg a slow kiss. Despite the tension she melted into it, feeling her whole body liquefy, leaning forwards just as he stepped back. 'My coat's somewhere in here.' His eyes were dark as he studied her, still looking concerned. 'I've got treats in my pocket that Morag gave me a few days ago. If I can find them he'll probably settle down. It's either that or a long walk.' He gave the dog a stern glare, but Cooper just stared back. He probably knew Tom was lying.

She stood, letting her hands fall to her sides. Her heart was thumping now as she tried to find the words, a way to gently tell him she knew. If they had any future together, it was going to have to start now. She'd have to tell him the truth – because he clearly wasn't going to do it.

She followed Tom across the room towards his coat, mulling over how she'd begin as he pulled a packet of biscuits from the pocket, opening the top and feeding a few to Cooper. As he did, a piece of pink paper fluttered to the floor. She bent to pick it up, recognising the black handwriting immediately.

Meg held it up between them, shocked. '*I promise to get a divorce.* That's my mother's writing. It's written on one of her pink Post-it notes.' She swallowed. 'Where did you get it?' She took a step back as her stomach dropped.

Tom frowned. 'Kitty wrote it? The paper was in one of the broken baubles we found under the Promise Tree a couple of weeks ago. I picked it up. It didn't feel right to hang it again so I was going to throw it away – I forgot it was in my pocket.' His forehead puckered as Meg shook her head.

'You didn't say…' she said. 'I was standing right there and I asked if there were any more promises, and you looked me in the eye and said no. Have you been honest with me about anything this entire time?' She screwed up the paper and put it in her coat, wondering why the whole thing made her so mad. Why that one small thing felt like such a betrayal. Perhaps because there was so much more layered on top of it? This was how relationships crumbled until there was nothing left.

Tom frowned. 'What do you mean?'

Meg swallowed and looked up, straight into those dark brown eyes, and tightened her palms into fists. 'I know who you are,' she said, feeling her heart fill with pain when his expression turned to shock. Even though she knew who he was, somewhere inside she'd been hoping it was a mistake. Or that there was a simple explanation – amnesia perhaps, a secret twin, maybe even alien abduction? 'Tom Riley-Clark. You wrote this…' She pointed a finger in the air just as the song ended and something jazzy came on. 'You were the lead singer of The Ballad Club. You were famous. Only you never said. Which all adds up to a whole load of lies.'

'You knew.' Tom took a step back as his expression clouded. 'I thought you did that day in the post office – you were buying the gossip magazine and you stared at me.' His lips thinned and his face changed as understanding flashed across it. 'Emily always looks at me too much when she's checking her phone. You played my Christmas song' – he waved a finger in the air and nodded – 'almost *every* time we met. Encouraged me to play the guitar… *interrogated* me about my life.' His cheeks paled and his mouth flattened. 'I should have known. I should have seen it.' He shook his head. 'It was never about me… it was always about who I was.'

'I only found out last night.' Meg kept her tone firm, even though the way he was looking at her turned her stomach. 'I didn't even guess when you played your guitar, although I suppose I should have, but I believed you. It never occurred to me you wouldn't be honest. I didn't lie to you: I didn't know.'

'Your whole life is a lie, Meg,' Tom said on a sharp exhale. 'You hide from your feelings. You want everything and everyone to be perfect, to fill your world with people who agree with you on all things. And when they don't, you pretend, just like you are now.' The words were delivered with such coldness she shivered. 'You're just like everyone else.' He shook his head. 'You wanted me for what I could give. Not the man who can fix a tap, or set up a stage.' He looked around the room. 'Fame, power, money—'

'Mean nothing to me,' Meg cut in. 'If you can't see that, you don't know me at all.'

Tom shook his head. 'I see a woman who wants Christmas, magic and glitter every day of the year, and a man who wants a life as close to normal as he can get. You're right, Meg.' His eyes hardened. 'We weren't right for each other after all.'

Chapter Twenty-Five

Meg slammed the door of her Christmas shop and stomped along one of the aisles, waving a hand in the air and smiling as Cora said hello. She'd been fighting the tears since she'd left Tom in the marquee and hadn't let one fall yet. But they were threatening to tumble over and she wanted to be alone when they did.

She clomped up the stairs, intending to head for her bedroom, but as she got into the hall she spotted her mum in the kitchen, drinking coffee and looking at her laptop.

'What's this?' Meg asked, feeling her tears dry up as a wave of unexpected anger took over. Instead of pushing it down and locking herself away, she put the pink piece of paper onto the table. 'You wanted a divorce? I thought you left home to figure things out?' Hurt and anger were searing a hole inside her and she didn't know how to make them stop.

Kitty stared at the paper and picked it up, twisting it in her fingers. 'I did. But what I thought I wanted when I got here turned out to be wrong. I guess even when you do everything in your power not to make mistakes – as you know, I made a career out of it – you still do.' She stretched the note out so she could read it. 'I'm glad you found this. I've no idea how you did, but I've been worrying about that bauble for a few days now. Cora said something about the Promise Tree being magic because of the wishing well and, God… I started to believe her.' She shook her head, her face a picture of disbelief. 'I've walked up to that tree dozens of times trying to see if I could spot a flash of pink, but there are too many baubles now.'

'You did?' Meg asked, her temper cooling as she pulled up a chair. 'But you don't believe in anything like that.'

Her mother gave her a sad smile. 'Not for a long while now. I've spent the last fifteen years trying to follow the safe path, to be pragmatic – then I came up to stay here and did something as silly as that. I almost threw away my marriage. I thought it was over, but it turned out I was wrong.' She traced the words she'd written with her fingertip. 'Being in Lockton seems to have changed everything.'

'Does Dad know you wanted a divorce?' Meg asked quietly, sitting down. She glanced back towards the hall but no one was listening.

'Not entirely,' her mother confessed. 'He may have guessed when I came up. When I avoided going to the marriage guidance meeting he'd set up. I think that might be why everything changed. We skirted around it last night. In truth, I think we both just wanted to move forwards. There was so much else we needed to discuss.' She picked up the paper and ripped it into tiny pieces, letting them flutter onto the table. 'Got a match?' she asked, smiling when Meg drew in a breath.

Meg nodded and picked up a Santa ornament from beside the kitchen window, then pressed a button on its back. A bright orange flame shot out of its pointy nose, making Kitty gasp. 'I don't have a fire extinguisher in the flat though,' Meg warned.

Her mother frowned. 'For now we'll take a risk, but we'll discuss that later. I need to draw you up a health and safety plan.' She shook her head. 'All those fairy lights and glass baubles.' She shuddered as she stood and grabbed a pan from the cupboard beside the sink, before dropping the pieces of paper inside it. Then she took the snowman from Meg's hands and set them alight. They took instantly, the pink paper curling up as the flames flickered high. 'Now that's gone, I can relax.' Her eyes drifted up to Meg's as the paper transformed into a scatter of black ash. 'Perhaps I need to hang a new promise today, or is the twenty-first of December too late?'

'It's never too late,' Meg said softly. 'What promise do you want to make?'

'To drink more whisky with your father,' her mother said, a hint of amusement in her eyes. 'And to worry a little less.'

'You want to hang it now?' Meg asked, trying hard to ignore the feelings simmering inside her. Perhaps a walk to the tree would help her process them. A bit of fresh air cured almost anything, apparently. Perhaps it would even work on a broken heart?

The Promise Tree was quiet when Meg and Kitty arrived, but the quantity of decorations hanging from the branches were of legendary proportions. Meg watched her mother stretch up to hang the new bauble, before standing underneath and staring into the sky as snow fluttered down on either side of her.

'Okay?' Davey asked softly, walking up beside Meg and making her jump. 'Because you were gone when I came back into the marquee earlier, and Tom's been hammering everything he can find very loudly since. Even Cooper's abandoned him for Johnny – and Tom has the biscuits, so things must be bad.' He stamped his feet into the deep pillows of snow on the ground and sighed.

'All good,' Meg sang, still watching her mother. Then she turned and took in Davey's pale face. 'What's wrong?' She reached out to grip his arm.

He frowned. 'I needed a walk. The airports are talking about closing because of the weather – there's another big storm due tomorrow – and there are massive delays on the trains. I've just heard from both of the acts for our concert.' He pulled a face. 'Two calls in quick succession. Neither can come. They're really apologetic, but it's just too much of a risk. They could end up stuck in Lockton and all of them need to get back. We've almost three hundred people heading to the pub in three days and absolutely no one to entertain them. We'll have to cancel.' He raised an eyebrow. 'Unless you or your family have a talent you've kept secret from me.'

Meg narrowed her eyes. 'Why don't you ask Tom? I hear he's pretty good on the guitar.'

Davey closed his eyes and nodded. 'So that's it…'

Meg turned away, but not before a tear slid down her cheek.

'Tom's an idiot,' Davey said. 'But a good idiot. He's just confused.'

'What about the fact that he used to be famous? Because from where I'm standing, he didn't seem to be confused about that. He'd just decided not to share,' Meg said. Her mother was still staring up at the tree and Meg wondered what she was thinking.

Davey sighed. 'If you'd known his wife, seen how she screwed him over… He's a good man, Meg.'

'I'm not sure that's an excuse for lying to me,' she replied.

Davey spun her around so he could look at her properly. 'Marnie used him, made him feel worthless because he worked so hard, gave her less of himself than she required. Love was a transaction to her. It was about what she could get – money, clothes, parties, that's all that mattered. Not him.' He looked sad. 'She wanted to rub shoulders with the rich and famous, to be in gossip magazines, for people to hang off her every word. And they did, at least for a while. But then that wasn't enough.' He sighed. 'Tom had to be famous for her to have all those things, but she resented his music. Then, when he wasn't famous enough, she just plain resented him.'

Meg swallowed.

'Tom loved her. I think for a long time he believed that's what love was all about. His mother dumped him and just walked away, you know that?'

Meg nodded, determined to squash the sympathy that was building around her heart.

'Music saved him. Literally. Music and his grandparents. They were probably the only people he's ever had in his life who loved him for who he was. Then his grandmother died and Tom wasn't there, and he blames himself for that too. He's been punishing himself for three years now. He's afraid of being used, or loved for something he isn't, so he's turned his back on music, and everything and everyone who could care for him.'

'He turned his back on me,' Meg whispered, as a second tear spilled onto her cheek and melted a snowflake there.

Davey nodded. 'I guessed that much. The question is, are you going to turn your back on him too?'

Meg mulled over that for a moment. 'I don't know if it's up to me. Or if I can forgive him for all those lies. He hurt me, made me feel stupid. Worse, he didn't trust or care for me enough to tell the truth.'

'Love isn't perfect, Meg.' Davey shook his head, looking sad. 'No matter how much you want it to be. People make mistakes, do the wrong things. It's what makes us human.'

'So everyone keeps saying, but I'm not so sure,' Meg muttered.

Then Davey looked up as they heard the crunch of footsteps and saw Lilith approach. His face transformed into an expression of pure need as she glanced at him and frowned. 'I'd better go,' he muttered. 'Things to do. Don't forget what I said, Meg.' Then he waved a hand at Lilith and sauntered back towards the pub.

Lilith watched him walking for a moment, her dark eyes filled with confusion and regret, before she held up a small box. 'My Bellagamba oil arrived. Morag called this morning. It was misdirected to a post office near Edinburgh, apparently: someone found it and sent it on.'

'Just in time,' Meg said, imbuing as much positivity into her voice as she could muster.

'Not quite. My parents cancelled.' Lilith lifted her chin. 'The weather's a problem and my brother has decided to stay home, so they'd prefer to spend Christmas with him. Most of my guests have abandoned their bookings and the hotel is almost empty from tomorrow. So…' She shrugged. 'It'll be Christmas alone for me. Which is fine,' she added quickly. 'I've plenty of tiramisu.'

'You can come to mine,' Meg offered. 'My family are staying but there'll be lots of room.' It would be a good distraction.

Lilith pursed her lips. 'You didn't get your promise either?' Her eyes darted to Meg's mum just as she turned away from the tree and spotted them talking.

Meg shrugged. 'On this occasion, I don't think I mind.'

'So everything worked out?' Lilith asked.

'Not entirely.' Meg sighed.

'Ah…' The Italian read her face like a book. 'We should have stuck to the agreement we made when we toasted in your cafe. Life without men. Now we are both heartbroken.' She nodded and smiled. 'In that case, I will come for Christmas. As Papa likes to say, "misery loves company". But you should know I don't like mince pies, roast potatoes or turkey.'

Meg nodded and her lips rose despite the ache in her chest. 'I wouldn't have expected anything less, Lilith. Then again, someone once told me differences can be good. Perhaps you can bring some of your tiramisu instead?' She smiled again. But still, her mind drifted back to Tom.

Chapter Twenty-Six

Tom chucked two pairs of jeans into his suitcase and followed that up with some of his clean dark T-shirts. There were clothes in the wash-basket but he'd finish packing those later on. Cooper sat on the floor of his bedroom wearing the Christmas jumper Meg had given him, sporting the dog equivalent of a frown. 'We're leaving after my shift tonight,' Tom said sharply, heading downstairs and opening the kitchen cupboard so he could gather the tins of food he'd bought since he'd arrived. He set them carefully onto the counter, noticed the sprig of mistletoe hanging above him and grimaced. Had Meg known who he was when they'd kissed that first time in her shop? Pain clawed at his chest and he tried to ignore it as he went into the sitting room. He'd been an idiot to trust her. He'd been an idiot to trust himself.

Davey's guitar was sitting on its stand by the tree. Tom considered putting it back in the boot room, locking away all those feelings that had started to emerge, but as he picked the instrument up his fingers traced the strings. The low hum that came from them punched a hole in his gut and he put it back down. Being here in Lockton, opening himself up to Meg, had given him his music back. He'd have to think about whether he could keep it now.

His mobile rang, and Tom gulped down the bubble of dread that climbed up his throat when he saw his grandad's name pop onto the screen. 'Are you okay?' he asked, picking up immediately.

'Great,' Jack soothed. 'I rang the pub and Davey told me you'd gone home. I wanted to catch you.' There was a honk in the background, and Tom heard the clink of glasses and laughter. 'Sorry, I know it's early but it's after sundown somewhere in the world – and on the boat I barely keep track of the time. We're having a party. It's been wild. Someone played one of your songs last night, and I wanted to call and tell you. This boy with dark brown hair who looked a lot like you did once. His voice wasn't as good. But he hit almost all the right notes – and it was like you were here. The people I was sharing a table with started talking about you and your band. How talented you were and how much they loved your music. One woman said her granddaughter is a massive fan and she's so disappointed you upped and disappeared.' He cleared his throat and his voice dropped to a whisper. 'I didn't tell them I was related to you, of course. But I remembered how proud your grandmother and I were, and I realised I'd forgotten to tell you that recently.'

'You tell me you're proud of me a lot.' Tom let himself sink into the sofa. Whether his grandfather meant it was another thing.

'It made me think about when you were younger, how much happier you were once that music teacher got you into the guitar. How playing always made you glow. It was the moment I think you really found yourself, began to get over your mother leaving.' He cleared his throat. The memory was painful for both of them. For his grandparents, his mother had been proof that the world wasn't perfect. That you couldn't save or fix everyone. Some things in life you just had to let go of.

'I…' Tom tried to remember how he'd felt, but he'd blocked out a lot of those memories years ago.

'You know, Marnie left your guitar at mine after she cleared the house. She said she didn't feel right about selling it, which means perhaps there is something beating in that icy black heart. I've been meaning to tell you. But every time I bring up the band or your music, you change the subject.' He paused. 'I've never interfered in your life, Tom – that was your grandmother's job. But… well, she's not here, and a woman last night was talking about how much every generation needs the other. How families should be there when people get lost – like stars helping you chart your next course. And I thought… well, I've not been doing my bit. I've been leaving you to it. Letting you drift, hoping eventually you'd bump into the thing you most needed, or that perhaps your grandmother would find a way of sending you a sign. Except you're really off course now and—'

'I'm not lost. I know exactly what I want and where I'm headed.' Out of Lockton in the direction of the Yorkshire Dales in a few hours. Something spat in the fire, a loud snap and crackle, as if someone or something wasn't happy with that idea. There was probably a song in that somewhere – one his subconscious would do its damnedest to write later on.

'I remember how proud your grandmother was, how much she used to boast about you.' Jack paused, as emotion. thickened his voice. 'I could almost feel her touching my shoulder while they were talking, telling me to call. We both know I was always too afraid of her to say no.' Tom nodded and smiled. 'So I'm calling to say, I think it's time you got back on course. I know you're eaten up with guilt about not being there when your grandmother…' He cleared his throat, trailing off. 'Despite me telling you that nothing about what happened was your fault. You've made some changes, some of them good – but you need to find your music again, sonny. Without it in your life you're turning your back on something very special. Blocking out a part of yourself. I'm not sure you're letting yourself live, and I'm calling to say you should take every moment you have and live it to the max – because you never know when those moments will disappear.'

There was laughter again in the background, and a woman shouted, 'Jack!'

'I've got to go, they want to check out the casino.' He laughed. 'I'm loving this trip, Tom, it's like a new lease of life. I've been missing your grandmother so much these last few years, I'd forgotten how to enjoy myself. Next year I hope you're going to join me. There are lots of pretty girls on this ship, and if you brought your guitar…' He coughed suggestively. 'Let's just say, you won't be lonely.'

Tom smiled. He'd not heard his grandfather laugh like this for years. 'I'll think about it,' he lied. 'Try not to lose too much money – I'll call you on Christmas Eve.' His voice broke a little.

'You do that, sonny – and we'll raise a toast to your grandmother, wherever she may be. Perhaps when I get back home, you'll come and visit?'

Tom found his head bobbing. 'Yes,' he promised, meaning it this time.

His doorbell rang just as they were saying their goodbyes and he hung up the phone. Cooper skidded towards the front door and

Tom paused before he went over to it, feeling a strange combination of hope and fear. Was it Meg? Coming to confess something else… or to tell him again she hadn't known. Should be believe her? A part of him wished he could.

Davey was standing on the doorstep, looking frozen. The weather had taken another turn for the worse and snow was falling in thick, fast droves. He stood back and let his friend come in. 'You disappeared from the marquee and I couldn't find you,' Davey said, taking a moment to shake ice onto the mat and pull off his coat before looking up into Tom's face.

'Sorry. I needed to get back before my shift later, to feed Cooper.' Tom wandered into the sitting room. The fire was burning and the Christmas decorations still sparkled from this morning, so he went to switch them off. He didn't want any reminders of Meg.

Davey went to the windowsill and picked up the empty Christmas bauble before putting it back down with a long sigh. 'I saw Meg by the Promise Tree earlier, in case you're interested.'

Tom shook his head.

'So she knows who you are?'

'Of course she does.' Tom spun on his heel. 'Why else would she get involved with me? There were so many clues, it was obvious. But I missed them all.' He squeezed his eyes shut, trying to block out the jumble of feelings, the anger burning in his chest.

'I'll tell you she didn't know. Meg's not a liar. My guess is whatever she told you is true,' Davey said.

Tom swallowed but didn't argue. There was no point now.

His friend's face fell and he shook his head. 'She's not Marnie, Tom. No one in Lockton – including Meg – cares who you used to be. A few might be nosy, want to poke into your past because that's village life, but no one cares if you're famous, or whether you play that guitar like Jimi Hendrix or a two-year-old.' He put his hands in his pockets. 'Except for me.' He pulled a face. 'Which is why I'm here. I need a favour.'

Tom walked up to the fire and poked it with a stick, just to give his hands something to do. 'What is it?'

'The bands have both cancelled.'

Tom turned, took in Davey's face and felt his insides sink. He drew in a sharp breath. 'You want me to play?'

Davey's chin jerked up. 'I know it's a lot to ask. I know you don't want to.' He glanced at the guitar and his forehead wrinkled in confusion – perhaps because the last time he'd visited it had been hidden away in the boot room? 'I wouldn't ask except all the fridges in the pub are filled with food, the marquee's hired and we've got over three hundred people arriving on Christmas Eve. If we cancel now, we'll lose the village hall because the roof won't get fixed, along with a fair amount of money. I'd probably live with those things…' He swallowed. 'But it would be the first Christmas Promise the village has broken in over two hundred years. I'm not sure I can bear being responsible for that.' His shoulders drooped. 'Just two hours, Tom. I wouldn't ask if I wasn't desperate. I've called around all my contacts and no one can make it. Worse, Johnny's been threatening to play the spoons…'

Tom chuckled despite himself. 'Okay. Fine. I'll do it. I owe you a lot – you've helped me out when most wouldn't, stuck with me through everything. Besides, I've got nothing to lose now.' Meg knew who he was; Morag too. It wouldn't be long before the whole village was in on it. Which was another good reason why he had to go. He closed his eyes. They'd all look at him differently. He'd no longer be the guy behind the bar, the man to call if your tap was leaking. It would be all about the man he used to be. How long would it be before they got bored of that? Before it wasn't enough for them either? His chest felt hollow. 'I'll stay in Lockton until then. But as soon as the concert's over, I'm going to leave.'

Chapter Twenty-Seven

Apple Cross Inn looked beautiful. Meg had spent the last three days decorating the pub, car park and marquee with as many Christmas baubles and as much tinsel as she could find, with Emily playing lookout. If Tom was working in the bar, or there was a sniff of him getting close to the pub, she'd headed back to her shop to hide. She knew she was avoiding him, but wasn't ready to see him yet – had no idea what to say. He'd lied, then accused her of doing the same. They were so different, they might as well be from opposite sides of the universe – and those differences still terrified her despite everyone's advice. But her heart still ached when she thought about him, and she'd barely slept or eaten since their fight. Because she couldn't stand the idea of not being with him either. She just didn't know how to put things right.

'It's busy,' her mother said as they walked into the pub and up to the bar, and Meg's stomach clenched even though she knew Tom wouldn't be there. She'd heard on the grapevine that a mystery act had agreed to play the concert when the other bands had pulled out, and guessed he'd decided to stand in. There hadn't been an official announcement – other than that they were in for a surprise – and she'd supposed Tom had been worried about all the attention.

Although what he'd do after the concert, when they all knew who he was, was hard to figure out.

'Looks like it's going to be a good night,' her dad said, giving Emily a big smile. 'I've not been out for a night like this for years. Feels like old times.' He grinned at Kitty and she blushed. Her mother had worn make-up tonight, and a pink dress. She looked pretty and happy for the first time in years, and there'd been no dark silences or fights. But Meg was still on tenterhooks, not quite ready to trust the changes. Her parents still hadn't kissed or hugged in front of her, and she wasn't sure what that meant.

'Do you want to find some space in the marquee – see if you can get close to the front?' Meg asked, looking around the room. It was filling up fast and she didn't want to risk missing a good seat for the concert. If Tom was playing, she wanted to be front and centre to support him, despite everything. She knew he'd be tense now, probably wishing he hadn't agreed to step in. She wished she could go and see him, or at least feed him some cheese or a chocolate bar, but knew he wouldn't appreciate the contact. She knew he'd been avoiding her for the last three days too. 'Here are your tickets.' She pulled a couple of slips of colourful paper out of her pocket and pushed them into her dad's hands. She knew Morag was standing at the entrance of the marquee taking them – and woe betide anyone who tried to get in without one.

Oliver nodded. 'We'll save you and Emily a spot. A double whisky for me, please, Meg.'

'Me too,' Kitty added, surprising her, then followed him towards the back of the pub.

The bar was deep in customers and Meg could see Davey and Matilda working hard on the other side of the wooden counter, along with a couple of young women Meg didn't know. Johnny appeared from the back carrying a couple of plates piled high with steak and chips, which he quickly delivered to one of the tables. Then he stopped as he passed on his way back to the kitchen, just as Lilith walked into the pub, and waved before striding over to join them. She was wearing her trademark heels again and the spikes were covered in snow.

'It's crazy,' Johnny said, grimacing when the door opened again and a crowd of five entered the pub. 'Davey's set up another bar in the marquee and we've hired extra staff from Morridon, but a few of those haven't turned up.' His gaze drifted to the windows. Even from here Meg could see thick snowflakes falling. 'I'm guessing they're not going to make it. I heard the roads are getting harder to navigate because of all the drifts. Even with the snowploughs working overtime, they simply can't keep up. They closed the airport and train stations an hour ago. Grant, Fergus and Agnes were meant to be driving to pick Evie and Callum up from Inverness; I just hope they made it and their plane wasn't turned back. They're not here yet and I know they don't want to miss the concert.' He frowned. 'Although the rest of Scotland seems to have arrived just fine.' He sighed when the door opened again and two more people strode in, their coats and boots covered in ice.

Lilith scrutinised the bar and put her hands into the pockets of her jeans. 'You need help?' Her dark eyes flicked towards Davey as a young couple moved away from the counter with their drinks, and a gap appeared before someone else filled it.

'We need a miracle. Failing that, experienced bar staff. These guys are keen, but they're clueless,' Johnny groaned.

'Where's Tom?' Lilith asked, looking around.

'He's… a little tied up. He's not going to be serving at the bar this evening.'

Lilith glanced at Meg with a quizzical look before turning back to Johnny. 'I can help.' She tapped a knuckle on her chest. She was wearing one of her silky shirts again. This one was midnight blue and made her eyes appear even darker. She glanced at the bar again as Davey looked up and spotted her, and her cheeks went a luminous shade of pink.

'You've done bar work?' Johnny asked, frowning.

Lilith raised an eyebrow and her eyes lit up. 'I run a hotel, I've managed a deli and have been known to pull a pint. Although I prefer serving a decent Barolo.' She paused, glancing over at Davey again, who looked flustered as he placed three glasses of wine in front of a customer and took the money. 'I think I can manage this. You helped me. Perhaps it's not just your brother who can rescue people, *si*?'

Johnny chuckled as a broad grin spread across his face and he nodded a few times, his eyes sparkling. 'Seems not.' He gave her an appraising look. 'I'm thinking, Miss Tiramisu, you might be just the woman our Davey needs. Yes please to the help. If you mean it?'

Lilith pushed her long hair over her shoulder. 'I wouldn't offer if I didn't.' She waved a hand towards the door of the kitchen. 'Lead the way.' Then she paused for a moment and eyed Meg and Emily. 'If you sneak to the front, I'll serve you first. If people get in the way, do what I'd do – *push*.' She grinned wickedly. 'Remember what you told me, Meg, because I have. Sometimes our differences can be good, *si*? Perhaps it's time to consider that and go after what you want, just like me.' She winked, before flicking her head in the air and marching after Johnny.

Morag took Meg and Emily's tickets at the door of the marquee. She was wearing a pink, yellow and blue dress and leaned heavily on her walking stick. 'It's busy, lassie,' Morag called over the din, pointing towards the stage. 'Your mam and da got seats right at the front so you'll get an excellent view. I saved a spot on the row behind for Agnes and the rest of the family when they get here.' She winked at Meg. 'I figure we'll all want good seats for the big surprise.'

Meg frowned. 'You knew?' Her stomach dropped.

'Ach, lassie, Tom didn't so much as give me a hint.' Morag patted Meg heavily on the shoulder, almost spilling one of the glasses of whisky she was holding. 'I spotted him in one of my magazines. Told him to stop all that fibbing, but I think he was worried about what people would think. Man's an eejit, but I've a soft spot for him. He knows what's important in life.'

She opened her mouth and Meg nodded quickly. 'I know. I should give him a chance. I got that.' Her eyes darted to her parents who were sitting in the front row. Their heads were close together and they were giggling. 'I might even agree with you,' she said on a sigh, glancing at the empty stage. She'd hung about a hundred silver baubles onto the ceiling above it and drenched the marque walls in tinsel, so the whole thing glittered like something out of Cinderella's ball. 'I just have to figure out how to convince Tom to give me the same.'

'Ah, lassie, you'll find a way.' Morag grinned. 'Anyone who can make Christmas last three hundred and sixty-five days a year can do just about anything they put their mind to.' A couple walked up behind them and Morag gently nudged Meg and Emily on. They weaved their way through the crowd of people. There were rows and rows of seats facing the stage. Many were already filled, and overhead the multicoloured baubles and fairy lights twinkled as huge black speakers pumped out 'I'm Dreaming of a White Christmas'. Meg jumped as someone tapped her on the shoulder. When she spun round she saw it was her best friend, Evie Stuart.

'We made it!' Evie punched the air. 'I thought our plane from New York was going to have to turn around when we got close to Inverness, but we landed just before they closed the airport. The drive here took hours.' Evie rolled her eyes and gave Meg a quick hug as they stood to the side to allow people to pass. Evie's bump had grown over the last couple of months and her cheeks glowed pink, clashing with her shiny red hair.

'I missed you.' Meg sighed into her friend's shoulder, squeezing her tight.

'You must be Meg's sister?' Evie asked as they pulled apart, and Emily nodded. 'Ach, it's glorious to meet you.' She looked around the marquee. 'And *so* bonnie to be back in Lockton. We need to get together, Meg – Nana Agnes tells me we have a lot to catch up on. I hear there's a new hot toddy in town who you didn't mention once in our emails or calls.' She raised an eyebrow as Meg pulled a face. 'Looks like there's *lots* for us to talk about.' She tapped Emily's shoulder. 'I also heard you're thinking of becoming a vet?'

Emily nodded. 'How did you know?'

'Nana Agnes – she said she might have sorted you some work experience.' She grinned. 'Which means you'll be staying here too for a while?'

Emily's eyes darted to Meg. 'If that's okay?'

'Of course it is,' Meg said, grinning for the first time in days. 'But I'm not telling Mum.'

Emily laughed. 'It's okay. I already have. She was fine about it.' She frowned, looking across at her parents. 'She's so much more relaxed, I almost don't recognise her.'

'Lockton has that effect on people,' Evie explained. 'My nana also told me about the wee chappie you found in the barn on Buttermead Farm.' Emily nodded. 'You'll be pleased to hear we saw a herd of reindeer in a field somewhere between here and Morridon on the drive from the airport, so I think he may not be alone for long.'

'You did?' Emily yelped. 'I saw something about them on Google but no mention of them since. I didn't realise they were so close. Did you drive right past them?'

Evie nodded. 'The roads are awful though. I thought for a minute we were going to have to hop out of the truck and climb onto one of them for a ride.' She snorted. 'I'd have done it in a heartbeat, but Callum was scared.'

'Really?' Her fiancé arrived behind them at that exact moment along with Grant, Evie's mum Fiona, Agnes and Fergus. He shook his head sternly, but swiftly grabbed Evie's hand and kissed it on the back.

Fergus frowned at the crowd. 'And I thought all the blethering from the Jam Club was bad,' he moaned, shaking his head and glaring as a couple shoved around them.

'Morag saved us seats at the front, Fergus.' Agnes winked. 'There's a bar in the corner if you're hankering for a whisky.'

'We'll get the drinks,' Grant interrupted, nodding at Fergus and Callum. 'You lot go and get our seats. Evie needs to sit down.'

A drum roll sounded above them as more people entered the marquee and sat. Meg and Emily approached the front row just as Davey hopped onto the stage and the crowd hushed…

Chapter Twenty-Eight

Tom's heart was thundering like a runaway train as he walked in from the side of the marquee and stood facing the stage. There was glitter everywhere – baubles hung across the ceiling and tinsel climbed every wall. The room contained more sparkles than he'd seen at any of his previous gigs, and he knew the whole thing was down to Meg.

He looked around the crowd, balling his hands into tight fists because his palms were so damp. He'd practised on the guitar yesterday evening in front of all the empty seats, but this felt very different and every part of him wanted to turn and run.

'Our surprise act for this evening is Tom Riley-Clark!' Davey's announcement was followed by loud whoops, and a few dozen people in the crowd who'd obviously heard of him stood and clapped enthusiastically as he approached the stage. A few whipped out their mobiles and took photos, surprise filling their faces, and Tom gulped back his desire to hide. 'I want to thank Tom for agreeing to step in last minute when the scheduled acts couldn't make it due to the weather. Many of you will know him as the man behind the bar in Apple Cross Inn, or the person to call in an emergency if something needs fixing. What you may not know is that Tom's a talented songwriter and guitarist – or that he was the lead singer of The Ballad Club.' A roar of approval erupted from the audience and Tom bounced onto the stage to join Davey. 'In fact, he penned "If Every Day Was Christmas", which is even now working its way up the charts.' The crowd hooted again and Tom stood, looking down, letting his eyes roll over the front row to where Meg was staring up at him.

He hadn't seen her for three days now, had been avoiding running into her by living between the marquee and his house. But just one look and his heart seemed to expand. She was clapping like the others, but she wasn't smiling and her face looked drawn. She wore a black dress which hugged her curves in all the right places but somehow looked wrong – he was so used to the sexy elf outfits now. Glitter decorated her cheeks and her hair hung around her face in golden waves; she looked beautiful and sad. He tossed his head, lifting his face up to the lights as he hooked the Gibson around his shoulder and let his fingers run over the smooth wood. The feeling was so familiar it was like coming home, and he wondered, not for the first time in the last few days, how he'd ever been able to give it up. Or what would have happened if Meg hadn't come along and encouraged him. Then he closed his eyes and let his fingers run across the strings as the audience began to clap...

Tom made his way down from the stage an hour later to a roar of applause. His shirt clung to his back and his hands were aching, but there was a new lightness to his step.

'You were brilliant, mate,' Davey said, taking the guitar from his hands and pressing a bottle of cold water into them. 'You had everyone in the palm of your hand. I'd almost forgotten how good you are with a crowd.' He patted him on the back and pointed to the exit.

'It was… more fun than I remembered. I guess I was more relaxed. Perhaps because I knew so many of the faces,' Tom admitted, taking a swig of the cool water. 'And I didn't lose myself once.' Every time he'd found himself getting lost in the music, he'd looked down and seen Meg staring up, like an anchor in a sea of waves. He just didn't know what that meant.

'I promised to get you straight out of the crowd,' Davey said, leading the way towards the edge of the marquee just as Morag blocked their path.

She smiled, her face almost cracking with the effort, and Tom's heart thumped, searching for the change in her eyes. 'I still hate that Christmas song,' she grunted, frowning. 'The whole thing sets my teeth on edge.' She bared them as if that would prove it. 'But the rest of tonight was all right. At least, it was a lot less painful than I expected. Johnny's still calculating, but we think we've raised more money than we need for the village hall roof thanks to you – plus I've a whole new topic to gossip about once my Christmas Promise is done.'

'Okay,' Tom said, smiling despite himself. 'I guess that's good.'

She shrugged, frowning a little. 'The gate at my house that you fixed is holding up, but the fence beside it has begun to lean a little. I wondered if you'd come to mend it, laddie, bring Cooper with you again? I got more biscuits. I'm planning to adopt a wee dog in the new year. Perhaps they'll be friends?'

'I… I'm leaving tonight. I'm sorry, Morag,' Tom said, his heart pitching a little. 'But I heard the weather's due to ease soon, so I'm sure someone else will be able to come.'

'Aye.' Morag nodded but didn't smile. 'I guessed as much.' She shrugged. 'If you change your mind though, lad, you know where I am – and don't forget to bring the dog.' She leaned onto her cane and spun around before walking away, passing Cora and Marcus as she headed towards the pub.

'That was amazing,' Cora gasped, her eyes lighting up as Marcus nodded along. 'I love your songs. I've been a fan of The Ballad Club for a few years. I had no idea…'

'Aye, she's a fan all right. Even has a few of your albums. I can't believe I never realised it was you. Seems to me I need to pay a lot more attention from now on. I didn't even spot Cora making doughnuts in my own house until she put one in front of me.' Marcus looked baffled.

'But now you like jam?' Cora said in a sing-song voice, and Marcus grinned just as Agnes and Fergus came up to join them. Tom looked behind them, his eyes seeking out Meg, but her seat was empty, as were Emily's and her parents' – which meant she'd obviously already left. It was probably for the best. He knew for his own sanity he had to walk away. There was no reason to make it any harder.

'Have you played any Simple Minds?' Agnes asked, stepping in front of him too. 'Because if you ever have a hankering to give one of their songs a try, I've a parrot at Buttermead Farm who'd appreciate hearing it.'

Tom nodded sadly. 'Thank you for the offer, but I'm retiring after tonight and I'll be leaving Lockton in a few hours.'

Agnes gave him a strange look. 'You'd better watch out if you're driving. You never know what you might run into. I'll see you again soon, laddie,' she said, squeezing his shoulder before following Fergus as he trailed Morag towards the bar.

Tom let out a long breath and followed Davey into the small section at the edge of the marquee which had been screened off, before anyone else managed to corner him. He grabbed his coat and tugged it on, suddenly keen to get away.

'You're really leaving?' Davey asked, looking surprised.

Tom nodded.

'But no one's going to treat you any differently.' He bobbed his head in the direction of the flap behind them where the crowd were still chatting. 'I think we just saw proof of that. You could leave tomorrow. There are Christmas carols around the Promise Tree at midnight. You could at least come to that? Say goodbye properly,' Davey said.

'I think it would be better if I went now,' Tom insisted.

Davey sighed. 'You fit here, Tom. You've been happier than I've ever seen you. I didn't spot one person out in that crowd who's going to treat you differently after this. You're still the man who can. Nothing's going to change that. So a few journalists might come up to see if they can get an interview, but they'll soon lose interest. My house is yours for as long as you want it. Or there are a couple of similar ones I know of for sale a little further up the road. Why not stay?'

'I've got to leave.' Tom picked up his backpack, blocking out the nagging voice telling him he was mad as Davey tried to hand him the guitar. 'It's not mine.' He pushed it away.

'You ought to hang on to it.' Davey handed it back. 'Seems to me a talent like yours shouldn't be wasted, no matter where you decide to take it next.'

Tom exhaled but took the guitar and nodded, before he shook hands with his friend and headed for the car park without looking back.

Meg was standing by Tom's car. He could see her in the distance as he crossed the snow, and his feet faltered as he approached. She wore a thick coat and woolly hat with long, sexy boots which stretched right up to her knees. The glitter on her cheeks sparkled despite the darkness, and snow was falling around her in thick masses. She didn't say anything until he was facing her. He could see her teeth were chattering so he unlocked the car and motioned for her to climb inside. His heart thumped as he put the guitar into the boot and took a deep breath. Then he got into the driver's seat and switched on the heater. They sat for a moment, staring at the windscreen in silence as the wipers swiped the deep pile of snow off the glass and more splattered in its place.

'I came to ask you to stay,' Meg said quietly, still staring forwards. 'I heard you were leaving tonight. I know you think I lied…'

'Davey told me you didn't.' Tom's voice was husky and he wondered if it was from the singing. 'I'm sorry I didn't believe you. Call it a kneejerk reaction, or call me an idiot. You'd be right.'

She let out a long sigh. 'Was it because of your wife?'

Tom nodded, surprised.

'Davey explained.' She swallowed. 'And I'm sorry. I've been getting a lot of advice over the last few weeks. I've been told to trust in differences, to stop worrying if we don't completely fit, to forgive.' Tom started to say something but she wagged a finger. 'Please let me finish. My parents' marriage taught me all kinds of lessons – many of them wrong, it turns out. I've been hiding for a long time now, trying not to make the same mistakes. And yet in some ways I've made them anyway. Perhaps they were different ones, but they were still mistakes.' She turned to face him. 'I wanted to escape into Christmas. For every day to be perfect. For the man I fell in love with to be perfect too. But there's no such thing, is there?' She stared at him. 'You rarely smile, you hate Christmas and you won't make promises.' Her lip wobbled as she tried to smile. 'But none of that matters. I've spent too many years focusing on all the wrong things. Looking for someone that didn't exist. Because I was afraid. Terrified of being hurt. But it happened anyway. I… have feelings for you.' Tom saw her frown even though her face was in shadows. 'Strong feelings, and I think…' She swallowed. 'I think you have feelings for me too.'

Tom didn't say anything. He couldn't. But there was a pain circulating in his chest. A bubble of need rising which he refused to acknowledge.

'I'm just asking you to give this' – she waggled a finger between them – 'a chance.'

Tom swallowed as his mind filled with his mum, Marnie and his grandmother. All those memories. He didn't deserve Meg. He couldn't do it. 'I'm sorry.' His voice dropped. 'I'm so sorry, but I can't.'

The roads out of Lockton were treacherous. Cooper whimpered in the back seat and pressed his nose to the glass, staring into the fields. After Meg had blinked back tears, then jumped out of Tom's car and headed for the pub, he'd driven straight to Davey's house and packed. He couldn't stay in Scotland for another minute. He wouldn't be able to stop himself from heading back to Apple Cross Inn to tell Meg he was an idiot and cared for her too.

But he wasn't an idiot. What he was doing was right. He had his music back, but he couldn't risk his heart. Couldn't risk letting someone else down that he cared about.

His car jolted over a drift, and the empty bauble Tom had flung onto the passenger seat as he'd left the house – because he couldn't face leaving it – wobbled and almost fell onto the floor. He pressed his foot on the brake, slowing to a crawl. He passed fences of baubles and knitted decorations and forced himself to shift his eyes to the front, just as his mobile went off and Cooper began to bark.

'I know,' Tom said. 'It's a miracle.'

'Sonny.' Jack's voice filled the car. 'I've called so we can make our toast. I know it's early here, but I wanted to catch you before midnight.'

Tom swallowed and glanced at the clock. It was half eleven. 'I'm sorry, I was going to call when I got to Morridon.'

'You're driving?' Jack sighed. 'On Christmas Eve?'

'I'm heading for my next adventure. I played a concert tonight,' he confessed, beaming when he remembered how it had felt. How all those feelings had poured out of him. It was as if he'd found his voice. Now lyrics were forming, the words effervescing in his mind. And this time he wasn't pushing them back.

'You're going back to the business?' Jack asked, sounding surprised.

'Nope.' Tom shook his head. 'I'll never do that. But I'm going to write songs again and play the guitar.'

'Did your grandmother send you a sign?' His grandfather sounded hopeful.

'Nope.' Not unless the sign had been Meg.

'Maybe she's waiting until you need to learn something else?' There was a shout in the background. 'I've got to go. That boy's going to sing… I'm raising my coffee now, Tom, to your grandmother, the love of my life – and to you, my grandson, a man I couldn't be prouder of. I'm glad you're finding your way back. All you need now is a woman who deserves you – someone to put the sparkle back into your eyes.'

Tom cleared his throat as emotion threatened to choke him. 'I'll be raising a glass to you and Grandma later too – and I'll be coming to see you as soon as you're home.'

He hung up, feeling empty. The snow was falling more heavily and he had to slow the car again as large round flakes hit the windscreen, obscuring almost everything in the distance. He couldn't see more than a few metres ahead and even that was hard to make out. He pushed his foot onto the brake as a series of random shapes seemed to materialise in the middle of the road.

'What the—?' He parked up and peered through the windscreen, but the nature of the shapes was still impossible to make out. He sighed and opened the door so he could step out of the car, and pulled up his hood as wind and ice blasted his face. Even from here he couldn't tell what was in the road; he just knew there were about thirty of them. There was a strange clicking sound as he slowly approached. In the back of the car, Tom heard Cooper barking. Wind whistled around his head, whipping the snow into his eyes. He almost tripped on a drift as he drew closer – then his breath caught in his throat. Because standing in the centre of the road, blocking his path and staring at him, was a herd of reindeer.

Chapter Twenty-Nine

Meg was cold. She pulled her coat tight around her and tugged at the ends of her fluffy green scarf, fighting back tears as she tried to sing 'We Wish You A Merry Christmas'. The villagers, all wrapped in puffy coats, hats and scarves, along with a few stragglers from the concert, were huddled around the Promise Tree holding songbooks – and their combined voices were just too loud. She swallowed and looked up into the snow-laden branches at the hundreds of sparkly baubles, wondering if Tom had ever made his promise – and if he had, what it might have been. To get out of Lockton before Christmas, or to avoid letting himself fall in love? She closed her eyes for a moment, blocking out the feelings of rejection. She knew Tom cared for her, but his wounds were just too deep for him to take a chance. In some ways she could relate, but that wasn't going to mend her broken heart and neither was this. For the first time since Meg could remember, Christmas wasn't going to fix anything.

Across from Meg, standing at the front of the large circle of people, Lilith and Davey were pressed close together, and the tinsel draped around their shoulders sparkled prettily in the moonlight. The Italian's cheeks went pink suddenly when Davey winked and grabbed her hand. She was singing and giggling and Meg wasn't sure if she'd ever looked happier. The image made her heart throb, but she was glad they'd settled their differences. At least one romance had begun to bloom.

Emily stood to Meg's right, warbling loudly, stopping every now and then to get closer to Agnes so they could talk about vets and work experience above the singing. Meg's mum and dad had been absorbed into the crowd and she couldn't see them now. After insisting Meg agree to meet up the following day to talk, Evie had reluctantly gone home with Callum after the concert because she was jetlagged. Meg had never felt more alone.

'Look!' someone shouted suddenly, and the singing began to falter, petering out to a few lone voices as the crowd all looked up from their songbooks and began to turn. Meg pivoted to look in the same direction – back down the road, deep in snow, which headed past Apple Cross Inn, the post office and her shop towards Buttermead Farm.

'It's my reindeer!' Emily cried, and she hopped up and down so she could see through the throng. The brown reindeer from the barn was trotting slowly up the centre of the road, heading towards the Promise Tree. He stopped suddenly and jerked his head up to sniff the air before making an odd clicking sound.

'Perhaps he's looking for more baubles?' Marcus joked from somewhere behind Meg.

'Or maybe he's just lonely,' Emily said. 'I read somewhere they're pack animals. He's probably looking for company.'

'Aye,' Agnes agreed. 'I suppose we all need that.' She reached for Fergus's hand.

They watched as the reindeer took a few more steps and sniffed the air again. Then there was a sharp beeping sound from the opposite direction and the horde rotated to look towards the road that led to Morridon. Meg stepped forward, but there were too many people for her to see what was going on. She went onto her tiptoes as the crowd surged in the direction of the noise. Then there were a few gasps and happy whoops as they scattered and parted.

'There are more reindeer!' Cora shouted, her voice filled with delight. 'It's a herd. It's got to be the wee laddie's family.'

Then Meg saw Cooper scampering through the snow, dodging the groups of people until he was close enough to press his wet nose against her leg. She reached down to scratch his head, feeling her heart lift as she looked up and quickly searched for Tom.

Was he here? Had his car broken down? What did it mean?

'Aye.' Agnes moved closer and clasped Meg's hand. 'Looks like your hot toddy is back, with no interference from me.' She grinned at Fergus.

Meg's heart was beating faster, and she swallowed the emotion as Tom emerged from the crowd. He was walking slowly towards her, and following behind him, like some kind of mirage, was a herd of about thirty brown reindeer. Meg waited, her heart in her throat, until he was standing right in front of her. His hat and coat were plastered in snow, but his eyes were warm and she had a sudden urge to kiss him.

'Why are you here?' she asked softly.

'You were right,' he said quietly, his brown eyes scanning her face. 'I do care. I care a lot. I was just too much of an idiot or too afraid to take a chance.' He closed his eyes and opened them again. 'I suppose I'd have figured that out in the end. But I've come back to say I'm ready to take one now, Meg, if you are?'

'What made you change your mind?' she asked, and her voice cracked a little. 'Because you were pretty determined to leave me behind less than two hours ago.' She watched as something like wonder passed across his face.

'My grandmother.' The edge of his mouth lifted. 'I know that sounds crazy. But my grandad's been telling me for months she was going to send me a sign.' He shrugged. 'I didn't believe him. But then I ran into this lot.' He pointed to the reindeer herd, who were slowly weaving their way past. 'I met them on my way to Morridon. They were blocking the road and just staring at me. In that moment I realised I should be doing precisely what they were. Coming to find my missing piece.' He reached out and traced a finger down her cheek. He had gloves on, but when he turned his hand over, the wool sparkled. 'The woman who brought me back to life, the person who gave me back my music, and helped me to feel. I was right about the glitter – it is catching.' He waggled his fingers and smiled. 'I was just too stupid or too afraid to realise it. We're different.' He nodded. 'I know that. You wear elf outfits, love tinsel, Christmas and mince pies.' He shuddered. 'But none of that matters. I've spent too many years hiding from my feelings, running because I was afraid. I didn't want to open myself up to music again, or to my feelings for you.' He took her hand and grasped it in his. Then he reached into his pocket and pulled out the empty bauble she'd given him. 'I didn't use this. But for some reason I couldn't leave it behind. So now I want to make my promise – is it too late?'

Meg glanced at her watch. 'It's five minutes until Christmas Day, I'd say you have time.'

'You got a pen?' He smiled.

She shook her head.

'Has anyone got a pen and some paper?' Tom shouted. A few people said no, someone offered to see if they could find one in their car, then Meg's mum appeared out of the crowd, walking hand in hand with her dad.

'Here you are.' She rummaged in her pocket, then gave Tom a pad of pink Post-it notes and a black pen. She winked at Meg as he knelt so he could rest the paper on his knee as he wrote. Tom opened up the bauble and tucked the folded pink paper inside.

'What did you promise?' Meg asked as he stood, then leaned down to kiss her firmly on the mouth. Her heart kicked up a notch and she smoothed a hand down his cheek, letting herself fall into him, before he gently eased her back.

Then Tom crunched up to the tree and hung the bauble onto one of the lower branches, before standing back and taking her hand. 'I promise…' He turned to Meg and smiled, his eyes darkening. 'To make every day with you feel like Christmas. The kind of Christmas you deserve.' Then he tipped her chin and bent her head up so he could pepper soft kisses across her mouth, before the kiss deepened and grew hotter. Meg tugged him closer, pushing her fingers under his hat, her heart beating fast, the blood pounding in her ears as her cheeks heated. Around them, the crowd began to whoop and cheer.

Then Tom pulled back and they both twisted round as Cooper barked. In the distance, outside Meg's shop, the herd had merged and the lost reindeer was now being nuzzled by his family, who were taking it in turns to crowd round. To the side of the street, bathed in a pool of soft yellow light coming from one of the lamps at the edge of the pavement, Meg's parents were locked in a gentle embrace.

A Letter from Donna

I want to say a huge thank you for choosing to read *If Every Day Was Christmas*. If you enjoyed it, and want to keep up to date with all my latest releases, just sign up at the following link. Your email address will never be shared and you can unsubscribe at any time.

www.bookouture.com/donna-ashcroft

If Every Day Was Christmas took me back to the magical Scottish Highlands at Christmas time. I so enjoyed being back in Lockton and seeing my favourite people again – from Meg and Nana Agnes to Morag, Fergus, Davey, Cora and even Lilith. Did you enjoy getting back together with the crazy locals in the snow? Meeting Meg's family and Tom, the gorgeous but conflicted hero, as he found his way back to his music? Did you guess who the mystery vandal was? Or think up your own special Christmas Promise to hang on the Promise Tree?

I hope you enjoyed the journey and festive escape. If you did, it would be wonderful if you could please leave a short review. Not only do I want to know what you thought, it might encourage a new reader to pick up my book for the first time.

I really love hearing from my readers – so please say hi on my Facebook page, through Twitter, or my website.

Thanks,
Donna

DonnaAshcroftAuthor

@Donnashc

donnaashcroftauthor

www.donna-writes.co.uk

Acknowledgements

Thanks firstly go to Peter, who took up marathons and triathlons when he was in his forties and provides a fair amount of inspiration for my stories. When I write about wild swimming, sea swimming or any general sports craziness, I'm probably thinking of him. And to the family who fit him so perfectly, Christelle, Lucie, Mathis and Joseph.

To Chris, Erren and Charlie – the family who fit me perfectly too. Thanks for being on the roller coaster and not jumping off.

No acknowledgements would be complete without a big Prosecco cheers to my writing buddy Jules Wake, or Jackie Campbell (thanks for the yoga treat when edits were bringing me down), and Julie Anderson (thanks for the cocktails and enduring positivity). You guys keep me going.

To Hannah Bond, my fabulous and very patient editor, her cat Zora (who had a cameo in this book), Peta Nightingale, Noelle Holten, Kim Nash, Alexandra Holmes, Alex Crow, Claire Gatzen, Rachel Rowlands and everyone else in the wonderful Bookouture team! Not to mention all their hugely gifted authors.

To Mel and Rob Harrison of the very talented Thinking Fox, who created me a fabulous new website during lockdown which I LOVE!! I can't tell you how much I appreciate it.

To all the lovely people who message me and leave such wonderful reviews – a huge thanks. This includes: Kirstie Campbell, Mags Evans, Pam Fryer, Claire Hornbuckle, Anne Winckworth, Alison Phillips, Amy Deane, Kim Holt, Soo Cieszynska, Jan Dunham, Tricia Osborne, Lynda Cardoza, Maria Rixon, Amanda Baker, Sue Moseley, Giulia Pitney Coope, Caroline Kelly, Sarah Marsh, Clare Seeley and anyone I may have forgotten. And to all the incredible bloggers who support me each time a book comes out, I am so grateful to you all.

As always, thanks to Katie Fforde, the Romantic Novelists' Association, Mum, Dad, Lynda, Louis, Auntie Rita, Auntie Gillian, Tanya, James, Rosie, Ava, Philip, Sonia, Stephanie and Muriel.

Finally, to the readers who have bought my books – many of whom have written reviews – I wouldn't be here without you. xx

Printed in Great Britain
by Amazon